Lost in *La La Land*

Tara Brown

Copyright © 2017 Tara Brown
All rights reserved.
Cover Art by Hart and Bailey Design
Edited by Andrea Burns

ISBN-13: 978-1542963367
ISBN-10: 1542963362

This book has haunted me for years.
I hope it haunts you as well.

Thank you to my team of insanely awesome beta readers, this one is for you!

What if you could enter your favorite novel?
Would you?
Even if it meant never coming back out?

Manhattan, New York, 2020

My reflection in the mirror isn't what it ought to be. There's a flash of something I vaguely recognize, a person I used to be or someone I will eventually become.
She's tired and haggard, she's probably dying.
She's there one moment, sitting in her chair, blankly staring out the window. And then she's gone. And I am me, normal me.
If I lean in and stare closely, directly into the flecks of my eyes, I still see her. It's the reflection. The window she stares from casts her back at me in the mirror. The gray day outside the window where she sits, the gray hospital gown she wears, the gray pallor of her skin. I blink and it plays live, clouds floating by, trying to animate the day and the woman I have become.
If I look close enough, I see the exact instant I will become her, become lost in la la land.
I can pinpoint the precise second that was the beginning of the end.
It's funny when you look back and see the end. To you, it disguised itself as a beginning, but it was a path to destruction. I craved that destruction, that end, that finality.
The end started the night I decided to change my work, to create a new machine from the one I'd been working on.
I was at a friend's, sitting in the dining room, waiting for her to bring dinner to her massive wooden table. Being the only one

seated, I was alone there amongst the eight chairs.

From the kitchen she giggled, obviously reacting to something her husband had said. I felt like a voyeur, listening in on the intimate moment occurring in the other room.

Being alone was hard enough without couples giggling and kissing, as was their prerogative. But it reminded me that I too used to kiss and giggle. I used to lean into someone, placing my whole heart on a shoulder.

Instead of hating them, I distracted myself by pretending to peruse the new apartment. I made a list of things I could mention when they came to the table. Normal people did that, discussed art and tables and area rugs.

My eyes scanned the walls and furnishings, and I happened upon a new painting. It was one of those art pieces that spread across the wall, continuing on several canvases as if the painting had been sawed into three or five or eight. This particular one was broken into five long thin panels.

The eye-catching work was of a beach at sunset with a boardwalk and long wispy sea grass. The clouds were thin, suggesting the air was warm with a slight breeze coming off the water. It was the sort of scene that made you want to step inside and walk off into the fading light of dusk.

If I let my eyes drift out of focus, I could hear the waves crash as I forgot for five seconds that my entire world was gone.

The smell of him and the burning house was stuck in my nose, despite all the time that had passed, but it couldn't fight against the overpowering scent of the sea and the windswept salt.

The taste of him and my tears was still on my lips, but it couldn't compete with the flavor of the sunscreen I would have spread over my arms as I roamed the sandy dunes below the boardwalk.

The sight of him, his smile and his back entering that smoky house, was lost in the blinding brightness of the beautiful beach and the way the water sparkled under the sunlight.

There had never been a competition inside me for what I felt more, my grief or anything else. He was always the winner, until that moment.

For a few minutes I sat there, free of every burden his death had laid upon me. For the first time I breathed deeply, imagining the air was crisp and clean and I was someone new. I was clean with the breeze.

I don't know how long I sat staring at the painting that stretched across the wall, broken into five scenes. Mentally, I hopped from each canvas, heading further and further into the work of art, fleeing my broken heart.

And like all scientists, I wondered what if.

What if I could make that picture come to life?

Even better, what if I could go into a painting made from my own heart's desire?

What if I could go there and he would be real again?

Would I care that he was just a dream?

I was the worst dinner guest from that moment on.

We ate salad with battered fish and crusty bread, and I tried to engage in conversation but everything was halved. Half an attempt at a smile. Half a conversation. Half a distracted stare as the painting caught my eye more than once.

Normally, I would have lingered over my plate, closing my eyes and tasting everything, dragging the crusty bread through the balsamic and Parmesan dressing, savoring the olive oil on my tongue as it mixed with the fish. I would have spent a few seconds paying homage to the fact I could taste and smell and devour all of it, and he could not.

It was my way of making sure he saw me living on—saw me appreciating things he no longer could. It was an act I wished to do well enough that he might believe I was living without him.

But that night I didn't live without him. I plotted. I was preoccupied as my eyes roamed the canvas, strategizing and arguing the scientific possibility of what I was contemplating.

Marguerite and Stanley were the perfect hosts, ignoring my absentmindedness. A fault they no doubt blamed on the loss of the only man I could ever love. It afforded me many transgressions. Every time I did something people disagreed with, they blamed him. I could have gotten away with a great many evil things with him as my justification.

I left that night, arguing equations in my mind.

My feet carried me through the damp streets of the Upper West Side.

I crossed at the wrong times, ignored the voices of others on the road, my heels clicking on the cold cement until I paused, realizing I was lost.

Still in a frenzy of sorts, I glanced up at the office building in front of me and grinned. I had walked to work.

Pulling my keycard from my purse, I didn't hesitate or contemplate the road I was about to take. I scanned the card and entered the building, leaving behind common sense and rationality.

Those were things I had lost in the fire anyway.

Chapter One

Manhattan, New York, 2024

"The storm got worse. I hadn't seen it coming. It came out of nowhere and the wind was so harsh and Dorothy was shouting at me. I ignored her and ran inside the house. I could taste the straw in the wind as the granary was lifted first. Sand and debris hit me in the face, but I closed my eyes. Toto snuggled into me, curling into my arms like he knew he'd be safe there. It was insane. There's no other word for it." Her eyes lit up as she spoke of the trip. "The floorboards rattled and the walls waved and buckled, and I swear I floated for a minute. Then I landed with a hard thump, the same as the house did. It was so dark and then this light came and it was a woman with a beautiful face and golden hair. She helped me up and was smiling when she told me I'd saved them all." She closed her eyes and sighed. "It was magical, Emma. Just magical."

The words are a form of bliss. My bliss.

Mrs. O'Leary waited with rosy cheeks and a satisfied expression on her face as I removed the sensors and IV.

When freed, she got up and wrapped her arms around my neck. "You made a dream come true today. Ever since I was a small girl I've wanted to see how magical Oz was and now I have. I really and truly have." She hugged hard and then walked for the door. "I will never forget this." She waved and let herself out as another customer came in, as if she had been waiting outside for the shop to open.

"Hi. Welcome to Lucid Fantasies. Can I help you?" I smiled.

The older woman beamed back, "I hope so. A friend of mine said she came and spent the most wonderful afternoon with you. She went into *Far from the Madding Crowd* and told me it's the best day she has ever had. And that includes having kids and getting married." She blushed and shrugged. "I was hoping I might give it a go. I don't have an appointment. I saw the 'appointment only' sign on the door. Could I make one?"

"Of course. I do have an opening right now if you have the time to stay. I just need to sit you down and have a conversation about some of your medical and personal history first. And we'll take it from there. My name is Dr. Emma Hartley, but call me Emma."

"All right. I'm Meredith Burks. Lovely to meet you." She made her way in and took a seat on the couch in the foyer as I locked the front door and got us both a hot cocoa.

When I put the mug down in front of her a wide smile crossed her lips. "I haven't had a cup of cocoa in ages." She lifted the mug and sniffed the steam. "Thank you."

"You're welcome." I sat and studied her face, trying desperately to guess what book she would pick. My mind flitted through old volumes of Sherlock Holmes. Or maybe it would be Nancy Drew. But when she opened her mouth and spoke I sat stunned.

"I would like to enter *Lady Chatterley's Lover.*" Her cheeks filled with color as she glanced down, clearly ashamed and yet somehow brave in the same respect.

"Of course." I smiled, wanting to reassure her there was no judgment on my behalf. Who was I to judge anyone? I couldn't even enter the machine, the one I'd created for myself. "But, before we consider a Lucid Fantasy, let's get past the formalities. I don't enjoy this part but it's very necessary."

"All right."

"It's a small questionnaire so I can determine if the machine and you are compatible."

"Okay." She sipped the cocoa and nodded.

"Do you have any history of mental illness in the family?"

Her brow knit as she contemplated those words. "No. I remember one of my aunts having dementia before they cured it, but I think that's it."

"Do you smoke, drink, or participate in recreational drugs?" I had become quite good at detecting if they were lying when answering this question.

Obviously, she was not when she scowled and shook her head. "Lord, no. Maybe when I was a girl, but it was the late sixties and everyone was doing drugs and smoking and drinking. They didn't know it was bad for you then."

"Of course." I laughed. "And have you ever lost someone you love?"

"Oh. Uhm—" A sad smile crossed her face as her eyes took a journey into the past. "Of course. We all have, haven't we?" She sighed and sipped the cocoa again. "My mother and father are both gone. My eldest sister is as well. My husband passed away last year. He was seventy-eight and riddled with cancer. I have never said this aloud, but it was a blessing to see him go. The peacefulness on his face when he passed was remarkable, as if watching the pain fade from him until there was nothing but calmness left. For a whole minute after he died he looked like the man I married. The boy I met." Tears filled her eyes. "It was nice, which is so odd. But he had been in pain for so long."

That was the answer I was looking for. She'd had a lifetime with a man she loved, but she wasn't searching for him. She might even want to be young again and try something new.

Satisfied, I continued with the questions, certain she was exactly the sort of candidate the machine required.

When we finished, I put her into the machine for her first session. We always started small, two-hour sessions. We would then build up to four hours. The most a person could stay was six hours. Very few people could last that length of time hooked to a machine, dreaming.

She went into *Lady Chatterley's Lover* and came out sparkling with secrets and satisfaction. Her cheeks flushed as she left the store with a new pep in her step.

Like a vampire or succubus, I gleaned something from it all. Her experience became mine. Her satisfaction fed me. Every one of my clients did. Their eyes sparkled again and their mouths twisted in revealing grins, never betraying everything they did in the book, but suggesting it was all more than they ever imagined possible.

I lived off that, the smiles and the sparkles and the happiness, and I imagined what it would be like to go into the machine and see him. I lived through them, closing my shop each day with a sigh of satisfaction.

Chapter Two

Manhattan, New York, 2025

    Lana's eyes lingered too long on the poster, before she finally spoke, "I'm ready, Emma." She lay back in the chair, relaxing. It was the same as always for her, the mayor's wife, Lana Delacroix. She never changed up her story. She came daily some weeks and always stayed as long as she could. The service had become something I had to book for the wee hours of the morning or after everyone had left, so I could fit in other clients.
    Every time she arrived she seemed happy and paid her money, which essentially was all I asked of anyone. But no one came nearly as often as she did.
    She had started a year ago, telling me she was obsessed with *Gone with the Wind* by Margaret Mitchell and needed to feel the book come to life the way it did when she read it. I told myself she was simply lost in the gowns and glamour of life before the Civil War. I told myself she hated her marriage and enjoyed living a dream.
    Maybe I lied to myself a little.
    Lana slipped her hands into the gloves that monitored her vitals as the forearm clamps clicked into place.
    The microbiosensors, glowing pale blue and pulsating softly in the syringe, were pushed into her arm under the clamp when I

pressed the start. I placed the mask over her eyes, putting her into a state of light deprivation. It helped with the dream.

The microbiosensor computers resembled a dot, or a tiny cluster of explorers under the skin, flashlights all pointing in the same direction. The moment my fingers touched the screen, starting the *Gone with the Wind* program, the nanobots deployed. The glowing small blue dot under her skin was gone.

They hurried to attach to the dorsolateral prefrontal cortex of her brain, hijacking the area, creating the world from within.

When we sleep and dream, our bodies go "offline" for lack of a better word. The primary motor cortex and primary somatosensory cortex are disconnected, so to speak. Since all dreams come from within us, my nanocomputers hooked into the dorsolateral prefrontal cortex with the story already programmed. The whole system was linked to a virtual world, based entirely upon a novel. There had to be a base of control. Early on, I discovered when people were put into a dream, completely in their control, it usually involved nightmares.

We were slaves to our own fears.

No, the journey required a controlled environment where patients were placed into a world they knew and were comfortable with. They were limited to a select group of options, centered on the base story within their chosen novel.

My research had its humble beginnings as deep-brain stimulation for patients with severe disabilities and disorders. Being a romantic and a widow trapped together in the same body, clashing and fighting each other's desires, prompted me to find a use for my life's work. Neuroengineering had so many opportunities as far as careers went. However, watching Lana's face when she entered the world created by a beloved author made them all seem so bland.

My system still improved the lives of the disabled and diseased, but in a whole new way. It not only gave them their families, but also the option to leave all that behind and enter a made-up world from the books or movies they loved.

Inside a work of fiction was a type of beauty we didn't have in the real world. It was mixed in a balanced way with chaos and romance. It was planned to be perfect. A precise amount of pain, pleasure, beauty, and horror. It was specifically what you desired, and that escape was in a controlled environment. Real life was nothing, compared to the possibilities I had brought to light with the technology.

If all you truly wanted in the world was to storm the beaches of Normandy or kiss Mr. Darcy, you could. The book set the parameters, but your actions allowed changes within the novel. I had set it up as a Choose Your Own Adventure, using the same concept as the children's series I had found in my grandmother's cellar when I was a girl, but I kept the possibilities for change limited. Back then, I had loved the idea of choosing my own possibility and outcome. Sometimes I died. Sometimes I lived. Sometimes I won. Sometimes I lost. But no matter what, when I opened the book the real world was gone.

As an adult, I saw the need to limit personalization, to avoid confusing reality with fiction.

All of life's mundaneness and boredom was replaced by excitement and possibility.

In the worlds created by authors there was hope.

But in the end, it was fiction. A true escape. No repercussions or costs.

In a story, nothing was like the real world where the pain was forever and getting past something was impossible. Your wounds might eventually hurt less, but they would never leave you. They would kill you slowly, a type of disrepair never to be righted. The journey in a novel was the opposite: over the minute you opened your eyes or closed the cover.

I sat back in the recliner, closing my eyes and letting my brain wander, and as always, my thoughts turned to him. In my heart of hearts, I wished someone would write the story of our love, and I could live there forever. A story that ended differently than ours had. A story that included the thousand things we had planned for and not the one thing we hadn't.

If I were any kind of writer I might have done it.

Being a scientist, this was the closest I could get to a happy ending.

But it would never be my happy ending, not my real one.

No.

I never entered the machine.

When I started the original testing of the idea, I discovered that people with my level of loss should never enter a world where they could rekindle their lost love. My one test subject, whose children had been killed in an accident, went mad, obsessed with being inside the machine again and again and again. She lost her zest for life. She lost her desire to be in reality. She became depressed when in the real world. I knew, from the moment I turned her away for the last time, I could never enter the machine.

No, my happy ending was helping people like Lana who were lucky to have only normal amounts of boredom in their lives.

Her worst problem was her loveless marriage to her asshole husband, the mayor of New York City, Marshall Delacroix, jackass extraordinaire and not a fan of my shop, Lucid Fantasies.

Not a fan of me in general.

His wife had been a client for a year, and he had tried to stop her from coming for the last four months.

Lana was a nice woman who deserved better than someone like Marshall. She deserved a marriage like mine.

A smile crested my lips as I remembered our wedding day, our beginning.

It was perfect.

Sort of like our end.

Perfect.

Perfect irony in a perfect disaster.

Aneurisms in men married to neuroengineers were like God mocking our entire species. I had always believed in science and evolution and the big bang theory. I had always believed in the miracle of the human brain.

But the moment he ran back into the house fire to save our dog, I believed in God. I believed my love had gone there with

Him—to heaven. My husband had gathered my heart with his and brought them to the safest place in the world, to be with a God I became convinced of in a matter of seconds.

I believed it because I refused to consider that my heart had died off when the house collapsed. When his heart stopped beating and his lungs no longer took in air. No, our love continued on.

My heart concluded there was no way he was gone forever. His energy hadn't shifted into something else; he had gone somewhere and held my heart hostage there. I called it heaven and even prayed it was the sort of place that I could join him.

Lying in the chair, my mind fought the image of him forcing me out onto the lawn. His dark-blue eyes squinted in the smoke as he nodded, reassuring me our dog would run from the house. We stood there, on the damp grass of our prewar home and waited.

But she didn't come.

The last look I gave him was a fearful one. The small fire was nothing, just a kitchen fire. Had the stupid extinguisher worked he would have put it right out.

When his eyes met mine, he nodded and kissed my nose. "I'll be right back."

That was the last thing he ever said to me.

He ran back inside to get the dog.

Moments later, my beloved Lola, a spicy little papillon, ran out to me. She leapt into my open arms. Holding her trembling body, I watched the doorway, waiting for him to come back out. The smoke was worsening, billowing from my back door. But it didn't bring him with it. I ran for the steps but hands grabbed me, pulling me back. I should have noticed the sound of the fire trucks and the flashing red lights in the thick smoke. I should have noticed the shouting and the hoses.

But my eyes were locked on the back door.

I barely noticed when the men went in.

I did however see when they came running back out because they carried him. That was when the house collapsed. The house, my heart, and our dreams all collapsed.

They wouldn't let me see him or touch him.

They took him in an ambulance, telling me nothing.

There's no feeling like the one of having no control over the world around you. I felt like a ghost. I wondered for a moment if I had died in the fire, if it had been worse than I thought, and I was dead and stuck to wander purgatory.

Lola and I trembled in each other's embrace, watching everything we had loved burn to the ground.

There were lies I told myself, like if he had not run back in, I might have been able to save him. But having his well-timed aneurysm as he went inside the burning house had secured his death. There was no way everything could have happened so perfectly.

It was a perfect disaster.

It had started with the kitchen catching fire just as we began the renos on the house. And ended with the dog not running out after us. No. It ended with the aneurysm. No. It ended when I sat alone in the hallway of the hospital, clutching my dog and wishing the man speaking to me would go away. No, it hasn't ended yet, but it will. It will end with me staring at gray skies and drifting clouds.

Every day since then, I wished I hadn't let him convince me to buy the older home or gotten the dog he didn't want, or we hadn't started the renos at a chaotic point in both our careers. I lied to myself and said those events killed him.

I killed him, if you considered the facts all spread across the board.

That was the thing that would kill me slowly. It was also the reason I would never go into my machine for my happy ending.

I would find him in there and never leave.

Hating the path my mind took whenever I closed my eyes, I opened them to discover Lana's heart rate was a touch low. The machine wasn't making note of it yet, so I reached out and touched her bare arm. Her heart returned to a normal rate, recognizing the stimulation.

When her time was up, I touched the screen, sending in the next set of nanocomputers to end the dream. They were the cannibals of the biosensors. They sent a signal to the ones attached to her brain, beckoning them like a siren or a pied piper. They led the computers to their death, her stomach. She would pass them in a bowel movement and not even know.

Slowly she started to come around, moaning and moving her lips as if still in the dream. When her huge lashes fluttered, her eyes dilated and then returned to normal. She yawned and stretched peacefully. "That was the best one yet."

"You seemed really into it."

Lana nodded. "I was." She cleared her throat. "I was at a ball, dancing and having fun. It was remarkable."

I unclamped her forearm and smiled. "Excellent."

"It was." She sighed again, seeming completely blissful. "I wish that were the real world and this crap was just a dream."

"I hear that." Instead of agreeing, I should have heard the warning signs in her wish.

I should have noticed her attachment to the machine.

I should have convinced my husband to buy a brand-new house.

I should have let Lola figure her way out of the fire.

But I never did many things I should.

Instead, I walked her to the door, sent her out into the rain, and locked up for the night.

The same rain that Marshall Delacroix would come walking through to find me.

I locked up the shop and headed to the water to stare out at the full moon from the docks. On a normal day, you could barely see it with the pollution levels being what they were, but if I were lucky I might get a glimpse. I always believed my husband could see the moon too. Maybe it was bigger in heaven than it was in New York. Maybe the moon was a vacation spot, somewhere to go and sit and read the paper. My husband loved to read the paper. It was why he hated Lola. She crumpled the pages and tried to chew it, thinking it was a game.

"Dr. Hartley?" a man's voice called from off in the distance, joining the sound of shoes walking on the docks.

When I turned I winced, outwardly. It was rude to greet my own mayor that way, but I despised him. "Mayor Delacroix, to what do I owe the pleasure of this intrusion on my private time?"

"I need your help."

Narrowing my gaze, I waited for the rest of the sentence.

"You have to stop seeing my wife." His voice didn't have its normal condescending tone.

"Why is that?"

"She's addicted. She isn't living in the real world anymore. She is hooked on that machine of yours and the stories she visits. Exactly as I told you she would be." It was accusatory but without being rude.

"I've told you already, people cannot become addicted to the machine. It doesn't give off anything. There are no chemical reactions to the dreamworld. It's no different than sleeping or reading or daydreaming, sir." My back stiffened in my trench coat as he drew near enough that we could speak at a civilized volume.

"Well, plainly speaking, she lied to you. She's addicted to drugs and does them before she comes to see you." He offered a smug grin with his nonchalant way of explaining.

"No, she isn't. I do random drug testing on my clients. It's something they have to agree to upon signing up."

"I didn't want to have to do this, but if you don't stop letting her come, I will shut you down. I will revoke your business license and end your career. They will find drugs in your apartment and a dead man in your trunk. I will do everything I can to stop you." His eyes flickered in the dim glow of the streetlight above us. "You don't want me as an enemy." He glowered one last time before turning and walking away, leaving me there with the ultimatum of the century.

Chapter Three

"Dr. Hartley, open the door please! Emma!" Lana's desperate voice outside my storefront made me sick. It had been weeks of her coming every day, begging me to let her in, but I never did.

Remembering her husband's threats, I shook my head. "You have to go home, Lana. You need to spend some time away. Your husband says he'll frame me for murder if I let you in. Surely, you see I can't have that."

Tears streamed her pale cheeks as she shook her head, frantic for me to open the door. Her eyes were filled with despondency as she pleaded, "Please, Emma. *Please.* I need this. There is nothing in my life. It's empty. Please don't make me live this way. I need to be that girl, the one who's happy."

I lost my battle then.

My fingers knew that word "need."

Slowly they made their way up the door, gripping the handle.

The desperation in her face broke my heart.

My fingers made a terrible choice.

They turned the lock against my better judgment.

They ignored the promise I had silently made to myself, swearing to never open my door to her again.

But her hopelessness and need spoke to my own.

Again, my brain whispered *what if?*

What if she needed it just one more time because this was

the thing stopping her from running back into the burning house?

What if this were the one time that cured her obvious depression and convinced her to leave the moronic bastard she was married to?

What if she simply needed one last time, for closure's sake?

What if I was living vicariously through her, and as hard as it was for her to say no to herself, it was equally as hard for me to say no?

What if?

I opened the door, ignoring the men in the car across the street—the men who watched my shop because they watched her. She was more or less a hostage or a victim of her marriage and that made me want to help her even more.

The moment the door closed though, she became the addict I had convinced myself I didn't see.

She scrambled to the chair, shaking her head of dark hair back and forth, preparing for the ride of a lifetime. Most people came because they wanted to live out their love of a novel. Most thought it was like a ride at a fun park for the literary people of the world. A fun park based entirely upon your own imagination and pleasure.

Lana Delacroix saw it as an escape.

And I saw her as an escape.

She was mentally fleeing a situation she deemed hopeless.

I was mentally fleeing my own mind.

I clamped her in and pressed the screen, bringing light into the small room. The man in the other room, who was enjoying Moby Dick, was nearly done, so I left her as she drifted off into her slumber and woke him up, smiling as he sighed. "You really are a genius, Emma. That was incredible."

"Thank you." I bowed slightly. "Thank you, Mr. Frank. I am so pleased you enjoyed yourself."

"It was inconceivable. I feel the need to wipe the seawater from my face. I can't believe the reality that is party to it all. It's overwhelming and at the same time enchanting." He got up and left, cheerful and waving. I locked the door after him, noticing the car across the street was gone.

I suspected it wasn't something I should be relieved about. Their absence was ominous.

But I let her stay in the machine a bit longer than normal, allowing her to be free for a while longer. This was definitely her last time.

When I woke her, her eyes didn't have the same relaxed look. Her pupils didn't go back to the right size, and she didn't stretch or yawn. She sat there, staring at the ceiling.

"You all right?"

"Yeah." She nodded but it took several tense seconds for her to blink and speak, "I just wish it were real."

"I can't let you come back, Lana. Ever. This was the last time, okay?"

"I know." She got up and left, no thank you or goodbye. She unlocked the door and walked out into the rain. She truly was the drug addict leaving the dealer's house, perhaps hating both of us for her needing and my enabling.

It felt a little off. I had made a mistake in letting her back in.

Instead of allowing the guilt to linger, I fell back on my go-to answers to justify my actions. The research had proven it was nonaddicting because the reward system in the brain, the limbic system, is tricked into shutting down. The neurons cannot send neurotransmitters, specifically dopamine, because they have been fooled into believing there is nothing worthy of a reward going on in the brain. That section of the brain is blocked from enjoying the process to the point of euphoria since the euphoria is falsely created for the subject. It cannot affect the body, only trick the brain into creating feelings that aren't there. If the dopamine and neurotransmitters aren't there, one cannot become addicted to them.

That was the theory, but seeing her face made me think otherwise.

The map of the machine started to flutter about in my head. I wondered where I might have gone wrong. I suspected the false euphoria was the problem.

There was also the possibility that the nanocomputers, microbiosensors, had changed or evolved. They could be tricky to control since they were highly adaptive. It was conceivable that they had mutated. I had to take the machine apart and see. But I needed some fresh air to contemplate it all.

I closed the shop and left through the back door.

During the short walk to my apartment I was seemingly on autopilot as I considered the places I might have gone wrong. One fearful thought played in my mind: what if Lana had gained more control than was intended? What if she was not only choosing her own adventure but also creating a new story from within?

Or what if the nanobots had taken over inside her and were doing it for her?

Jesus.

The possibility made me laugh as I entered my building, imagining evil robots taking over the world in a zombie-apocalypse-styled raid, like in a videogame. Nanocomputers taking over people, controlling them.

Had I made the first zombie?

Lana had acted like one when she left.

When I got inside, Lola was panting at the door. She leapt at me, still amped from the neighbor taking her out for her one of her scheduled walks or bathroom breaks.

"Hello, my love." I kissed her soft head, inhaling the perfumed smell of her doggy shampoo. She had been to the groomer only the day before and was as fresh as a flower. "How was your day?"

She tilted her head, contemplating my question and me.

I placed her down, getting her dish of food. I scooped the saucy meats she loved into the dish. "Look, bison tripe. Who's excited?"

She ran around in a small circle, doing her saucy-meat dance. The dog was a charmer. Her tricolored body was mostly white with small spots and stripes of beige and brown. She had the huge elephant ears papillons were known for and the curly tail. I adored her dainty feet and tiny beak.

I stroked her back as I placed the dish on the floor. She lapped at the tripe and crunched the kibbles I had stirred in.

After watching her for a few minutes, I grabbed a dinner from the freezer, pad Thai, and started heating it up.

My mind wandered.

Had I done something that now, five years later, I should take a closer look at?

Lana was the first and only patient to come on a regular basis. I should have paid more attention to that—studied her. I adored the joy she got, and I had lived vicariously through her on each journey.

Every time she went in, I closed my eyes and imagined it.

I too was Scarlett, descending the beautiful staircase at Twelve Oaks, excited to see Rhett. Only he wasn't Clark Gable. He was my dead husband, Jonathan.

That was where everything went wrong, even in a simple daydream.

Jonathan would then smile at me coyly, maybe smirk a little before turning and walking from the room. Like Alice was with the white rabbit in *Alice in Wonderland,* I would need to chase after him. But the dress was so grand and the stairs so high, I wouldn't be able to. In my head, I took the stairs slowly, my eyes always searching for him.

He would be the white rabbit, misplaced in the story of Miss Scarlett and her Rhett. Jonathan would be impossible to nail down to get a clear glimpse of. He would lead me around the rooms. It would end up more frustrating than exhilarating. A puzzle that couldn't be solved or escaped from.

And now it would all be over because, no matter what, Lana wouldn't be back. I would keep my promise to the mayor.

She was addicted, and as much as I wanted to study that, I had to respect the fact she was a regular person and not a test subject.

I curled up on the couch with the news on, flashing images and words, but my brain was lost in the sea of possibilities and problems. I crawled around inside the machine mentally, trying to find the flaw.

My stomach growled.

I glanced back at the microwave, sighing. I'd forgotten my meal again. I poured a bowl of cereal and ate it, leaning against the counter and visualizing my problems on the wall.

Lola barked at me, scratching at the door.

I searched for my coat, realizing I was still wearing it.

I was losing my mind.

Grabbing her leash and my keys, I darted out into the hall, only to discover I'd forgotten her in the apartment. I sighed, cupping my face with my hands and taking in several breaths before getting her and heading for the walk.

We had a private park in the back of the building, specifically for dogs. It was a safe place to walk at night in Manhattan.

I paced and strolled, tapping my fingers as she scampered about, sniffing and peeing.

"Dr. Hartley?"

I turned, wincing when I saw the mayor again paying me a visit alone. "Mr. Mayor, to what do I owe this pleasure a second time?"

"You swore you would keep her from your shop." The stricken look on his face made me less defensive than I could have been.

"She needed one last time. I had to do it. We never told her it was her last time before. She needed to go in once more knowing that; she needed closure. It was cruel to cut her off."

"She's nonresponsive. I hope you're happy now."

"What?" My heart leapt in my chest. "What do you mean? Did she hurt herself?"

"I took her to the hospital, but they can't find a thing wrong with her." His words were calm, the creepy kind, until he lashed forward, grabbing my arm roughly. "WHAT DID YOU DO TO HER?"

"Nothing!" I shoved him back. "Nothing! Sir, get control of yourself."

"YOU WILL TELL ME WHAT YOU DID!"

"Nothing." I shook my head but my mind wandered. She had

seemed different. "It was just like every other time, but she seemed sad. Take me to her." I had to see her to understand it. Part of me believed she might be faking it. She hated her husband more than enough to do that, and she was mourning her loss of the fantasy.

"You will never see her again!" He grabbed my arm once more, his grip tightened, shaking me as he sputtered contradictory outbursts, "I will fucking kill you, and I do mean gut you like a fucking fish. You won't see her again. You have to fix her. If she isn't normal by tomorrow I will burn your whole shop to the ground with you in it," he contradicted himself.

"Sir!" My insides tensed as I took each word he threatened me with seriously. "Stop!" I pulled back, trying to escape his clutches. "I need to see her. I understand you're upset but attacking me will not fix this. I need to see her to fix it."

He turned to drag me.

"Wait!" I pulled back. "My dog, Mr. Mayor. Stop. Please. I will put my dog inside and meet you downstairs, out front." He seemed about to say something, but I changed my tone to a nonnegotiable one, "I want to help her. I see your wife has become addicted, I see that now. I agree with you. It's impossible and yet she has. She's had a reaction that shouldn't be possible. I want to solve it as well."

He lifted a meaty finger, sticking it right in my face. "You better fix this, Doctor. Or I will kill you. I'm not playing around." He turned and left the garden. His grief and anger made him sound like a mobster. He was an ass on a good day and this was not a good day.

My hands shook when I picked up Lola and carried her to the apartment. I didn't get my purse or anything else. Clutching my keys and cell phone, I turned and left.

Lana was nonresponsive?

How?

Was she stuck in the world of the novel?

Was that possible?

Could the nanocomputers have remained in her brain,

attached, instead of flushing themselves from her body upon following the pied pipers down the chute?

No.

They were computers. I needed to stop making them the monsters. They didn't plot, except in horror movies. They did the one thing they were programmed to do. And she was the only person unable to move past it all after being unhooked. Everyone else who used the machine enjoyed the trip. They left smiling and peaceful, the way she used to.

Jesus, had I turned her into a zombie for real?

Was the horror movie coming true?

Had the nanobots evolved into something terrible?

Were they the monsters?

I walked out the front door, nodding at Andrew the doorman.

The mayor's driver got the door for me, scowling like I was the devil herself. I climbed in the backseat, trying to ignore the tension and hatred being directed my way.

"How is this possible, Doctor?" the mayor asked from the dark of the car.

"I don't know." I shook my head. "It isn't. The program runs in a way to prevent addiction or even a bodily response. Everything is shut off and disconnected. The nanocomputers commit suicide, so to speak, when the program has run its course. It's scientifically impossible. This is akin to coming home to find your computer has decided you're having pizza for dinner and taken the liberty of ordering for you."

"And yet, she is in a vegetative state. She doesn't speak. She doesn't look around, almost like she has no control. Her eyes don't dilate. She is a corpse with a pulse."

"Zombie," I muttered.

"What?"

"Nothing. I need to see her to understand."

"Your shop is going down. It's dangerous, just like I always said it was." He pointed his meaty finger in my face again. "You are a dangerous woman. You're going to be shut down and your pseudoscience is going to burn."

I cocked an eyebrow at him. "Point that finger the other way. I didn't drive her to come to my shop every day of the week. How bad is your marriage that she needs the escape?" I regretted saying it the moment I did, but the expression on his face made it so much worse. He looked like he might strangle me so I moved closer to the door, turning away from him but keeping his movements in my peripheral.

When he finally did speak, his voice was thick with emotion, "You have no idea what you're talking about."

"Possibly. But I suspect we're both carrying some of the blame." I stared at the seat ahead of me, frightened and confused.

When we arrived at the private hospital I didn't wait for the driver. I got my own door, hurrying to the front of the building as my insides became a scrambled mess and my heart raced. I marched down the stark hallway and pressed the button for the elevator, although I didn't know where I was going. I just needed to be away from him. I pressed the button for the floor I knew the patients with brain injuries went for testing.

I hurried to the nurses' desk. The girl at the desk glanced up at me, but she immediately focused back on the computer screen.

"Lana Delacroix, please."

Her eyebrows lifted. "Who are you?"

"Her doctor."

She raised one eyebrow, lowering the other in disbelief. The heavy steps of the solid and angry mayor behind me vibrated through my body. I pointed a thumb in his direction. "Ask him. I'm her doctor."

"LET HER THROUGH!"

The nurse jumped, pressing a button for a large door to open. "Room 8."

I walked quickly, hoping to escape the wrath of the titan following me.

In Room 8, I found exactly what he had described. Lana was in a bed, staring wide-eyed at the ceiling. I paused in the doorway, turning back. "Let me see her, alone."

He appeared as though he might argue or throttle me right there, but he nodded once and folded his thick arms.

I turned back toward her and walked in slowly, watching to see if she moved in any way that might reveal the fact she was playing possum for her husband's attention. I settled next to her in the chair and continued to observe her for several moments. She did not move except to breathe.

Having touched her a thousand times, the intimacy of the moment didn't hit me until afterward; I stroked her hair from her face like a mother or a sister would. "Lana, tell me what's happened. It's Emma."

A tear slipped from her eye—a response, though nonverbal.

Her eyes stayed fixed on the ceiling, her lips didn't move, but an emotional crisis was obviously burning its way through her. I continued to rub her dark hair from her clammy forehead. I had to know if an attachment had somehow formed for her, if she had somehow become part of her story but was unable to walk away. "Tell me what's wrong. Do you miss Rhett?" Her eyes didn't budge. "Ashley Wilkes?" Again, she did not respond. "Have you fallen in love with something inside *Gone with the Wind?*"

At that moment, she twitched. Her eyes darted about the ceiling as her lips formed a word, actually two, "Danny Jacobs."

I honestly didn't recall all the characters. It had been years since I'd read the novel or seen the movie. "Did you somehow fall in love with it all? Or just Danny?"

"Danny." Her eyes fluttered for a moment before she lost responsiveness, and she was again stuck staring at the ceiling.

"Did she say anything?"

I glanced back at the doorway, nodding. "Danny Jacobs, one of the characters in the book, I assume. She must somehow be stuck in the story. I don't see how this is possible. I'm worried she may have had a stroke during the program or something. I can check my records for her vitals, but I doubt there is anything there. My sensors would have picked up even the slightest change unless maybe they've glitched. I mean, it's possible. I'll go over everything again. She shows signs of being in shock or possibly the nanocomputers haven't left the system, which should be impossible, in theory, but there could always be a glitch. Nothing is perfect."

The mayor's eyes became slits, dark angry slits. "What did you just say?"

"What?" I hesitated to repeat it. "Which part?"

"Did you say Danny Jacobs?"

I nodded, completely confused. His rage took over.

He flew toward me, ripping me from the chair and gripping my arms. My head jerked back and forth like I was being murdered in a martini shaker. His screams owned all the air around us. I screamed in response and when attendants and nurses filled the room, he was pried from my body.

"Stop!" I blinked through tears.

"GET HER OUT OF HERE! GET HER OUT!" he screamed and pointed, hitting women and men alike.

I scrambled to my feet, racing from the room as they pinned him against the far wall in the hallway. I didn't wait for the elevator. I took the stairs, sprinting as fast as I could. When I broke through the doors at the front of the hospital, I dropped to my knees, gasping for air and sobbing.

I had no idea what just happened.

Chapter Four

Running my fingers across the machine, I considered a thousand possible outcomes. Two stood out the most.

If she'd had a stroke, why hadn't the machine caught her body's reaction to the program or the fluctuation in her vitals?

If indeed the nanocomputers were still adhered to her, she needed the pied pipers, the sirens of doom, to enter her body again to beckon them.

My only option was to sneak the syringe of nanocomputers into the hospital, inject her, and run the pied piper call through her body once more.

If that wasn't it, and the tests they ran on her brain didn't show a stroke, I would have to face the music. It could be a complete mental breakdown because she possibly had a preexisting mental disorder I wasn't made aware of, and I had put her at risk the entire time, slowly degrading her mental stability.

I would be liable in some ways, but if she had lied to me, the form she signed at the beginning would waive any responsibility on my part. Not that it would make me feel better. She was still sick in some way and my machine was partly to blame.

The mayor's response to Danny Jacobs made me curious too.

I sat at my computer and ran his name with hers in Google. It took a lot of sorting through different social media sites until there it was: the most important key to her addiction to the machine.

"Danny Jacobs dies in terrible crash." The words left my lips with horror and shock.

How had I missed this?

The moment I asked her the question flitted about my mind. She had laughed and shaken her head, completely relaxed and at ease.

She had lied like it was her job.

The headline gave me chills but the article made me sick to my stomach. I burst from my chair, grabbing a syringe of the pied pipers, the tablet I used to run the program, and darted for the door. Hailing a cab in the cold and dreary weather was nearly impossible. Every one of them already had a passenger. Finally, a cab stopped and I jumped in, shouting, "The private hospital on Saint Nicholas Avenue!"

The driver hit the gas, sensing my urgency.

I held up my card for him to scan when we arrived, fleeing the cab the instant the light turned green on the machine. I didn't take the elevator, hoping to sneak into the room when no one was looking. The six floors up were murder.

I was gasping for air and wheezing when I cracked the door open, scanning the nurses' station and surrounding area for people. The lone nurse had her head down, reading or sleeping. I couldn't be sure which. There wasn't a single other person in the area.

Something sounding like a radio went off, causing the nurse to lift her head. She got up and sauntered down the hallway, opening the door I needed to get through. I took my chance, springing from the stairwell and dashing into the room where Lana continued to lay perfectly still.

I closed the door behind me and injected her immediately before I hurried to the other side of the bed to slide down the wall and wait for the nanocomputers to link to my tablet. I tapped the start of the sirens' call, setting the pied pipers into motion. The program to dislodge any and all nanocomputers from her brain ran exactly as it had before, signaling it had completed its task. In a perfect world, I would have already created nanocomputers to take a tour of the brain, scanning for any rogues that had hung on. Or perhaps added a tracking device to each one, but that might have increased the size of them.

I would have to think about the changes I needed to implement at a later date.

Glancing up at the expression on her face, I winced.

There was no doubt in my mind that Danny Jacobs was to her what Jonathan was to me—her soul. They had just celebrated their engagement when his car went off the road with them both in it. He had saved her from the vehicle and swam her to shore where she managed to crawl from the icy waters, but he hadn't been able to do the same. Exhausted from saving her, he was swept away with the river, his body found much later, frozen on the banks.

She married the mayor two years later, but the wedding photos showed the hollow stare of a girl still lost in the current, still clinging to the body of her love. A girl who had also loved a man destined for the other world, the one we weren't allowed to go to. The one where our hearts were held hostage.

The mayor's face was not the same as hers. He obviously loved her. Her desperate sadness and desire to escape came from the very same place that told me to avoid the Lucid Fantasies machine. My Choose Your Own Adventure would be overpowered by my broken heart.

Had I known about hers, I never would have let her use the machine.

I should have done a more thorough check into her background. I should have researched her. I should have listened when the mayor told me she couldn't come anymore. I should have let my dog die in the fire.

I should have done a lot of things I didn't.

Focusing back to the problem at hand and leaving the past and the "should haves" where they belonged, I gazed up to watch her for a while, staring, motionless. She didn't move and barely breathed. I began to drift off until I was startled by her gasps for air. She sat up, shuddering and coughing. She turned and frowned at me. "Why are we here?"

"Danny Jacobs."

She winced. "What?"

I nodded. "You lied to me."

She lay back, confused and continuing to breathe heavily. "What about him?"

"When I first thought about making the machine to hook up to books or art, it was only to have someone write a certain story that I could live in, a story that was once real before it took a wrong turn. I wanted to fix the wrong turn and escape this world."

She turned her head, staring at me like a ghost. "But you never go in."

"I can't, Lana, don't you see that? I know what would happen to me if I went in. I wouldn't get lost in the perfection of that world. I wouldn't care about the story of the book or the characters. I wouldn't even notice the plot. Because I lost someone once who meant more to me than anything in the world, I have always feared I would find him in there, waiting for me. I would never leave if he were in there. I would become addicted to the machine. Or I would force my body to remain in a coma so I could stay and be with him." As much as I hated her for making my machine look like the guilty party, I understood.

A tear slipped down her pale cheek. "He was there. Danny. He was always there. We danced and talked, and he was just as I remembered him being." She closed her puffy eyelids, squeezing them shut. "He was warm and alive. And then it got harder and harder to find him. I could chase him around and finally find him. And we would . . ." Her cheeks flushed.

My heart broke for her. "And of course you got addicted to seeing him."

"And heartbroken every time I left him." She quivered.

"You can't go in there ever again, Lana. You have to grieve and let him be where he really is." My words stung inside me where the darkness was. I knew the words. I knew their meaning. I knew I needed to hear them, no matter how painful they were.

She didn't answer me. She sobbed quietly.

I got up, taking her cool hand in mine and squeezing. "Take care of yourself."

She sniffled and heaved, and yet I left her there. I had enough of my own misfortunes; I didn't need to see hers too.

I went home to snuggle my dog and contemplate the places I had gone wrong in everything.

And that maybe the mayor was right. My science was dangerous.

Chapter Five

Manhattan, New York, 2026

The paper crinkled in my hand from the force of the wind and my grip. My eyes couldn't leave the one word I refused to believe: lawsuit.

Instead of telling the mayor the truth, Lana let him believe my machine had caused her mental breakdown. She never mentioned Danny Jacobs to him, and I believed it was because she was angry with me for refusing her the journey into the story again.

I crumpled up the paper, tossed it into the garbage pail, and stormed into the shop. The phone rang, lighting up on the wall, revealing the face of the doctor ordered to test the machine for me. They had been calling for days.

I contemplated not answering again, but I knew they wouldn't stop until they were able to test it. Pressing the button, I sighed. "Hello."

"Hello, Dr. Hartley. We're hoping this afternoon works for the assessment of the Lucid Fantasies machine."

"Fine." I nodded at the man with the beard. "It does. I have cleared my appointments for the month to go through the system anyway."

He smiled like we might be friends or colleagues. "Excellent. I will see you in a few hours."

I pushed the "end call" button and slumped onto my desk, staring at my picture of Lola. As I was already in my late thirties, I had to assume my dog would be the last love I ever had and, unfortunately, she was in her last decade of life.

I pressed the screen on the desk, bringing up the live feed of her at doggy daycare. She was wrestling and growling at another toy dog. She was such a savage. She was my savage though, so she was cute and fuzzy while being hateful.

Jonathan had hated her more than anything. She was a diva, and he had always envisioned himself with a large dog. I spun the ring on my finger, remembering the last time we argued over the dog before finally getting her. I'd told him we might not be compatible, like a fool, because we were never going to want the same things. It made me smile now. We were so opposite, we had gone full circle and ended up matching anyway.

He was my rope dropper, a trait I always thought I hated.

At any point in our relationship if I tried to have an argument or a tug of war for power, he refused to engage. He would drop the metaphorical rope and walk away. I tried so hard to fight with him, but he never participated. He laughed at me or just tolerated whatever rant was going on. He was calm and cool and loaded to the hilt with common sense. And somehow, through it all, he loved me. Me, being spicy and passionate and moderately insane like all scientists. In the end, by some small miracle, he let me win the argument over the dog.

I closed my eyes and let the story of us cloud my head.

When I woke, surprised I had slept, the door buzzer was screaming. Stretching and yawning, I sauntered to the front door to find three doctors: a woman and two men.

"Dr. Hartley, I am Dr. Williams. This is Dr. Brielle and Dr. Dalton."

"Hello." I opened the door wider. "Please, come in."

"We are extremely interested in the machine. We of course know of your work with brain injuries and physically disabled patients to create lucid daydreams, generating lives where they feel fulfilled and not stuck in their broken bodies. We have obviously followed that from its origins. But this—this is something far more interesting. Taking books or movies people love, works of art even, and transplanting sleeping people into them. It's fascinating," Dr. Williams gushed. "The last few years have been very exciting for you. And all of us in neuroengineering."

The woman, Dr. Brielle, gave me an equally intrigued smile. "We have been petitioning to be the people who would test the machine with you since it came under fire. When the mayor started his claims against your work last year, was coincidentally the same time his wife became a frequent client of yours. We knew he would start a witch hunt against this."

Her words made me feel a touch better. Despite the fact they couldn't fix the guilt I had over not knowing the mayor's wife was in love with a ghost.

"Don't get us wrong though, we have to be unbiased, as hard as that will be," the quiet man, Dr. Dalton, added with a less than pleasant demeanor.

"Of course." I tried to be polite. I didn't want them to hate me and punish my machine for it. "What exactly would you like to see with the machine?" I hoped they would ask to enter a book so they could experience the full genius of it.

"We will of course be testing the machine to the fullest." Dr. Brielle's eyes widened. She looked like a kid in a candy shop. Maybe she was a true book lover. "I'd love to go first, and the book I would just about die to experience is *Loving* by Henry Green." She almost sounded giddy, maybe a hair shy of it.

"I need to ask each of you the necessary questions first." All three faces appeared confused which made me smile. "I check to ensure people trying out the machine are fit to use it."

"Are there any dangers?" Dr. Dalton narrowed his gaze.

"No. It's like any fun ride at a park. If you have a bad heart or a personality disorder or a drug addiction, lucid dreaming in a forced environment might not be the healthiest decision for you. Paranoia, hallucination, and even nightmares could result from any of those preexisting factors in combination with the machine."

They all nodded, Dr. Dalton clearly less convinced than the other two doctors.

After we finished their surveys, I winced and gave Dr. Williams a look. "I'm sorry, but with your meds and prior alcohol addiction, you aren't a prime candidate."

He smiled softly. "Have you done tests on subjects who have addiction in their past?"

"Yes. We did a year of test studies, working with a broad spectrum of patients. We found anyone with addictions took each ride as an escape from reality but their addiction, being part of who they are, reared its ugly head in the dreamworld. Smokers crave a cigarette and don't find the sensation of smoking in the dreamworld as real. Their bodies actually enter withdrawal, the same as alcoholics and drug addicts. And past addicts come out of the machine wanting whatever it is they are addicted to. It is very much a unique experience to each individual person. We also found that people who don't like books didn't enjoy the experience. They didn't find the connection to the characters, nor pleasure in being transported into a new world or time or anything. They were bored in fact." It was the same speech I'd given many prospective clients.

"That impresses me. I like that you've done the research and have done your due diligence. You didn't rush this, as you could have, and you've maintained a strict code of ethics as far as the machine is concerned."

"Except with Mrs. Delacroix of course," Dr. Dalton added.

"I never knew of a reason to refuse her. She passed all my tests, paid, liked the service, and she was an all-round pleasure to work with." I didn't add that she had also lied about one small detail. I didn't want them to know I suspected tragic loss may cause an unnatural dependency.

"She came every day some weeks. You never saw this as excessive?"

"Some people have a glass of wine every day. We don't call

them alcoholics. She was truly enjoying the ride. I believed she just wanted to be inside the book. The colors and the dancing and the dresses were real for her. And the book is lengthy; she would need time to get through it." And she was meeting her dead lover so that was clearly a draw.

They all nodded and waited for me to continue.

"This way to the machine." I stood and held out a hand for Dr. Brielle. She would go first.

Many hours later, I unhooked Dr. Dalton and expected him to smile but he scowled. "As I am not a fan of fiction, I can confirm your findings in the other nonreaders. That was boring to say the least."

I laughed, unable to stop myself. His inability to filter himself was endearing in some strange way.

"Oh, it's too bad you can't go, Henry. You would love it." Dr. Brielle turned to Dr. Williams.

"I'm sure I would. I do tend to love the odd escape from reality." He winked at me and then gave Dr. Dalton a disapproving headshake. "You are a disappointment. How can you not enjoy fiction?"

Dr. Dalton shrugged it off. "I have never enjoyed the imagination. I believe in science and tangible proof. I despise when I read a novel and the science is so far-fetched there's no way it could conceivably happen, and I am meant to dumb myself down and suspend my intelligence for the hours I suffer through the lies within. No. I can't be bothered. But I see how someone with no knowledge of how the world works could enjoy this contraption." He let his real feelings be known then. I'd suspected he was on the mayor's side when he arrived, but this assured me there would be no kind words for me in his review. "Now we need to observe you in the machine and we will be on our way."

"Oh, we've done four hours already. Surely you don't want to sit through another two hours of my being hooked up to it." I started to sweat.

"We need to observe as a group to ensure there is no bias in any of the opinions; all three of us must observe one patient together. We believe the maker of the machine should have the expertise to give us the needed evidence to prove the machine is sound." Dr. Williams smiled wide.

My heart raced. My mouth dried of all saliva. My stomach cramped. But I pushed on. I forced a smile across my lips as plans formulated in my mind. In a flash, I bounced ten ideas to avoid this, from sabotaging my machine to faking an epileptic seizure, but nothing would work. There was no room or time to do anything but hook myself in.

"You did say the machine essentially runs itself. It is a simple program and does everything needed with little effort from you. If we detect problems, we'll run the siren program from the tablet." Dr. Dalton grew smug. "Simple."

"Very." I got into the chair, forcing my legs onto the rests. Every second seemed like it stretched across time.

"Are you all right?" Dr. Brielle gave me a concerned look.

"I am. I just never go into the machine. I'm always doing it for everyone else." It was the best I could come up with as my heart was in my throat and my stomach convulsed. "I don't have anyone who can run it for me." I nearly wiped the sweat from my brow but didn't want to be obvious.

"Of course, that makes sense. No one to monitor you and your vitals whilst you're in."

"No. And after spending hours taking people through it, I sort of just want to go home at the end of the day." I wanted to go home right then and there.

But I didn't.

I lay back, pretending to be relaxed, and watched as Dr. Brielle hooked me up, copying everything I had done to her. She did everything precisely and at the end checked it over twice. "I think you're ready. What book?" She grinned excitedly for me. Of course she couldn't know how the journey would be for me. And I couldn't let on that it would be the best and worst day of my life. Reliving the heartache was going to be brutal, but I would get through this. I would!

"*Persuasion*, please. By Jane Austen."

"Of course. Captain Wentworth." She bit her lip, lost in the thought of him for a moment before tapping her way through the system to pick the novel.

"He's my favorite," I added, not sure why I was divulging that. I hoped he was enough of a distraction that Jonathon might not be one.

"Oh, mine too. The dedication and devotion he had to Anne, even after all that time—it was so romantic. A true mark of a gentleman."

A silly smile, regardless of the fear I was nearly crippled by, smattered across my face. There was no fighting it. I loved that she sounded different, having spent two hours in a novel. She was excited for me the way I always was for everyone else. "Exactly." I nodded and closed my eyes, ready for the light-deprivation mask.

I took a deep breath and waited for it all to hit.

I had been in the machine in its early stages, back when the science was for ALS, MS, and Parkinson's victims. I knew the sensation of falling that occurred moments after it was initiated. I was prepared for the way the breath pushed from you in a forced exhale when you landed.

Everything was still dark.

The world wasn't done loading.

It was unsettling to be there, in the waiting room before the show. I should have created something a bit more pleasant than complete darkness. I felt as though I'd been swallowed up by the nothing.

It only lasted a moment and then a light hit so bright it blinded me.

I winced, covering my face, shielding myself from the intensity of it, but it didn't help. The light was so powerful it flashed through my eyelids.

Blinking, struggling to see, I wondered how no one had given me feedback on this. How had they forgotten to tell me about the terrible first two minutes of the ride?

But when the light faded and the world took form, I forgot what I had been thinking about.

I forgot my name.

All I knew was the house—no, estate—in front of me was the most beautiful place I'd ever seen. It was out of a movie.

Standing in the terraced garden, I was stunned by the cobbled walks and layered fountains. The spray made the whole lush garden sparkle like diamonds floated in the misty air.

The house, a handsome estate based on Haddon Hall in Derbyshire, was stone and brick with old Tudor windows that gave the impression one was barred into the home.

The arched doors were solid, made of heavy lumber with sturdy and weathered handles.

Brightly colored vines grew up the sides of the great building, smattering pink blooms to complement the green and gray stone.

Mossy gardens with perfectly shaped bushes lined the pathways. One went to the house and another led farther into the garden, giving me the impression there was a maze made of hedges.

The sky was blue and white and the wind was warm as it brushed against me, carrying with it the scent of the garden and fields.

On the other side of the sculpted hedges, opposite the house and maze, I could see clear across the rolling hills dotted with perfect little outcrops of trees or bushes. Everything appeared as a painting, which it was. Digitally painted to appear this way.

My mind brought the painting to life.

Taking a step, I winced at the feel of my shoe pinching my toes. When I glanced down at my foot, I paused for half a second, unsure of the dress. It was a pale green Regency day dress with a straight skirt, simple hem, and gathered bodice to create a slightly ampler chest. It was exactly the sort of thing a lady would wear midday.

Even my brain was different, allowing for English vernacular to become part of my inner dialogue. We never used Austen's language and strayed from using too heavy of a British baseline but instead tried to refine the American English so the majority of our clients weren't left behind. A true Austen aficionado would have been a little disappointed.

I wanted to tilt my head back and let my arms float so I might let the entirety of it sink in.

I made this.

It was mine.

My creation based on the words and works of others, but still mine.

Jane Austen and I had created something magical, together. We were partners. Sort of. Jane had made up the story and I created the script, having my digital design team shape the scent of trees and flowers and the pinch of old-fashioned shoes. It made the dreamer live it all.

A tear streamed my cheek as I took another step, my plain brown shoes no longer pinching, as if my feet had become accustomed to the rigidity of them.

The soft, damp grass smelled strongly of fresh rain and I sank in when I walked.

The cobblestone pathway to the side of the house was perfect. It was aged, exactly as it would have been if this were truly an estate home built hundreds of years earlier with only minor renovations or improvements. Additions and refurnishing were much more commonplace back then.

As if on a secret or spy mission, I crept up the cobblestone and peeked in the windows. They were hazy and small with lead bars, done in the Tudor style.

The parlor was decorated in a shabby chic style.

This was where the young ladies took tea in the afternoon and did their artistries—crocheting, needlepoint, reading, or painting.

Biting my lip and feeling as if I were new to the world, a young girl again and not a woman in her late-thirties, I snuck to the door, taking the heavy cold handle firmly in my hand and turning it so I could enter silently.

Everything was right.

Every part of this world was right.

Scents of fresh-baked bread and musty furniture hit me as

the indoor air made its escape, rushing past me.

Piano music softly played from somewhere in the house. Maybe one of the servants was practicing.

I knew Anne Elliot had two sisters: Mary, the complainer, and Elizabeth, the wretched snob.

Mary would be at Uppercross with her family and Elizabeth wouldn't be practicing the piano, not unless she was on show for some wealthy prospect. It could have been Anne, but she was busy no doubt, undertaking the family's misfortune. For that was where the story started, in the midst of the Elliot financial ruin.

When I closed the door, I sighed, contented in a way I hadn't been in years. The reason I hadn't been peaceful didn't cross my mind.

Nothing more than exploring and seeing everyone interact crossed my mind.

"Anne!" a shrill voice shouted into the silence.

Footsteps, not thumping ones but hurried nonetheless, sounded above my head.

"Anne! Lady Russell has come!" The pitch and disrespect in the tone suggested it was Elizabeth shouting. When I left the parlor, I paused, seeing Lady Russell at the base of the stairs with a servant and an elderly woman in a fine riding dress.

Lady Russell was exactly as she should have been. In her late forties or early fifties, with perfectly coifed hair and a sharp look to her eyes. She was dressed just so and forcing a soft smile on her lips.

Elizabeth was also what I had expected to find. She had a pretty face but a disdainful smirk on her lips and an apathetic temperament. As if nothing pleased her. Her hair was styled suggesting she might attend a ball later, but in truth she wouldn't be leaving the estate. Her dress was fancy for an afternoon of lying about, seemingly her attire did the boasting of their fortune for her.

Her eyes drew to mine, narrowing as she forced something of a pleasant smile to her lips. "Cousin Jane, did your turn about the garden serve its purpose? Are you much refreshed?"

"I am," I answered quickly. Of course. When we'd loaded the book, we added Jane, the cousin. In every book, the person enjoying the story from my machine was named after the author. In this case, obviously, I was Cousin Jane. If this were *The Shining* my name would've been Stephen or Stephanie. If I were a boy in this story, my name would've been John. The side character always ended up becoming the important person in the tale, taking over for the actual main character. In this version of *Persuasion,* I was Lady Dalrymple's daughter, which meant Elizabeth and Sir Walter Elliot would both vie for my approval and time.

But I could choose how I acted.

So instead of tolerating any more of Elizabeth or Lady Russell, I turned and gazed up the stairs for Anne. I suspected us to be fast friends. She was a girl of common sense and a kind heart.

When she got to the landing she smiled politely at us all, curtseying. "Lady Russell, Cousin Jane. How are you both?"

"I am well," Lady Russell spoke quickly, taking the space in which I was meant to reply, and then attempted to offer me a kind expression but failed. The hawk eyes ruined her smile. They were sharp and knowing. Judgmental, as they should have been.

"Oh, I'm well as well." The sentence sounded stupid. Though not very good at it, I was improving on my accent with every word, thought or spoken.

"Shall we all take a turn about the garden before tea? The sun is warm today." Anne wasn't pretty. She was all-right looking, if I were to be completely American about her appearance. But she was so kind that her genuine smile lit up her face and improved her looks.

"I just came in, but I'd love to meet you out there."

Elizabeth gave me a stare. "Have you come to a decision on whether you will join us in Bath?"

"As you mentioned before, Anne will be needed in Uppercross. Therefore, I will go with her. Thank you. I wish to see more of the countryside."

Her jaw dropped in horror, but she quickly snapped it shut

again. "Of course." She turned and gave Anne a smug expression. "I did forget to pass along a message. Mary has taken ill again and requires you there. Thus, you will be going to Uppercross to remain with her until she is quite better." She started up the stairs, pushing past Anne. "After you have bid our farewell to the tenants and secured the house, of course."

Lady Russell's jaw tightened, but Anne's did not.

"I will remain and take care of that with you, Anne. And then I will go to Uppercross and care for Mary if you wish to go to Bath." I said it because staying behind meant seeing the story unfold, and I desperately wanted to be a part of that.

"There is nothing for me in Bath. I would rather for a small house nearby. Your company shall be an added pleasure." She smiled wider, as if that were possible.

"Excellent." I was truly excited, despite Lady Russell trying to kill me with her death stare.

Chapter Six

Sir Walter Elliot, who turned out to be exactly the man I had imagined, a complete knob, waved at us from the carriage as they drove off.

"Strange that Mrs. Clay is with them to Bath. A simple widow of no fortune or connection. Unlike your father to be in such company," Lady Russell murmured, maybe thinking I didn't hear her mean-spirited words.

"She is Elizabeth's companion of choice." Anne shrugged it off.

"Over her own sister? I have to say, I find that discourteous in every way."

"I find solace in that she will be distracted and forget I am in the country still," Anne chided and gave me a look. "I have to close up the house and then we may leave."

"I am at your disposal. Tell me how I may assist you."

"You are too kind. Will you stay and meet with the new tenants of the estate, Admiral and Mrs. Croft? They will arrive at any moment and if I hurry I should be done bidding farewell to the others by this evening. When you are finished, bring the carriage to Lady Russell's and we will carry on to Uppercross from there."

"Of course."

Lady Russell's narrow jaw dropped. Of course, she had

expected to be the one to meet the new tenants.

Anne hurried, convincing Lady Russell to join her for at least part of the day, bidding farewell to their many tenants.

The impulse to choose a path in the story hit then.

I couldn't be sure what it was, but something called to me from outside at the same moment as something else called to me from the front door.

My adventure was letting me choose an outcome.

Turning, even though my post was the front door, I left through the parlor in the back of the house and walked into the garden.

My feet drew me across the lawns to a hillside.

The warm wind cooled, picking up enough to rustle my hair loose from the braids on top of my head. I contemplated going back but whatever called me from the hillside was too strong. It would surely turn out to be an important part of the story.

And I most likely wouldn't miss anything important. From where I stood on the hillside I had a full view of the driveway. I would see the Admiral and Mrs. Croft arriving five minutes before they did.

My steps lengthened, and after a few moments I was running, in a dress and shawl and the most uncomfortable shoes in the history of footwear.

When I reached the top of the hill, my breath hitched as I took in the spectacular view of the entire valley opposite the estate.

It was three hundred and sixty degrees of beauty.

I spun in a circle to experience it all until I grew dizzy and slumped to my knees in the soft field.

I didn't know why I had been compelled to come here until I saw the view. Surely this was what the effort was for.

But then I saw him.

I would have recognized him anywhere. We'd based the character on an actor I fancied.

He wasn't astride a white horse or even in his navy uniform. He was a regular man in a top hat and dress clothes that resembled a suit but with weird Regency pants and very tall boots. They were riding boots which made me think a horse might be nearby.

When he took the hat off and narrowed his gaze to see me better, I lost myself. He had the most dazzling blue eyes and beautiful face. He put the hillsides and estate to shame.

The way he strutted, as if he had a cause to saunter over with swagger, was mind-numbing.

My jaw dropped and my heart raced. Even with my mouth wide open, I could get no air. He had become everything in a matter of moments—footsteps.

His dark-blond hair, tanned skin, and plump lips caught my stare after the haunted quality of his own gaze had already claimed me.

He stopped mid stride and sighed. "Oh, I'm sorry to be so forward. I mistook you for someone else."

"It's all right. I'm Em—Jane Dalrymple. A guest of the Elliots."

"I know that last name. Your mother must be the viscountess, Lady Dalrymple."

"She is."

"I'm Captain Wentworth, Frederick Wentworth. I'm sorry to have approached you thusly. I—it was most ill-mannered of me, and I swear I *am* a gentleman. I mean to say, there is one in here, somewhere." He smiled and I gulped. "But I honestly believed you to be someone I am well enough acquainted with to be as bold as this."

"I'm Jane." I knew I'd said my name already but the smile that crested his perfect lips distracted me.

"Yes."

"Captain Wentworth, Mrs. Croft's brother?" I didn't know what else to say. He was too handsome.

"The very same. Do you know my sister or the admiral?"

"Yes—no. They're coming to let my cousin's—Anne's estate. I am to meet them in the yard." I struggled with words and his beauty and the fact I didn't speak this way even when I was alone and doing my best British accent with Lola.

Lola.

Her face brought with it memories. Thoughts I'd not had in some time.

Lola.

The fire.

Jonathon.

"Are you unwell?" He interrupted my suddenly distracted thoughts as I glanced around us, checking for Jonathan. I should have checked for him when I arrived but the desire just hadn't been there.

"I need to get back to the house. Your sister will arrive any moment." I turned and ran down the hill, hating my shoes increasingly with every step. Why did I write this into the script? Why didn't I let women wear Tieks?

"Miss Dalrymple, wait!" He ran after me.

When we were in the yard again he caught up, stopping next to me as I eyed the door and feared with all my heart that the man I loved more than anything was standing in the house, peeking around a corner, watching and waiting. "Allow me to escort you." He chuckled and breathed, heaving his words. "Please."

"Thank you. But I must go."

"Perhaps, since my sister is arriving any moment, I might also wait inside?" It was a dodgy thing to ask in that era, but I nodded, completely agreeing to his coming inside and chasing off my ghosts.

I had to stay focused. I had to show them the machine was sound and people like me could use it. Once.

He opened the door for me and we walked inside.

Suddenly the inappropriate thing we were doing hit me.

"Tea?" I asked nervously.

"Yes, thank you."

I hurried away from him to find a servant. When I did, I ordered the tea and snuck back to where he was. Lurking around the corner like I was his ghost, I watched him as he gazed at the paintings and furnishings. His nose wrinkled when he viewed the family. I couldn't help but laugh at that. Seeing Elizabeth and Sir Walter, I might have done the same thing.

He glanced back, noticing me. I popped from behind the corner, like an idiot, and took a deep breath and forced myself back into the room with my literary crush from about the age of thirteen. He truly was the absolute best a man could be. Making him a look-alike of one of my celebrity crushes might have been a mistake; I was giggling and grinning like a fool.

"Where are Miss Anne and the rest of the family?"

"Her father and horrible sister—" I paused and winced.

"It's not a crime to admit to one's true feelings, so long as the recipient of those feelings is not nearby. I shall share mine to make you feel more at ease. I too cannot bear them, either of them. To be in this house, except to relish the knowledge that they can no longer afford it, is more painful than anything imaginable. How incredibly dreadful is that?" He sighed and lowered his gaze. "They have never shown me kindness and I cannot be the bigger man, I'm afraid. Perhaps I lied when I said a gentleman lurks inside me."

"Bath," I blurted.

"Bath?" He wrinkled his perfect nose again.

"Sir Walter Elliot and Elizabeth have gone to Bath."

"Anne hates Bath."

"She's here. With me."

"Here?" His eyes widened.

"Not in the house now. She's visiting tenants. We close the house up today in anticipation your sister and her husband will take possession immediately."

"I see." He sighed. "That is likely for the best. I took a jaunt in the fields above the house in hopes of seeing my sister already in the garden." He said it in a way that made me suspect he wasn't telling the truth. Not the real truth. It was his version of why he'd been there. No doubt the one he'd chanted when he was walking up the hillside.

"Of course." Had Anne been the one to take a stroll in the field she would have come upon him and maybe the entire story would have come to its end right then and there. She would have seen him, been weak and showed him that she loved him. He might have returned the love and there would have been no need for the full tale.

As it was, this was a lucky turn of events.

I had been the one to see him. He had used me to get into the house and be near her. I knew this was the same as my using him as a distraction so I could prove my machine was safe, even for a person like me.

The sound of the carriage arriving at the house ended the stare we were stuck in, both thinking of another person.

He was the best sort of company to be with, someone who understood your distraction was because your heart was split. You had one half while the other piece remained with the person you loved where it was unintentionally brutalized.

"It sounds as if my sister has arrived," he spoke softly, nodding his head at the hall behind us.

"It does," I agreed.

He smiled weakly, not for me but through me.

That was how we saw each other, we didn't.

It was rather perfect for a moment.

Chapter Seven

Blinking into the dreary weather through the window, I longed for something so wrong.

It wasn't necessarily the captain.

It wasn't my husband.

It wasn't even the distraction from regular life.

It was the fresh feeling of being alive.

The story lingered, killing off whatever curiosity I had over the machine and my dead husband, and created a need to live again. Not just any life but the one I wasn't brave enough to live out in the real world. A life I didn't think actually existed out there.

I sipped my tea, hating that it tasted so plain, like every other aspect of my existence. In the story, tea came with fresh-made scones, hand-churned butter, and honey from the apiary out back. It all tasted the way my first-ever cup of tea tasted. I had it in England, at Harrods, fifteen years ago and used that experience to frame all tea in the stories.

But it wasn't simply the food and drink. It was everything about the meal.

The conversation was soft and pleasant and the food was rich and flavorful. The tea was dark, like the dismal day staring back at me through the window, only it was bold and robust.

Not dreary at all.

No, every aspect of that perfect world, the one I'd created, was bliss. Even if I ended up having tea with the Crofts and Wentworth, it wasn't awkward or uncomfortable. It was lovely.

I blinked and realized the phone was ringing. I didn't know how long it had been. I turned, answering with a fake smile and suppressed agony. "Hello?"

"Dr. Hartley, how are you?" Dr. Brielle appeared cheerful and fresh faced.

"I'm well, Dr. Brielle. How are you?" She was the only one I actually liked of the team investigating my machine. Liked, as in could imagine being friends with.

"Very well. I'm calling to let you know the inquiry into the machine is completed. You will be notified of the outcome soon." She smiled wide and I knew the answer, not from the smile but the stony look in her eyes. The smile was faked.

"The mayor won?" I couldn't believe it and yet couldn't believe I honestly thought Lucid Fantasies and I would be given a fair chance.

"I don't know, just that the outcome will be presented soon. The other reason I was phoning though, was that I was hoping to book a session on the machine. I was hoping to come in and have a chat about that." She swallowed hard, still trying to convince me that she meant no harm, but at the same time warning me of something I couldn't see or guess at.

"You wish to run through a book again?"

"Yes, much longer than last time. The two hours went by so quickly." Her eyes widened, again as if she was trying to tell me something.

"Of course. After you complete the two-hour trial you are permitted to try four hours. When would you like to come in?" I spoke as politely as I could but the strange stare in her cold eyes and the quiver in her soft voice told me this conversation was not to be trusted. Maybe she was not to be trusted.

"Is this afternoon clear?"

"Of course. I'll meet you there in an hour."

"Very good. I'll see you then, not to do the run-through but to try to pick a better-suited book for myself. Cheers." She hung up too quickly.

Something was off.

It didn't stop me from going to meet her.

I put on my raincoat and boots and kissed Lola goodbye, ensuring my dog sitter had read the message I sent. If something Machiavellian were lurking behind the appointment, I needed my dog cared for.

When I got to the office, I opened the blinds and turned on the heat, setting up shop like I normally would every day.

I gave everything a quick wipe and made sure the diffuser was plugged in. The soft scent of lavender was helpful to the sleeper. Also, it masked the scent of the old building.

I waited for an hour but she didn't come.

An hour and a half passed as I sat in the window, staring out at the droplets of rain hitting the puddles it had formed. My eyes darted to the machine several times, narrowing and contemplating putting myself into it, but I was stuck on who I could get to observe me. Dr. Brielle came bursting through the door. She locked it and leaned against it, soaked from the rain and winded.

"Dr. Hartley, you have to believe me." She gasped. "I had no part in this."

My heart thumped wildly as I shot up from the chair. "What is it?"

"The mayor is having the equipment seized. The inquiry was never a review. Dr. Williams and I were unaware at the time that Dr. Dalton was only here to assess the equipment, as in what benefit it could have in a military setting. The government is going to come and take it, seizing it under the protection act. It's bullshit." She sobbed without crying. "I booked the appointment to warn you. They'll be here tomorrow. They don't know I'm aware of the whole thing."

"My God."

"I was working early this morning, I always come in later. But today I didn't. I was in the coffee room when Dalton took a phone call in the hallway, speaking about the seizure of your equipment. I asked Williams if he knew anything, and he said the review was over and it sounded bad for you. He hinted that he'd just realized Dalton has been on the mayor's payroll from the start."

"Of course he has." I slumped, wanting some of this news to be a shock but none of it was.

"You have to remove this brilliant equipment and get out of here, away from Manhattan even. If you can." She glanced back at the door. "I need to get back. I will try to message you if anything else happens. I'm so sorry."

"It's not your fault."

"Nor yours." Her eyes sparkled with knowledge. "I know about the mayor's unhappy wife. Everyone does. She married him under duress, sort of how all decisions are made around him."

"She did?" I hadn't heard this story.

"You didn't know?" Her eyes searched mine. "Her family has a bakery. The building isn't worth anything but the land is right in the middle of a development prospect. Her parents refused to sell. Someone made their lives miserable, trying to coerce them into selling it. Suddenly, Lana marries the mayor and her family's bakery is protected. The building, though not quite suiting the parameters of the designation, became a heritage building and the development moved to another part of the city."

"I did not know that." My heart ached for Lana, even if she was suing me.

"Everything works that way for him. He's a bully and a criminal." Dr. Brielle scowled, her eyes revealing so many emotions, flashing one after the other. "Take care of yourself, Emma." She turned and unlocked the door, rushing back out into the rain.

I locked the door again and turned, plotting the removal of all my equipment and exactly what I would need to bring with me to protect my work.

It was going to be a long night.

And it was.

By the time I had everything packed into the back of

Marguerite and Stanley's SUV, I was exhausted.

"Thank you for coming to help." I offered Stanley a weak attempt at a smile as he closed the back door of the vehicle.

"Emma, I can't believe this shit."

"I fucking well can! I want to kick that pig mayor in the balls!" Marguerite blasted Stan and me. "The thing I find the most disgusting is that the scientific community joined in on bullying one of its own, and then allowed the government to plan to steal the technology to weaponize it. Or at least under the guise of weaponizing it. The government has officially gone too far."

"I agree." Stan wrapped an arm around his zesty wife as she frothed.

"And another thing, who the hell does he think he is, blackmailing some poor girl into marriage? What a psycho. How do New Yorkers not know this story?"

"I don't know." I sighed, exhausted beyond the ability to converse. "We need to get going though." I glanced behind us, checking the alley for spies, something I'd been doing all night long.

I never moved the chairs or any of the large equipment, just the computers and tablets and robots. I didn't need anything else. With my equipment gone, the space resembled every other dental office. What it had been when I came upon it. From the windows, it still looked like my office. The desk and chairs and magazines remained; only the important technology was gone. It fit into five boxes, not even large ones.

All my work, technically, could have fit into one box, but I had the equipment for four beds.

The drive out of Manhattan and across New York to Rhode Island was long—long enough to contemplate what my next step would be.

Arriving at the old house my dead husband's aunt left him, the one I'd never stepped foot in before this moment, made the question of "what next?" even more convoluted.

Did I dare to stay here, hidden and alone in the country like Miss Havisham? The house would have perfectly suited a pale old wig with ringlets and a tattered wedding dress. Or did I hide the equipment and return to the city to boldly face my enemy?

I needed to think on that.

I was bold, but also tired.

"Dear God, what a hot mess." Marguerite gave me a horrified stare. "You can't stay here. This place looks like an old insane asylum. I didn't even know there were old Gothic country houses out this way."

"It's been in Jonathan's family for over three hundred years. He was the last child in his family, so of course it passed to him, and now me."

"And never a stick of updating," she muttered and climbed out when Stanley parked.

"Em." He gave me a look. "Honestly. You can't."

"Let's just take a peek inside." I chuckled, pretending I wasn't terrified. "I think there was some updating done."

"Does it come with the ghosts or are they added into the purchase, like a sofa or table?" Marguerite joked.

"I suspect the ghosts are part of the security system." I pulled the old-fashioned key from my bag, a cut key with no microchip.

"How quaint." Her eyes darted to the old key.

"The locks are fifty years old." I sighed and put it into the lock, twisting once until it clicked, and turned the old handle. The house gasped, like a crypt unsealing as I opened the door.

"Spooky, Em," Marguerite whispered.

"Super spooky," I agreed and crept inside. The moonlight barely touched inside the house through the dusty old windows. What the beams of light did reveal didn't calm our fears, if anything they got worse.

Dust coated everything that wasn't covered in an old white sheet. Cobwebs and leaves were scattered about, making it all appear much worse for wear. The level of disrepair made the old house Jonathan and I were fixing up seem brand-new.

This was truly disturbing.

I flicked on a light switch, preparing for the old wiring to spark and light it all on fire, losing a second home.

But instead, it switched on, adding a soft yellow light to the room and creating more shadows than the old house needed.

"Not sure that helped things." Stan nudged past us and started removing the white sheets. "This is too scary. We need to get rid of these." He dragged them off quickly, making a pile on the floor. Marguerite and I didn't move. I didn't think I could.

Once the sheets were removed, we both stepped farther into the room, closing the door, and began to help get the lights on.

A trip around the main floor to turn on lights, revealed what the old mansion really looked like.

It was actually quite magnificent.

A grand sweeping staircase with a dark wood banister, the kind you could slide down if you were a kid, was part of the huge foyer. The large double doors were made the old way, thick and heavy. They creaked, telling a story of another time.

The windows were ancient and barred, in the old Tudor fashion, and covered with heavy drapes. I pulled those down, getting Marguerite to help me.

Dust filled the air, making the rooms hazy.

The wallpaper-lined walls were done to accent the room's décor. It made everything feel rich, but old money, where the wealth was all tied up in land and not available cash.

The wooden floors had marks etched into them, like drawings done to depict the times the house had been through. The furniture suited it all, heavy and expensive but not a taste people had anymore.

Jonathan's aunt Muriel had died a year after we were married. The house sat empty from then on, years of silence with the odd groundskeeper to check out the inside and power.

"This place is huge. It'll cost millions to fix up." Marguerite had made her mind up on the old place the moment we drove in.

"Maybe." Stan shrugged. "But it would be worth tens of millions if done nicely. What's the acreage?"

"Twenty," I muttered, glancing about, wondering about Jonathan's family.

"Yeah, tens of millions. The square footage has to be close to six thousand. Three on each floor, maybe four."

"Ten thousand." I turned to him. "Five thousand on each floor and a basement, but I don't think they ever fixed it up. The two top floors were modernized in the seventies."

"You can't talk about modernizing and then say seventies. That's nearly sixty years ago." Marguerite rolled her eyes. "It's settled, you're coming home with us."

"I have to pick up Lola after we hide the boxes."

Stan nodded. "I'll grab them. You girls figure out the creepiest place in the house to stash them." He left out the creaking front door.

"Honestly, Em. You should sell this monstrosity." She sneered and started searching for hiding places.

I wanted to agree. I really did.

Chapter Eight

Lola gave me a nudge as she whined and glanced at the door again. She didn't hate being at Marguerite and Stanley's house the way I did. They had kids and a backyard. They had the sort of life dogs needed. The sort of life I think I once whispered to her that we might have.

I hadn't been certain about kids until we bought the old house. Jonathan had always wanted them, but I wasn't sure. Then we got the old fixer-upper and something shifted. I found myself staring at the bedroom next to ours, planning on fixing it up but not to be the guest bedroom it was intended for. No. I saw yellow paint and animals lining the walls and a blue ceiling with clouds and a sun. And maybe a son. Or a daughter. Or maybe both.

I saw things, promises I had made to myself and to Lola and to Jonathan. Promises I would never keep.

Stanley and Marguerite's kids were the closest thing Lola would ever have.

I got up and let her outside to run about. She adored the huge yard and different smells and the cracks in the fence where she could bark at the neighbors for even daring to step a foot into their yard. Technically, they didn't have a yard. Their yard was an extension of Stan's, an extension of Lola's.

She was a bossy little thing.

It was one of my favorite things about her, the savage beast in tiny packaging. She feared nothing and everything and overcompensated for it all.

I stayed a week, taking up space and time and needing more than I helped. I hated being in a guestroom and being a guest. Maybe because I hated guests. I assumed everyone did as well.

On the eighth day, I packed my bags and called a cab, needing my own space and time.

"Leave the dog," Marguerite offered, not asking me to stay longer. "Don't go back into the city with the dog. She likes it here and we don't mind having her, to play with the kids. She's so good."

My dog was easier than I was. She didn't sit and stew on the predicaments in her life. She didn't stare at paintings and get lost. She didn't scratch itches that weren't real or long to be somewhere else.

"You sure you don't mind?" I did the obligatory thing. Leaving Lola would be easier, since I was going back to my apartment and wasn't sure what I would find there. I imagined the mayor would be sitting outside in his limo with his guards, his henchmen. They would grab me and place a black bag over my head. I would be carted away like in the old movies.

"No. God. The kids love having her here. And honestly, she spends too much time alone in the apartment. You're always having to hire someone to take care of her or put her in dog daycare. This is better." She hugged me as though she was ending the conversation, deciding for us both.

"Thanks. I appreciate everything. I'll come back for her once I have the apartment settled. I need to get it on the market and make some serious decisions." I squeezed her back, almost scared to be leaving. Her house had become a bit of a haven, even if I hated being a guest.

"We love you, Em. You know that."

"I know." I waved as the car arrived and carried my small bag out of the house. I hadn't packed much to leave with, wanting my apartment and office to look the same, as if I hadn't run off. I had even planted fake computers that were never used by me for anything. They were laptops of Jonathan's. I'd wiped them to sell but hadn't gotten around to it. They ended up being the perfect decoys.

Anything of value, anything that carried my work, was hidden with Miss Havisham's ghost at the old mansion.

The ride into the city was dreary, as always. Late fall was cold and wet and gray. It was my favorite season. Watching things die off had become a bit of a delight, like I wasn't so alone in that respect.

I got the cab to drop me off three blocks from my apartment, certain I would need to survey the area before committing to going up.

As I made my way to the apartment, I switched my phone back on, noting Dr. Brielle never messaged me back. In fact, I had no missed messages, not even from clients.

The shop had been closed long enough that people weren't calling anymore.

That saddened me.

Their joy had been my food, and I was malnourished and suffering from this famine.

The cars driving up and down the boulevard appeared to be regular traffic. Nothing stood out as parked with people inside watching the building. No vans or anyone lurking around corners. It appeared to be a normal Wednesday.

I went in the side door, one I never usually entered through, and took the stairs to my floor. I was winded by the time I made my way onto my floor.

The hallway looked and smelled the same as always, a mixture of the people living here.

My heart raced, my palms sweat, and my stomach ached, but I walked as if I'd done nothing wrong, head high and shoulders back. I took a deep breath as I slid the microchip key, listening as the lock opened itself as if I'd said the password.

When I opened the door and stepped in, I flinched, waiting for it.

But nothing jumped out.

The house had been gone through, there was no denying that. Everything had been opened and searched, but it wasn't in ruin. There was no real mess or chaos to it. I would close the cupboards and drawers and pretend none of this had happened, apart from the violated feeling, of course.

I closed the door and leaned against it, hand on the handle, ready to open it back up and flee. Holding my breath, I listened.

But no one moved.

Just as I sighed, relaxed and safe, a woman with messy dark hair and a dead look in her eyes strolled from the back hall. "About time you got back." Her voice and face were so altered I might not have recognized her. But there was no mistaking the huge ring on her finger.

"Lana?" I gasped. She had bandages on her wrists and needle marks on her thin, pale arms. "What are you doing here?"

"Waiting for you." Her words were soft, not angry—heartbroken or exhausted maybe.

"If your husband knew—"

"I left him. I filed for separation and hired a lawyer." She nodded, wiping away a tear from one of her eyes. "He's going to ruin my parents' bakery but they don't care anymore. They just want me away from him." She held up her wrists. "He faked my suicide." She started to laugh like bits of madness were slipping out. "Like I would be so averse to dying."

"Oh my God." My words were barely audible.

Her vacant, cold eyes darted around the room, making me wonder if she was on drugs or had actually escaped the mental ward. She itched her arm, scratching a scab, answering the question of drugs. "He's a monster."

"I know."

Her dodgy eyes met mine and we shared a moment before she spoke, "You're the only person I trust."

"Why? What about your parents?"

"You were the first one to see him, to know what I've gone through. You know me better than anyone."

"And I have the machine you're addicted to." I said it boldly, calling the spade in her pocket what it was. Because I was bold, even if I was tired.

The dead look in her eyes didn't change as the smile crept across her lips. "There's that."

"Was it you who rifled my apartment?" I scanned the area, careful not to leave her gaze for too long.

"No. I came after his men. They were here a week ago. I knew you wouldn't hide it here. You're a genius. He underestimates you." Her creepy grin remained. "Cocky arrogant men do that."

"I can't help you. The machine is ruining you."

"The machine is saving me." Her eyes lightened faintly. "It wasn't so hard for Marshall to convince the doctors I might have cut myself. Or that I might have wanted to kill myself." She scoffed. "I would never cut myself—I hate blood, but the doctors don't know that. I did take something a few times, before."

"You've tried to kill yourself before?" Jesus, did she lie through the entire questionnaire?

"Before I met you, I would check into a wellness center in Palm Springs every single spring. I hated watching everything coming back to life. All the things that had been dead with me all fall and winter, were reborn, leaving me behind. After the third time trying to die, I realized I couldn't spend spring with him. I needed something else. I went to the center in Palm Springs and stayed there, sitting in the rain room and taking antidepressants. I did that for years before I met you."

"I had no idea." Her depression rang true for me. In my own ways, I understood her sickness and hatred of spring.

"Of course you didn't. I made sure you didn't. The first time I went into your machine, I was looking for a miracle and I found it. I was cured; I felt alive for the first time again. At first it was me and Rhett and Ashley. We danced and had fun. Then one day, I saw Danny. He was watching me. We danced and laughed and he took me to his house, and we made love. I came out of there knowing that if I could get a small dose of it, I could get through whatever being married to my oaf of a husband could throw at me. I never took drugs again. I never took anything to hurt myself. I never went back to the center."

"You made love?" I cringed outwardly. "How is that possible?" I hadn't mentioned the no-penetration rule I had for the system. I didn't need to see people getting off more than they already did in the machine. Women weren't necessarily the problem, but I still had a no-sex rule.

"I don't know, we just did. It was magical."

"What changed? What made you sad again? Every time you left in the last few months you looked sad."

"The baby." Her eyes sparkled, coming back to life. She smiled and was herself again, like the old her but dirty and filmy and still slightly tweaked out. "In there, in the machine . . ." She paused and tapped her head. "I was pregnant, but I would come out and it wasn't there." She touched her belly. "I was just me again and the baby was gone."

"Baby? Impossible." I said that word too much around her. "You can't change the storyline that much."

"I did." When her eyes met mine again they were clear. "I had a baby in me and a husband who loved me and a life. Yes, it was hard to leave every day, but I always went back." She blinked and tears rained down her cheeks. "I told myself coming out of the machine was like going to work."

She had found a way to manipulate the nanobots?

My brain did laps, trying to figure out how the story could change so drastically and how I could have missed such a large problem.

"Take me with you. Please." She pled with her gaze.

I didn't know if it was the baby, or the fact I wanted to see how she did it, but I nodded. "Let me get some more things and money. There's a place we can go."

I should have told her no.

I should have regarded the insanity in her eyes.

I should have called the mental ward and reported her.

I never did do the things I should.

Chapter Nine

She was silent on the first train and the second.

I wasn't even certain she was breathing in the cab. She made no noise.

She was eerily quiet when we rolled into the small town a couple over from the one where my house was.

She didn't even ask a question when I got a second cab to take us to the next town over, or a third one to drop us two blocks from the house.

She didn't complain when we hiked the two blocks in the pouring rain or when I opened the old iron gates to the estate where we would be staying.

She walked up the driveway, eyes steady and face soft, without uttering a single word. I unlocked the gate and stepped up to the porch to open the front doors, swinging them wide. The house didn't gasp this time. It was ready for us.

The maids, who I'd hired, had cleaned it to the point that the filth was gone and the wood shined, but nothing would fix up the old look or feel. The furniture gleamed from the wood polish and vacuuming but the decor was still fifty or more years old.

The fridge was filled with food and drinks and the dishes were all washed and ready to use.

It would have to do for now.

Lana strolled about, analyzing or exploring, I wasn't sure

which, while I called and booked a realtor and stager to take on my Manhattan apartment. I gave up my lease on the dentist office that was likely being raided at that very moment.

I wasn't going back, not for a while.

Then I turned off my phone and went to get the equipment.

In the dark room of the basement where it was, I crept through the shadows the dim lights cast. As I grabbed a box a noise startled me. I spun, jumping when I saw Lana staring at me with her dead-fish eyes and mussed hair.

"I thought I would see if you needed help." She said it so flatly, I wasn't sure if she was being real or if she'd quickly come up with something while getting caught spying on me, plotting my death.

"Sure." I pointed at a box. "Grab that one and I'll grab this one. We don't need the other boxes right now."

She moved with no emotion or purpose. Like a zombie.

We carried the boxes upstairs to the top floor, to the bedroom I had designated the one we'd use for the machines.

I plugged the equipment in and glanced back at her.

She was staring at the glass container of nanobots, marveling maybe at the bright blue light that shone from within them. It reminded me of a bright blue lava lamp, only the nanobots had capabilities beyond the average human's comprehension. Apparently, also beyond my comprehension.

The glass container was pressurized and controlled by a compartment below, run on batteries that didn't require changing. The microscopic robots had been programmed to always keep their population at a set number, reproducing as they needed. Them and the container would outlast all of us. It was a genius invention, one I'd always admired.

I grabbed the second container, the sirens, and placed them on the dresser next to the others.

Once I had it all settled, as close to set up as I was going to get in the small room, I plugged in the lavender diffuser and closed the drapes. I lit a candle, creating dim lighting so I could watch her but not have it bright in the room.

"Thank you, Emma." She shook slightly as she spoke, her voice cracking. Her eyes had come to life again.

"Don't thank me, Lana. I'm going to experiment on you. This is a business transaction, nothing more. I'm paying you in trips inside."

"As long as I go inside, I don't care." She lay back, offering her veins, like a heroin addict handing over her arm. "I just need to give birth to this baby."

Seeing the mess she was didn't give me pause. It should have.

I hooked her up to an extra machine this time, using the old software I had from when I created Lucid Fantasies. It allowed me to track her, to explore with her. The nanobots would report back with visuals but also send signals from the different areas of the brain, showing the stimulation the experience was creating.

She took a deep breath, squeezing my hand like we were old friends, which in some ways we were, and then closed her eyes.

I sent her in, putting her to sleep, and watched the screen of the old laptop I hadn't used in ages.

My belief in my product had been blinding.

Sitting back, watching her nanobots start their journey, I expected the initial reaction. They sped for her dorsolateral prefrontal cortex and hooked in but something gave me pause. I sat up, watching the code popping up, realizing a small part of the cluster had strayed from the herd. They headed into a different part of the brain as if they were commanded to. Each nanobot moved with speed and efficiency as though heralded to the cerebral cortex.

My stomach clenched as I watched her run her own show. Her dreams were her creations. Her mind had evolved, not the nanobots.

She wasn't a zombie, she was a puppet master.

She had experienced them so many times she had changed to suit the skill set they offered.

She had a need and unconsciously solved the problem.

"No," I whispered, certain this was impossible. This level of long-term use wasn't something we'd tested against, but we hadn't thought we needed to. Everyone dreamed. Every single day people dreamed. They daydreamed. They read books and watched movies and imagined things. It was never hazardous. However, a forced dream, inside a forced world, apparently could potentially create a problem, as shown here.

I watched, in half horror and half fascination, as she used the nanobots to her advantage, masterfully creating the world in which her heart lived.

At the six-hour mark I brought her out, desperate to ask questions. She woke much the same as the last time I had put her in. She was partially awake and still stunned. I ran the sirens call a second time, forcing the biosensors to commit suicide. I made a note to up the dosage and the length of time the siren's call ran for Lana.

"Tell me how it works. I want the full explanation, from start to finish. How it feels going into the world and what experiences you have while there. I need to know what you recall from being there, what memories are formed, and how they exist in your mind. Be detailed." I grabbed a pen and paper and turned my laptop camera on, recording the conversation.

The screen image was fuzzy from the dim candlelight, but she nodded as she sat up. "Okay." She sounded different, still detached but less depressed.

The gloomy creepy-looking woman, who had hidden in my apartment for days on end, was gone. Old Lana was back.

"When I go in, it's dark and peaceful. It's quiet for a moment, like the world is building in front of me but I can't see it yet." She shuddered, wrapping herself in the blankets. I realized there was frost in the air when she spoke, and suddenly registered that I was frozen solid. I turned on the gas fireplace that likely used to be a wood-burning fireplace but was converted in the eighties.

She breathed softly, continuing the story, "Then it loads, all at once. I'm blinded and overwhelmed. I see everything, maybe too much for a second, and then it's normal. Wherever the story was when I left, it takes off from there. So now, my baby is about to be born. I'm quite pregnant. Danny's worried I won't survive labor.

He doesn't understand that this world isn't real and that he's dead." She chuckled.

"Sorry, what?" I cock my head, certain I've misheard her.

"I'm pregnant—"

"No, I got that part. Did you say the story takes off where you left it, exactly? Like the book is loading where you left off, like reading? Or the story you're creating is taking off?" The system was designed to allow a traveler to experience a book in chronological order, but this sounded like she was off story, big time.

"I haven't been in the book for ages. We finished it off and then created our own."

"So you aren't Cousin Mel, having a baby?" I gulped.

"No. Mel died. I am me."

"Margaret?" The character I created for *Gone with the Wind*, named after Margaret Mitchell.

"No. When we left the storyline, when I saw Danny and was able to connect with him fully, I stopped being Margaret."

"You chose to stop being Margaret?" My insides felt like water. My mouth dried completely as I tried to understand this.

"Yeah." She smiled, pleasant and calm. My insides threatened to burst all over the room and my brain was ready to explode, but she was calm.

"You weren't distracted by the novel?"

"No." She shrugged. "I mean, I was. It lasted like the first couple of weeks, I don't know. But then I thought of Danny and I stopped living in the dream. I found him and started playing a new storyline out."

"And from there, every time you enter, you are taking off where you left off?" I felt numb.

"Yes."

That was impossible.

"But you're present, you know you're in a story and it's fake?" I couldn't get a handle on this.

"Of course. It's just like living out a fantasy, one where I get to have everything I ever wanted."

"Is the story still set during the Civil War?"

"No." She wrinkled her nose. "Too violent. We changed it a while ago. Different setting. I decided on the sixties. He has a job as a salesman, and he goes to work in a blue suit and an old car. It's new to us though."

"We. Us. What the fuck?" I stood and paced the room. "Why do you even go into *Gone with the Wind?*"

"I assumed the control is part of that storyline," she answered hesitantly.

"We need to see. Lie back." I hurried to the machine, starting *Shawshank Redemption*. It was nowhere near *Gone with the Wind*, and I couldn't imagine Stephen King would be as easy to stray from.

She went in once more, her brain repeating an identical response as some of the nanobots strayed from the herd and went directly to the cerebral cortex again.

I let her stay in for an hour before pulling her out. Again, she was a zombie before I sent the sirens call a second time.

"Well?" I asked impatiently.

"Story took off the same as last time."

"Didn't the book load?"

"It did but I stopped it and made my world."

"Impossible," I muttered, stumped and yet fascinated.

Chapter Ten

"You're certain you understand?" I asked her again as I lay back, scared of her inability to work the machine.

"I've watched you hook me up hundreds of times. I could do this with my eyes closed!" Lana snapped.

"Right, but that's sort of the part I'm worried about. You aren't exactly the queen of focus."

"No, but if you don't come back, I won't be going back in, will I?" she snarled.

I parted my lips to continue arguing but paused, seeing her point. "Okay then. Don't let me die in here. Four hours, no more no less." I lay back, fighting to relax.

"I don't want you staying in longer than four hours. I want my turn," she growled and pressed the buttons, starting the procedure.

We'd gone over it a dozen times once I realized sending her back in wasn't ever going to lead me to the answers I needed. She was too far gone from the book and couldn't trace back her steps. I needed to go in and see if I could control the changes myself. You had to break it to fix it. I didn't want it to be me, but we couldn't risk the repeated exposure to another person's brain. Plus, finding a candidate like us, one who had suffered a great tragedy as far as lost loves were concerned, wasn't going to be easy.

It had to be me who went in, looking for the moment I would gain control of the story.

I expected it to be a flash or a second where the Choose Your Own Adventure lost its spark.

As I entered *Persuasion* again, the story started right where I had left it, the same as a favorite book I had put down.

The world loaded with me smiling at Admiral and Mrs. Croft as I was leaving the Elliot estate after having tea with them and ensuring they had everything they needed.

I paused, lost for one heartbeat before I lifted my hand and waved. "So lovely to have met you both." I glanced behind them to the captain, offering a slight smile. "And you as well, Captain."

"The pleasure was all ours." Mrs. Croft waved, clutching her handkerchief in her other hand. "Do visit again. The invitation is open."

"I shall. And as I'm just going to Uppercross, I suppose we will see more of each other."

Captain Wentworth bowed as the carriage left, taking me to Lady Russell's home to pick up Anne.

She hurried out of the house, all flustered and blotchy but not letting on as to what was wrong. "Sorry for my delay, Jane, dear. I'm finally finished. All our obligations have been met." Her eyes glossed over ever so slightly as she blushed again. "And were you able to meet with the Crofts?"

"I was. They're unpacking and settling in nicely."

"Lovely. I am grateful you could help with that." She said it so softly I nearly missed it.

As the carriage was one of the open ones, a barouche, it was bouncy and noisy, providing the perfect distraction. We didn't have to speak which was a nice break. Polite conversation was like modern-day small talk but with thoughtful pauses and intention. It got downright exhausting thinking all the time, especially aloud.

In our silence, my eyes darted about the forest, expecting Jonathan to pop out from behind a tree or bush, but he didn't.

We made it all the way to Uppercross just as my butt was getting sore. Men greeted us as we stopped, helping us down.

Several offered me the eyes, the ones that suggested I could take a roll in the hay with them if I so fancied. Never having been a hay-rolling sort of girl, I ignored the men and the slight option of the Choose Your Own Adventure. A romantic tryst with a stable boy had to have been a fantasy for some women, which was why we loaded it. With a fade-to-black ending of course.

"Anne!" Two awkward-looking girls came rushing down to us from a large house. Both had hands out and warm greetings for Anne.

"This is Henrietta and Louisa Musgrove, Charles' sisters. And this is my dear cousin Jane Dalrymple."

I curtseyed as they did, just deep enough.

"Dalrymple?" Henrietta's bright-blue eyes widened.

"Yes, I assume you know of my mother, Lady Dalrymple."

"Indeed." Henrietta's wide eyes glanced at her sister. "A viscountess. We are honored. You must come and meet our mother."

"Yes, she will be pleased you have both come," Louisa gushed.

"Of course. We will but please excuse us to see to Mary first. We will be along shortly, I'm sure." She turned to the small cottage to our right, next to the stables and then to me. "Jane, if you prefer, you are welcome to go up to the big house first."

"No, I long to see Cousin Mary again." I grinned, glancing at the girls. They snickered, and we all agreed at the ridiculousness of Mary, silently.

The girls hurried off, running back up to the big house as I followed Anne into the small cottage.

When we got inside I cringed at the smell and disorder of the home. Mary was lying on the couch, sleeping with a plate of half-eaten food on her stomach. She looked a mess.

"Mary, are you quite well?" Anne rushed to her, playing the doting sister.

My eyes drew to the windows as I scanned the courtyard for my dead husband.

But he didn't come.

"Anne? My God, what are you doing here already? I'm hardly prepared for visitors, I'm unwell, can't you see?" Mary moaned.

"Shall I make some tea?" Anne asked softly.

"Surely not. Though I haven't seen them yet, even in my state, we should have tea with the Musgroves."

"They've been by. You were sleeping." I couldn't help but say it.

"Cousin Jane, what a lovely surprise. I wasn't aware you'd be joining us."

"Hello, Cousin Mary. I'm sorry you're not well for my visit."

Her eyes narrowed. "The rest has revived me. I am quite well enough, I suppose, to go up to the big house." She handed her dirty plate and cup to Anne who took everything to the table for the maid to clean. Mary just barely got herself up, dramatizing the effort it took.

I disliked her more than in the book. I disliked manipulative people.

When she had her hair repinned and her dress brushed of crumbs, we started the slow walk up, Mary required, to the house. She was lazy on a whole new level. I was surprised she wasn't fatter.

"How are Father and Elizabeth?"

"In Bath with Mrs. Clay, a widow."

"Mrs. Clay?" Mary's eyebrow arched. "Elizabeth's companion or Father's?" She grinned wickedly.

"You're awful. Of course Elizabeth's. She's not anyone of importance," Anne mocked her father, not Mrs. Clay. I understood that. But Mary didn't.

"No, of course not. A baronet cannot allow for such company," Mary sneered, sounding like all the Elliots, except Anne. "I suppose I will have to visit them, I should really take the waters for my health." She popped something into her mouth and began chewing. I hadn't even noticed she brought food for the short walk.

When we got to the big house it was chaos: dogs barking and Mary's boys running around, hopped up on sugary treats, and everyone was gushing over Anne.

Mary stood in the corner, getting sicker and sicker as the seconds went on. I realized how much it must bother her to always play second fiddle, even with her own husband, Charles. He rushed to Anne, hugging her and kissing her on the cheek, lingering just a second too long.

No one paid Mary that kind of attention.

As they all spoke quickly and laughed loudly, I took my chance to gaze around the manor, searching for a pair of dark-blue eyes and lips I could still feel pressed against my own.

But Jonathan was nowhere to be found.

At tea, news came of dinner. The Crofts would be attending, as would the eligible Captain Wentworth. Anne paled at the news, appearing more uncomfortable than I had ever seen her. The Musgrove girls and Mary squealed in excitement as I sat in a corner having tea with Mrs. Musgrove, a kind and gentle woman.

"And as the cottage is so small, we were hoping you would be comfortable enough to stay here in the big house." Mrs. Musgrove spoke to me softly, obviously trying not to slight Mary in any way.

"I would be delighted."

"We have a lovely guest room and I've instructed the maids. They will ensure you won't need for a thing."

"Please, don't go to any trouble on my behalf. I am honored to stay with you." I gently placed a hand on hers, truly grateful. Besides the daughters trying to put on airs, something I assumed they did to annoy Mary, the Musgroves were lovely people.

After tea, we readied for dinner at the big house. Mary and Anne went to the cottage to ready. It took hours to get cleaned and dressed and have hair done.

As the sun went down, screams poured across the large yard between the house and cottage. I watched out the window, as torches were hurried over to the cottage. Of course, I knew the part of the book we were at. Young Charles, Mary's son, would have fallen from the tree, dislocating his shoulder.

Anne would stay with him, not seeing Captain Wentworth.

The rest of us would dine with the captain and his sister.

I felt bad for Anne, knowing she longed to see Wentworth, the same way I longed to see Jonathan. And Wentworth definitely wanted to see her.

At least he and I would forgive each other and tolerate the poor behavior and elusive stares filled with secrets that we inflicted on everyone else.

When my ladies were done with me I looked like a perfect Jane Austen character. My pale blue dress with a wide neckline and string of pearls reminded me of *Emma*. I suspected we had gotten the costume design from that movie.

I left the room, anxious to see the Crofts and the captain again, but also curious as to why I hadn't seen Jonathan yet. He hadn't even tried to come to me, or I hadn't conjured him the way I imagined I might have.

The dining hall was decorated for the dinner party with dishes of appetizers lining the buffets. I stood with my back to the fire, warming myself against the draftiness of the large manor home.

"Miss Dalrymple, you look lovely." Mr. Musgrove entered the room with a soft bow.

I curtseyed and smiled. "Thank you, sir. As do you."

"What, this old thing?" he joked, waiting for the laugh I tried not to let sound forced. "Can I interest you in some of my mulled wine? It's an old family recipe. Some say it's the best they've ever had."

"That would be lovely. Thank you."

I adored the dance that was civility but also the language of the time that we used. We didn't have it perfect, we didn't steal any of Austen's lines, but we tried to come as close as we could without confusing our modern patrons. The level of comprehension had decreased over the years. As technology got smarter, people relied on it more. It did our thinking for us. Common speak in 2026 wouldn't have been understood by people of Austen's time. Unfortunately, they were smarter even though we knew more. It was proof that knowledge was not intelligence.

"I won't be but a moment." He hurried away, fetching

someone to get me a drink.

As he left the room, Captain Wentworth entered. His bright-blue eyes landed on mine, forcing a smile from my lips and then his. "Miss Dalrymple, how lovely to see you again."

"Captain, please, call me Jane."

"If you'll call me Frederick." He bowed, as he got closer.

"I haven't earned my title except by being born, but you however have. I will address you as Captain, and you will address me as Jane. Please." I was firm and kind. I didn't want him getting the wrong impression. I was here for Jonathan—*no,* scientific research. And Jonathan. And the captain and Anne had to end up together.

"As you wish." His eyes twinkled with delight, not lacking the haunting expression they held earlier, but doing a better job at attempting to mask it.

"As you wish" was my favorite line from *The Princess Bride.* Wentworth saying it was swoon-worthy.

"Are you enjoying your time in the country?" I asked politely.

"I am. It's been a pleasant trip. My sister adores the house and gardens, it's . . ." He flinched. "Insensitive of me to be saying that, of course. Forgive me."

"Nothing to forgive. I'm sure Anne will be grateful that the house is being well cared for and loved. Your sister is a sweet lady. I'm certain it's an honor to have her there."

Wentworth's eyes widened. "Yes, well. I need to be more careful. I would hate to offend either Miss Elliot or Mrs. Charles Musgrove." He stepped next to me, warming himself by the fire as well. "And are you enjoying your time in the country?"

"Indeed. Very beautiful countryside."

"It is." He sighed, perhaps as uncomfortable with small talk as I was. "I haven't been here in so long. The sea has been my home this many years."

"Do you miss it?" I asked.

"No. And yes. I love the sea. No sailor worth his salt would dare travel her if he did not. But I am grateful to be ashore." A grin toyed with his lips or vice versa. "It's time for me to settle into a real life."

"Have you found a suitable match then?"

"No. I am at leave to match with anyone who will have me." He laughed.

"I hope I'm not being too forward in saying this, but Anne has mentioned your prior engagement." I glanced at him, offering empathy and hopefully friendship instead of obligated flirtation. "I was very sorry to hear it ended the way it did."

"You and I both." Wentworth's jaw clenched. "Her family's misfortunes have been perfectly timed, if you ask me. I haven't wished it upon them, but to see such a reversal of fortunes, so to speak, is all the irony I need."

"But you must still love her." I couldn't believe he would be so cold. "Surely there is a chance that the match could be rekindled."

"Love?" His expression changed from annoyance to anger. I had crossed a line. "Absolutely not." He bowed. "Excuse me a moment." He hurried from the room and I felt awful for prying.

He didn't come back, making it even worse later when we all had to sit at the table and his eyes didn't meet mine.

The night went by quickly, spent eating and drinking and laughing. When I excused myself to snoop through the back halls once more, in search of the ghost I was haunting, Captain Wentworth cut me off in the hallway.

The tense expression on his face had been drunk away, replaced by a charming smile. The one that made my stomach tense. "I shouldn't have spoken to you that way. You've been nothing but kind to me and I was rude in return."

"The fault is mine. I pried. I'm sorry."

"No, you acted as a friend would. You asked me if I loved her, since you wish to see your friends happy. I did." He walked closer, swaying slightly and leaning on the wall across from me. "In the beginning, all I thought of was being enough for her family. I ignored my heartache and pushed myself, trying to be a man they would approve of. I loved her then." His eyes glistened, telling me more of the story.

"I know your loss and I am sorry for it." I wished I could tell him how she still felt.

"How could you? Women cannot know a man's heart or pain."

"I was married once. A long time ago." I couldn't believe I was speaking of it, I never did.

"Was?" He furrowed his brow and I realized what I'd said. The daughter of Lady Dalrymple was never married, and I wouldn't be called miss if I were.

"In secret. It was an imprudent match," I lied. "I married in secret and he died before anyone knew." The lie rolled off my tongue too easily.

"I did not know that." He scowled. "Though I would not have; I am afraid I have been at sea for far too long to know the comings and goings of the city." His words turned to a whisper, "I am truly sorry for your loss."

"And I for yours," I offered quietly. "Please do not speak of my previous—"

"It will never leave my lips." He bowed softly. "And I am honored you trusted me with it. What was his name?"

"Jonathan. Jonathan Hartley. He was a lawy—barrister," I quickly corrected myself.

"If I'm not being too bold, might I ask how he perished so young?"

"Fire." I told two truths and several lies. Jonathan was never a lawyer but how did you explain PR executive?

"That is a tragedy." His gaze softened. "You do know my heart, perhaps better than I do." He pushed off the wall and sauntered down the hallway, away from me.

In the dark I stayed, alone and regretful of the lie I had created in this world. But I was certain I'd done it, I'd changed something, making it my own. I sensed the difference as I was pulled back, home.

Chapter Eleven

I sat in the window, sipping the tea, wishing it were more.
The day.
The tea.
The emptiness inside me.
The companionship.
All of it lacked true and exquisite flavor.
Even my pain was more in the machine. More colorful. More agonizing. More depth.
The tea might as well have been water and the broken heart might as well have been a splinter.
"Did you notice any changes in the story inside this time?" Lana asked as she sipped her tea.
"No," I muttered, realizing I'd forgotten she was even here. "I changed something though. I felt the change. I told a lie that wasn't part of the story and I created something new."
"Oh yeah, that happened a lot to me in the beginning. Trying to be normal and fit into the story but then saying things that made sense in the real world, but not in the book. I did that until I didn't have to. Pretty soon the lies I told became the world around me." She yawned and rolled her head as if her neck had a crook.
"You did?" I forced myself to hear what she was saying. "You

lied until it became true?"

"Of course. It was hard at first, keeping up with all the lies. But then the world sort of changed, like it was using the lies to make itself."

"Interesting." I contemplated that. Lies were known to create a different blood flow in the brain, causing more activity in the prefrontal cortex. If the rogue nanobots attaching to the cerebral cortex were somehow linking in with the imaginative and deceptive parts of the brain, the story could be changing from the lies. I'd read a thesis a few years back claiming that lying was made easier as the subject lied more and more. The emotional connection to the lie, the guilt, and regret eased off as the liar detached and the blood redirected, almost feeding the lies and starving the emotions. Lies got bigger but the liar felt less when lying.

Perhaps that was the difference in the story, and now that I had talked about him, I'd created him in the world. Maybe Jonathan would appear.

"I'm going in before you today."

"What?" Her eyes narrowed. "You can't. You know I'm in labor, right? The beginning stages. I've been having contractions for a day."

"Fine. But six hours, no longer," I conceded too easily. Not for her, but for me too. I told myself she was the addict. She was the one who needed it. I was just trying to figure out the fault in the machine.

And that was the truth, even if my motivations weren't entirely scientific.

"Have you ordered more food?" She puzzled as she stood and strolled toward the fridge.

As I parted my lips to answer, I paused, unsure. "I don't know."

"It's hard to separate eating in there and eating here. We should get protein bars and shakes and meal replacements. It's only sustenance we need, not meals." She wrinkled her nose at the open fridge door. "And this is dire. We're down to the veggies and fruits."

"I'll do it now." I grabbed my tablet and went to the store's website, ordering our usuals as well as her suggestion—a month's supply of protein and meal replacement foods. Eating inside the machine made it so I didn't crave food out here. In fact, I wasn't hungry at all.

The possibilities for the machine helping with weight loss for obese people fluttered around in my head. I had never thought of it, but Lana and I were both losing weight we didn't have. She didn't fill out her clothes the way she used to. Her hair didn't have the luster it once did.

Vitamin deficiencies were likely the culprit. I added vitamins and minerals and oils to the order. We needed to stave off scurvy and bone loss at this point.

"They'll deliver this afternoon, around three. We'll make the break between you coming out and me going in then."

"Three?" Her eyes widened. "You're going to go in at four for six hours? You'll come out at ten at night?"

"Yes, it means you'll have to stay up later than eight," I remarked.

"Fine. I hope you added coffee and tea to that order."

"Always." I chuckled. Coffee and tea was where most of my daily caloric intake came from.

"Marshall messaged me again. My parents' bakery closed today." She said it to the fridge, not looking at me.

"I'm sorry, Lana."

"I'm not. I'm not buying into his threats and blackmail anymore. My parents are retiring anyway. They sold the land to the investors, making a small fortune, and bought an inn in Virginia. They're going to have a bed and breakfast."

"We should visit them sometime," I offered before really thinking about the repercussions of something like that. How would we go into the machine if we traveled?

"Maybe." She nodded half-heartedly, obviously she also realized we wouldn't be able to use the machine. "I sent my lawyer the signature on the final amendments to the separation agreement."

"Will Marshall fight you on this?"

"Of course. He hates losing and a divorce is so public. I'm hoping he'll offer me a buyout to go away quietly." She took a bite of the apple she had pulled from the fridge and closed the door. The apple was past its peak, slightly wrinkled.

She handed me one in identical shape. I ran my fingers over the puckered skin, smoothing it out. "And what if he comes here?"

"We call the police, directly. We don't try to deal with him. We're taking the necessary precautions. The gates are locked. Our IP is diverted through several routers. We keep our electronics off except when we're sending messages and then turn them off. We don't talk to anyone apart from the grocery boy. What else is there to do?"

"Sell this old house and move somewhere far enough away that he can't reach us." I shrugged.

"He's got friends everywhere. This is our safest bet. We're out of state." Her eyes narrowed. "If he comes here, it'll be to take the machine away. He blames it. We need a backup plan for that."

"Okay." I nodded, taking my first bite of wrinkled apple.

She was right.

As she entered the machine after breakfast, I sat in the dark room, going through my old emails by candlelight.

When I found the one I was searching for, I read it over and over, saddened by the fact I was even considering it.

But this was a new place for me, a new low and high. It was something I had to consider. The changes in my landscape and expectations forced it. I pressed reply as a knot in my stomach twisted.

Answering the email was easier than I thought it would be, but sending was harder. My finger lingered over the "send" button, unable to press down. I was betraying myself. I was a traitor to my beliefs. I was selling my soul to the devil.

Lana stirred slightly, her heart rate lowering. I reached up and touched her arm, settling her with human contact. Without thinking, I exhaled and pressed "send."

It was what it was now. I'd agreed to a sale.

I was no longer the person to blame for the machine or the person who would be robbed when the mayor came to take it.

The technology would go to the highest bidder, and we would be left with the machines we currently had.

It was a solid deal, one I'd never considered before this moment.

Chapter Twelve

The carriage ride to Captain Wentworth's home, an addition to the story I wasn't sure if I'd created with my lies or if we'd written it into the storyline, was new to me. We should have gone as a group to Lyme, but we were going to Wentworth's, a home I didn't know he had.

Mary sighed and readjusted herself for a fifth time in a matter of minutes. "We must be nearing the house." She leaned forward and glanced out the window.

Cramped in the small carriage with the sound of horse hooves around us, I glanced at Mary and the Musgrove girls. "Why didn't Anne come?" She hadn't offered me an explanation, just that she didn't feel up to traveling. To hear her complain was odd and obviously a lie to avoid coming. I didn't know who had created it, Anne or me.

"She was unwell. Said she didn't feel up for the trip. She's off to Bath in the morning to see Father and Elizabeth." Mary yawned. "I'd say she made the right choice. This must be twice the distance to Bath." She switched around again, visibly annoying Louisa.

"You could have also stayed behind, Mary," Louisa muttered.

"You know very well I can't be without Charles. It's awful for my condition to have to shift for myself, alone in that cottage."

She said "cottage" like it was the worst word in the world.

I smiled gently at Henrietta and then glanced back out the window. The murky stains made seeing through difficult, but I noticed all the glass in England was like that.

Men shouting interrupted our awkward silence, making us all glance out the window on the far side from me, seeing what I had to assume was our destination. It was massive and creepy, clearly based on Sir Walter Scott's home in Abbotsford. I blinked and wondered if we'd added this to the story. The house was a favorite of mine. It was odd that this would be the house Wentworth lived in.

But my memories of the architecture of code and creation felt a million miles away, locked behind a haze I couldn't muddle my way through. The fact this was a story was becoming jumbled.

I made a mental note of that and hoped I would recall it all when I woke.

The moment the carriage stopped, we all groaned climbing out. My butt had never hurt this much in my life. My hips and joints ached as I forced my way from the tiny opening. I swear the carriage got smaller the farther we went.

The Gothic estate was better up close than anything I'd ever imagined. My eyes danced across the brick façade and staircases leading to gardens and patios.

We were surrounded by lush gardens filled with purple heather and carved hedges in strange shapes. One side of the shrubbery had a long path where the stone wall had repeating arches with vines crawling up them. The staircases did as well. But the home was clean and neat. Everything was tidy, even the gravel. Benches lined the pathways, providing places for ladies to sit and enjoy the sun.

The uneven rooftop was trimmed with small turrets and gables.

Wentworth beamed as he dismounted and turned to us. "Are you ready for the ride to be over?" he asked us, jokingly. He'd been in an increasingly better mood for days.

The four of us ladies nodded, ready to be as far away from

the carriage as humanly possible.

He offered Louisa and Henrietta his arm as Charles offered Mary his. I strolled behind them, gaping like a fool who had never seen a magnificent home before.

As we entered the large archway leading through the front door, my breath hitched.

"Are you ill from the ride?" Charles glanced back at me.

"No. I just adore architecture."

"I see." He chuckled.

I wasn't behaving as a lady of stature would, but I was stunned by even the entrance. As a Gothic revival of the late eighteen hundreds, the house couldn't be more wrongly placed in the story, but I didn't care. It was beautiful.

The ornate fireplace of the entrance hall captivated me as we were led past old suits of armor, family crests, and hunting trophies. When we got to the staircase and hallway, I got lost. There was too much to see, too many books and paintings and ornate tiles.

"If you wish to freshen up after the ride, Mrs. Humboldt will be happy to show you to your rooms." Wentworth nodded at us all expectantly.

"I don't need to freshen up," Louisa exclaimed boldly. "I want to explore. Is there a dungeon?"

"No." Wentworth half laughed.

"I am exceedingly exhausted," Mary remarked to the old lady awaiting our decisions at the bottom of the stairs.

"I would prefer to freshen up as well." I gave a soft smile to the old lady.

"As you wish. Follow me, please." She started up the stairs, moving much faster than I expected.

"Your things will be brought up," Wentworth added as he left us and disappeared down a dark hallway. Louisa and Henrietta giggled and ran off down the hallway we had come in.

The candles and lanterns weren't bright enough to light the house to the extent modern electricity would have, but the dim glow added to the spookiness of the corridors and dark wooden décor.

Shadows danced in obscure corners and along the hall where closed doors created mystery as we were hurried along the upper floor.

Mrs. Humboldt stopped at a heavy wooden door with a skeleton key in her hand, unlocking the large latch with a click. I was terrified to enter the room, scared of what she had locked in or if she was locking something else out. "This will be you, Miss Dalrymple."

But when I got inside the doorway, the daylight flooding through the massive windows took all the creepiness away.

The giant four-poster bed and ornate furnishings made the room too beautiful for me to be scared.

I crossed to the bed and climbed in, lying on my back and wondering how the days spent here would play out. If we would rest or ride or adventure around the gardens? I imagined the food would be sumptuous as the home was, rich and overly done.

Wentworth's history worked its way into my mind.

Was his family fortune meant for someone else when he asked Anne to marry him all those years ago, or did he come into money beyond what he had made in Spanish gold? The house was something he wouldn't have afforded before becoming a captain, and yet he had just landed back on shore. It was confusing but there was no way to ask him. I would have to discreetly ask the maid.

I snuggled into the feather bed, feeling blood begin to circulate back into my legs and butt.

I would have to live and die at this house. I was never getting into another carriage.

When I was certain I had spent enough time refreshing, I got up and forced myself to leave the haven of my new room. I didn't need refreshing, my hair wasn't budging, not with the amount of pinning it had required, and my dress looked exactly the same, well starched.

I crept along the corridors, slowly turning handles and feeling a bit like I was in the wrong story. This was much more

Northanger Abbey than *Persuasion*. But my lie must have altered things.

As I explored the entirety of the top floor, I found one door that wasn't locked. I turned the handle, my heart racing when it didn't stop at the latch. I pushed the heavy door open just a crack, taking a small peek into the room. It was furnished as if a man who needed very little lived here. A simple bed and bureau and two small candlesticks.

"Can I help you?"

I spun, gasping when I saw Wentworth hovering over me. His stare was intense, angry even.

"No. Sorry."

"Were you snooping?" He cocked his head, not removing himself from the path I would have to take to get away from him and this room.

"I was." I confessed, feeling foolish. "I was confused."

"By all the locked doors that you have no doubt tried?" His eyes sparkled, not with anger but with something else.

"Indeed." I burst out laughing.

"I inherited this house from an uncle with no sons, only a few months before we were to come ashore. I had not seen it since I was a boy, and all my belongings were brought here well before I was. I had never met a single person on staff beyond Mrs. Humboldt. I gave her strict instructions to lock everything up and only allow staff in certain parts."

"You thought your staff would rob you?" I furrowed my brow.

"I did. Why would they be loyal to me? They don't know me." He grinned after a moment of us staring too long. "And now I am to be mocked for wanting security?"

"You are not." I laughed again, making him smile. For such a gloomy man, his smile lit up the dreary space where we stood.

"You are laughing, madam."

"I was just surprised. I never would have imagined a servant robbing someone. I would think it hard enough to find employment, let alone keep it."

"I suspect that is a wealthy person's prerogative to assume

servants cherish their employment. But having been a servant in the crown's navy, I know bitterness and entitlement can breed in any set of circumstances."

"Will you keep all the doors locked so I have to find secret passages to complete my snooping, or will you allow for the doors to be opened?" I said it with the necessary hint of sarcasm required. "The curiosity of what lies beyond is likely to kill me."

"We can't have that. I shall give you the grand tour, if you like."

"I would love that. And just so you're aware, I adore old houses and creepy stairwells and secret passages. I wish to see it all."

"Of course you do." He laughed. "And as I am as in the dark about the house as you, we shall have to hire out the tour to a proper guide." He offered me his arm.

"But there's a door already open." I pointed to his room.

"Oh yes, be my guest. Have a look. Shall I wait out here so the invasion of my privacy is satisfying to you?"

"Please do." I grinned and entered the room, adoring the creak and groan of the heavy door as if no one had opened it this wide in ages.

The room was stark of clothing and furnishings, just a bed and a bureau. The window was dusty and the drapes tattered. There was far too much space, suggesting a need for more fixtures. The fireplace seemed so far from the bed, I doubted any of the heat from it would be felt.

"I think this is the worst room in the house," he spoke loudly from the shadows of the hall where he remained. "So naturally it's mine."

"Commonplace for wealthy people to improve their private room last. The rest of the house is open to the public. Logically, they would want to update places that are seen first, giving the impression the house was entirely beautiful."

"That makes sense and yet it does not comfort me to know I will be sleeping in the forgotten room." He acted genuinely wounded but I was sure he wasn't.

"You, who slept on a ship you described as barely fit for service, sharing your cot with other men and somehow survived?"

"Indeed. You were paying better attention than I believed." He chuckled, stepping into the room. I spun, meeting his gaze, both of us smiling. In that moment, something happened.

It might have been the way the dim light of the gray day hit his face or the way he smiled at me with that gleam in his eyes. I might have been that we had spent so much time together, talking and laughing and building a comfort I'd never known with another man.

Whatever it was, in that moment, my heart began to beat again—not the normal heartbeat one required to survive, but the one that fluttered and suggested I felt things I wasn't certain of.

"Shall we continue this tour before we have to explain our activities?" His smile suggested our actions would be frowned upon, as if there was something to them. A hint of feeling that neither of us was admitting to but also not denying. We spoke of it in looks and stares and side-glances that might not have been intended to be seen.

I had obviously ignored the feelings until this very moment, maybe distracted by it all. And now they were in my face and they were written on my face and they were controlling the heart in my chest.

I forced a calm smile across my lips and walked to him, taking his arm and pretending I didn't feel the heat of him next to me or the way my fingers trembled.

He walked to the stairs, shouting down them in the least gentlemanly way I'd ever seen him act. It was a common thing to do in one's house and yet completely uncivilized and lazy. "Mrs. Humboldt!"

"Sir?" She popped her head out from around a corner down the hall from us.

"We'd like all the doors in the house opened and a tour if you have a moment."

"Of course." Her eyes widened and she hopped to it, rushing to the doors, clicking open each metal latch and cracking the door for us. Silver light from the cloudy day slipped into the halls, revealing dust dancing on the subtly moving air inside.

Each room had a fire lit and a repeating theme: bed, bureau, and wardrobe. The windows were dusted and the drapes beaten.

Each room smelled of furniture polish and age.

When we made our way back to the housekeeper on the stairs after seeing all the upper floor's bedrooms, Wentworth narrowed his gaze. "And the secret passages?"

"What's that?" She didn't speak to him in the same manner as the housekeepers at Uppercross or Kellynch Hall did. She must have known him before coming here.

"Out with it, old woman. I know you know." He didn't speak to her the same way any lord of the manor did either.

"I've warned ya about calling me old woman." She turned on her heel and headed for the master's suite. "Are you coming?" She hurried down the hall and turned right when she entered the room, disappearing.

Wentworth and I hurried after her but paused in the doorway, confused.

She popped her head out from a wall that was made to look like it met the brick of the fireplace, when in truth there was a slight gap, enough for her to squeeze through. "Hurry up then. I haven't got all day."

Wentworth's eyes were wide when he escorted me to the gap and allowed me to go first, after the housekeeper. I glanced back nervously as I slid between the wall and brick.

He barely fit between, making a scuffing noise as he dragged himself through. When we arrived at the landing of a secret staircase, the narrow hall opened up.

"I had no idea." He spun in a circle. "Is this an escape route?"

"Aye, in case the house were to be invaded. Each room has one, a door behind the fireplace. The stairs all lead to the other rooms." She pointed at the many tiny staircases shooting off this one. "And this hall leads to the courtyard at the right of the house, nearest the stables."

"Fascinating," I muttered and walked to the other staircases, climbing one of them. When I got to a solid brick wall I grinned and pulled the unlit candlestick on the right, snapping it off the wall.

"What are ya doing?" Mrs. Humboldt shouted and came up the stairs behind me, pushing on the brick and opening the door. She snatched the candlestick from my hand and hurried off again, headed back down the stairs.

The room was mine, as I suspected it might be.

"Is this your room?" Wentworth asked, making me jump. I hadn't realized he was behind me.

"Yes." I laughed, clutching my heart. "It is."

"I like this room the best. The view of the arched wall is stunning."

"Did you come here often as a child?" I asked as I spun, inhaling sharply when I realized how close he was.

"A few times. I never imagined it would be mine. My elder brother, Edward, should have inherited. But he passed away while I was at sea. Just after my uncle did. I arrived home to a new house and all my belongings being shipped off." A haunted smile crept across his lips. "It was fortunate the house came furnished, as my belongings weren't enough to bother bringing the carriage over the long trip."

"What of the lady of the house? Your aunt?"

"Died, many years before. They had only two daughters, neither able to take ownership of the house nor needing it. They married well, both. The house would be a financial burden neither of them needed."

"And now Sir Walter Elliot, who cannot afford his own home and has snubbed you, even though you are in possession of a home that is at the least on par with his, is renting to your sister? What a strange turn of events."

"Indeed." His eyes met mine, making my stomach tighten again. Our faces were too close to be mistaken as anything but preparing for a kiss.

I contemplated whether I should or not, losing the argument almost instantly.

"Are ya coming for the remainder of the tour or shall I leave ya here?" Mrs. Humboldt shouted up at us from the bottom of the stairwell.

Wentworth winced. "Coming." He grinned at me and turned, hurrying down the stairs.

I smiled, enjoying the feel of the heat on my cheeks as I hurried after him.

Of course that was the moment my ghost showed up.

Chapter Thirteen

"You're certain this is what you want?" The lawyer, a friend of my parents from Los Angeles, scowled. "All your hard work going to line someone else's pocket. I thought you were against this."

"I am. I was. I am." I nodded and signed the paperwork without even reading. The only line I cared about was the ownership of the four machines I had developed and currently possessed and no liability over any prior situations. They would have to make their own machines, no doubt they would improve them.

"Do you need money? Your trust—"

"No, thank you, Mr. Bauman. I just want this to all go away. Lana Delacroix has vanished. She dropped the lawsuit and left her husband. The government won't be able to seize the equipment as the patent is no longer mine to protect and the company the complaint was originally lodged against has been dissolved. I am a private owner of equipment which I will keep for personal use only, while the plans have been transferred to a company the government wouldn't dare go after. I was an easy target on my own. I left the schematics of the machines I made for the ALS patients with the research company I used to work for and the government has never come after them. Just me. And only because of Marshall Delacroix. This buys my forgiveness and forces them to leave me alone."

"Sounds like you've given it some thought. But to see such beautiful work go to a massive corporation which will manipulate and mass produce the product, taking away the specialness of it all, breaks my heart. Your father's as well."

"Say hello to them for me." I smiled and signed the last page.

"I will. And I'll have the funds transferred into the account you've given me." He reached across the table in a moment of realness he and I never had before. "Take care of yourself. You look tired."

"Thank you. I will. Say hello to everyone back in LA for me."

"You should come and visit and say hello yourself. The sun might do you good. You're very pale."

"I've been hiding out a lot; hopefully this contract changes that. Regardless, now isn't a good time to come to LA. Mom emailed recently that they'll finish the year in Vienna. Maybe next year." I winked and got up. "Thank you for coming all this way."

"Please, you know I would do anything for your family."

"Thank you." I waved and left the restaurant. It was three towns over from my house and Lana. I was still discreet and careful, after all this time.

Even the old house had been sold to a numbered company Lana and I started. On the off chance something were to happen to me, it would be hers. It and the machines.

Over a year spent together, hiding and going inside the machine and guarding each other, had done a lot for our relationship. She was the sister I never had and the wife I never knew I wanted. We cared for each other. We loved each other. It was something the world wouldn't understand. Not unless they went inside and saw what we did. Experienced what we did. We knew this world was nothing, it was a half life.

The cab rides across the towns, hopping out of one and into another at a slightly different location, felt so unnecessary.

But as we hurried down the empty road in the second town, I noticed a car following us.

My insides clenched as I turned to the driver. "Can you pull over at the library instead? I think I might get some books."

"Sure." He pulled over a moment later, and as the car behind us slowed down, I saw his face. My throat dried and my hands began to sweat. Marshall Delacroix's eyes met mine through an open window.

I paid the cabbie and hurried into the library. Hiding behind the shelves of the travel section, I watched from between the books as he entered, reminding me of a mobster as always. As he drew nearer I saw the wear of Lana's disappearance in his face.

"Dr. Hartley, let's not do this cat and mouse game. I need to speak with you."

I turned on my phone and texted 911 to the number. When it delivered, I turned the phone off again, slipping it into the back of my skirt, in my underwear. The code meant she needed to turn the phone off and hide everything. She wouldn't even unlock the gate until I messaged her again, even if I showed up on the doorstep, she wouldn't let me in, not without the code to tell her it was safe to. She knew this meant that I'd been recognized.

"What do you want?" I asked as I slipped from behind the shelves, eyeing up the librarian who parted her lips to tell us to stop talking. She changed her mind when she saw the other men with the frightening-looking man staring at me with daggers.

"I want my wife."

"Your divorce will be final the moment you sign it. She doesn't want to be with you." I stood my ground, acting unafraid but lying.

"She has been brainwashed by you and that contraption of yours." His eyes narrowed.

"Haven't you heard, it's not mine anymore. I sold it." I wanted so badly to be smug but I couldn't. My hands were pools and the threat of urinating in the travel section was real.

"You think selling your plans and patent changes anything? I have doctors who will claim that you warped my wife's mind and altered her. Specialists."

"There was a clause I added to the purchase agreement. Any lawsuits became the sole responsibility of the purchaser. I am no longer liable for anything that occurred from inception of the machinery to this moment now or fifty years down the road." A little smugness escaped.

"What!" His eyes widened and the violent man he was masking, lashed out. "You deceitful bitch!" He rushed at me, lunging to grab me by the arms and shake me like he had before.

"Call the police!" I shouted at the librarian as he raged.

"You lying bitch! You're coming with me!" He dragged me to the doors but I fought.

The other men grabbed at me as I screamed. "Call the police!"

"Unhand her!" The librarian jumped up, shouting as well, as I scratched and bit, earning a slap across the face from someone. Stars took my gaze as I spun and slumped into the arms of the person grabbing at me. I shook my head to clear it and started kicking again, fighting.

The mayor grunted and clawed at me, hitting the librarian as she reached for him.

"Stop!" a new voice shouted. I couldn't see who it belonged to as my face was covered by a large hand.

"This is none of your concern. This woman is being taken into custody—"

"Let her go and back away, now!" the man shouted.

"I will have your job. Do you know who I am?" Marshall barked as I struggled free, excited to see a policeman with a gun drawn on us.

"I don't give half a shit who you are. You don't come into my town and start manhandling and abusing women. Now back up." The police officer waved his gun at the men.

"Thank you." I started to cry, sobbing with relief. "Thank you." I covered my mouth and sobbed harder.

The librarian, sporting a bleeding lip, crawled to me, grasping my bleeding arm. "You're hurt."

I hadn't noticed my forearm was gushing blood. I didn't know where the wound had come from. I felt the cold phone, safe in my underwear—that was all that mattered.

"You two go to the hospital. It's only a block over." His eyes met mine. "I'll have Stacey, one of our deputies, come and get a statement from you both." The police officer nodded at us as he reached one hand up and touched the radio on his chest, while continuing to hold the gun on the three men. "I have a situation at the library. I need all units."

"You're making a big mistake," the mayor muttered, his eyes making attempts to murder me with his stare as he spoke to all of us. The librarian and I moved slowly, getting more and more distance from the three men with their hands up.

"I need the newspapers as well. Send Andy over. We got the mayor of New York City sexually and physically abusing women in the library." The police officer grinned as he let go of the radio. "Almost didn't recognize you, Your Honor."

The mayor growled as the librarian and I got up, attempting to straighten our clothes and leave with some semblance of dignity. No wonder the police thought it was sexual abuse. My skirt was torn and my blouse was ripped open. I clung to my clothes with trembling fingers, visibly shaken.

I wanted it to all go away. I wanted to pretend it didn't happen. I wanted to get in another cab and go home, but this had to stop.

Even if it meant me being forthcoming about my location and offering an address, I would see this assault charge through.

The mayor would try to buy his way out of it, but this wasn't New York. And these people weren't on his payroll. It wasn't even his state.

I had to have hope that good would win against evil.

Even if this world was mostly evil.

Chapter Fourteen

I sat on my bed, staring at the fireplace and wondering if Jonathan would ever show himself to me. As much as I had desperately wanted to see him, his was not the face I needed.

I was eager to see Wentworth. I wished I could tell him about the horrible thing that had happened to me. I wished he would offer me comfort and protection. I wished he could come out into the real world with me, and maybe even kick the mayor's ass.

Instead, I stared at the brick and waited for a ghost to come.

The house was silent, as everyone else was sleeping.

The candles made for a perfect scene in which a haunting would occur.

Even my crisp white nightgown was exactly what a girl wore when a ghost entered her room at night.

But he didn't come.

So I went to him, certain I would see him in the secret passageway, certain he would be spying on me.

I pushed the brick as Mrs. Humboldt had, making a ton of noise as it slid open, dragging along the floor. I winced and glanced back at the door, hoping I hadn't woken anyone.

It was open enough for me to slide through so I grabbed a candle in a holder and carried it into the shadows.

The flicker of the light danced on the walls as I made my way down the stairs, casting my own shadows.

"Emma?"

I spun, seeing him standing on the stairs behind me, the ones I'd just come down. I must have walked right through him, considering I could see the bricks through him now. "Jonathan," I whispered. He looked exactly as he had the day he died, same clothes and all. My heart leapt at seeing him. It was the moment I had been waiting for all this time.

"You're here?" He scowled. "How?"

"I'm in my dream. I'm in a story where I created you with lies of an ex-husband." My explanation sounded insane. I hadn't thought it through well enough.

"Ex?"

"You're dead, my darling. You died. You left me. I came here looking for you."

"No. Impossible. I would never leave you. I love you." He rushed me, but his hands went through mine. He didn't sound like himself, but rather what I would want him to say to me, what I wanted him to say a long time ago.

How was Danny there for Lana, so real that she gave up everything to be with him, and I got Jonathan the ghost who spewed words like the hero in a romance?

This was not my funny and pragmatic Jonathan. This was not Jonathan but a cheap copy, a version my brain weakly made up to satisfy a lie I told. My own creation.

Somewhere in the back of my mind, fear whispered that my loss and grief and imagination were not the same as Lana's. I couldn't make Jonathan real. Maybe it was the denial. Maybe she had a much better case of it than I did.

Or maybe it was that my rational brain, my scientist's brain, saw through the façade.

"My hands." He swiped them through mine again and again, confused as to why we couldn't touch. "You're a ghost," he spoke softly.

I thought about arguing the fact but then I realized, the story was real to them and I was the ghost in the machine. I was the outsider. "Yes, darling."

"Is this the only time we'll see each other? Is this you saying goodbye to me?" Was it? Was that why, after all these years, I was having the least realistic interaction with my husband possible?

"I don't know." I stared into his eyes, lost in their unnatural glow.

"I came to Sir Walter Scott's house to wait for you. I knew you'd be back. It was your favorite place."

"Of course." The memory I couldn't believe I'd forgotten slipped back in. I'd been here before. I came on a tour with Jonathan once. We came to Sir Walter Scott's house, but we never saw secret tunnels.

That was why I'd linked him to this house—the lies in my brain told the nanobots about this place.

"How are you?" he asked so delicately.

"I miss you." Tears flooded my eyes. So many things were different now. So many things ruined.

"I miss you too. How's Lola?" He chuckled bitterly.

"Well. She's with Stan and Marguerite. They're taking care of her now. She loves the kids and the yard. And my lonely life isn't good for a dog."

"You must miss her."

"I do. I miss you both. I wanted to say sorry. I wanted to try to explain how sorry I am."

"Sorry for what?"

"That I let you go back in. I should have stopped you."

"In where? Did you sell the house?" he asked, clearly unaware of the fire. Unaware of how he had died. Unaware of being dead. Because this was not him and it was never going to be him. That bitterness of truth stung but I forced myself to see it, scared to go backward from it.

"Yeah. I did. I bought an apartment in the city and then I sold it too. And now I'm living in your gloomy old aunt's house. It's creepy and Gothic and sort of exactly what I needed."

"Are you fixing it up?" His eyes widened with delight.

"Yes," I lied. I didn't know why. This wasn't his ghost and the real Jonathan wasn't going to see the house. For some vain and shallow reason, I wanted him to think I was doing better than I was. As if giving away my beloved dog, moving from my cozy apartment, selling my prized company, and living in his dead aunt's run-down mansion wasn't a sure sign things weren't going well.

But this wasn't Jonathan. He was dead.

So dead that I couldn't even make him real in my mind.

I called it preservation and told myself it was because I didn't want to mourn him again. I'd nearly died last time. But I really did want to say sorry.

"I always dreamed about fixing that old house up. I imagined it beachy and more Hamptons than scary with old wallpaper and smelling like dog piss." He smiled. "I'm glad I got to find out you're fixing it up. And that I got to see you again." Was that what he would have said? Or did my mind make him say it? Would he be glad to see me but not be able to touch me? How had Lana made this transition so smoothly?

"Me too." That was true. While I was grateful to see him, even in this form, I couldn't trick myself into believing this was him. I saw this for what it was, my imagination. In Austen's book, I could play along and be convinced of everything. Everything but Jonathan being real. He was a man who made snide comments and joked constantly and laughed when he should have cried. He was something I could not create. I could not fake my way through.

I wished, only allowing myself a second, that he were real, that we could kiss and touch and he would make me smile.

But instead he faded. "I love you, Em. I will always love you."

"I know," I whispered back as he became nothing but a figment of my imagination, the remnants of something once great. I made my way back up to my room, closing the fireplace again and slipping back between the sheets.

I lay for a long time and stewed on how final it all was. Jonathan was dead. He was really dead. He was never coming back. I was never going to see or touch or hold him again. We would never kiss. I would never be able to tell him I was sorry for letting him go back inside. Sorrier than I had ever been about anything.

And while this machine didn't bring back my husband and didn't trick me into believing he was still with me, it had done something else.

This story had saved me the way it had saved Lana, differently though. She was saved finding the man she missed, and I was saved finding joy.

I blew out the candle and sighed, exhaling so many things beyond a bit of air.

When I woke, I felt rested in a way I hadn't in ages. A servant brought in tea for me to drink while she readied me.

"Did you hear the news, miss?" she asked softly, glancing back at the door.

"What news?"

"Captains Benwick and Harville, ma'am, they're on their way. They're coming to stay."

My eyes widened. "They are? What about Miss Anne Elliot? Have we heard anything from her?" I no longer wished for Anne Elliot to join us. She was now competition.

"Just tragedy in the last letter Miss Mary received. A Mrs. Smith has passed suddenly, pneumonia. Miss Anne was devastated and her father was disinclined to attend the funeral, leaving her alone."

"How tragic." Mrs. Smith was the widow friend of Anne's in the novel. She was the one who saved Anne from marrying Mr. Elliot, her cousin. I wondered if she had been able to tell Anne of William Elliot's cruel nature and social climbing ways. Or of his affair with the treacherous Mrs. Clay. "I need to send a letter." I cringed at the thought of interfering, but I also couldn't sit by while poor Anne was heartbroken and ruined by a horrible marriage. She might have been competition, but she didn't deserve that fate. No one did.

"Of course. I'll send for some paper and ink. Or would you rather dictate it?" Her eyebrows lifted in hope.

"No, thank you. I will write it myself. I appreciate the news as always." I lifted one side of my lips in a slight grin.

"Yes, ma'am." She curtseyed and left me.

I went to breakfast, lost in what I should do for Anne and unsure if writing the letter was really a good idea. Wentworth greeted me with a wide smile. "Good morning. Did you hear?"

"Yes, how exciting. Your friends are joining our party." The story was twisting and turning, and I was the one driving the crazy train taking us into uncharted waters.

"I am expecting them this afternoon. Were you made aware of the other sad news?"

"I was. Poor Mrs. Smith. Poor Anne." I sat, picking at some grapes as tea was poured for me.

"And to be there with only her father and Elizabeth to comfort her. It's awful. I had Mary send word that Anne should join our party as well."

My stomach sank. "Certainly. That was kind of you."

"Do you think it sensible of me to do such a thing? I don't want to be misleading in my intentions."

The fact he was confessing this to me was a crushing blow to our obvious attraction to one another. Of course, I should have known he was still in love with Anne, and I should have realized I was nothing more than his friend and confidant. "Yes. In polite society, a respectful invitation should only be considered sent as a courteous offer. No one would think you having ulterior motives beyond helping an old friend." It was a lie but I hoped a genuine sounding one. Surely, Anne and her awful father would believe this to be the rekindling of the relationship between Captain Wentworth and Anne. And now that the Elliots were broke, the captain was suddenly a good prospect.

I didn't want him to think me under an illusion as to our time spent together and what it meant. He hadn't given me reason to believe there was anything beyond companionship in our own personal tragedies. And if the one-sided relationship was nothing more than a crush, I didn't care. As least I told myself I didn't.

Mary and Charles lumbered in, sounding like ten people

instead of two. "What a peaceful sleep, so good for my condition."

Charles rolled his eyes. "Yes, what a wonder it is for one's mental state, being away from one's children."

"The noise of them aggravates my ailments." Mary sat, wiping her noise with a handkerchief before sipping the tea. She wrinkled her nose and added two lumps of sugar, stirring and marveling at the room. "What a lovely breakfast room, Captain. Your aunt had an eye for décor."

"Yes." The captain lifted his brow, amused.

"Are we going to have a hunt when the other men arrive?" Charles asked, taking a large bite of sausage without cutting it. "A hunt would be capital." He spoke and chewed like an animal.

"We shall. I was thinking tomorrow after they have rested. Harville tires easily."

"Right, of course he does."

"And if you don't mind not mentioning the death of Harville's sister, I would appreciate it. It's a sensitive subject for poor Benwick. He loved her so." The captain's eyes darted to Mary's and then mine. "Are Louisa and Henrietta coming down?"

"They've already gone outside for some air." Mary scoffed as if the notion were something disgusting.

"Is Anne going to come?" I asked Mary, half hoping she would say no.

"She is. She'll be leaving Bath within a fortnight. She sent word this very morning that we should be expecting her."

"Excellent." I smiled and sipped my tea. I couldn't shake the displeasure in the news that Anne was coming, even though I had only intended to warn her myself. It was selfish and awful, but I wanted the captain's attention and I didn't want to share it with Anne or the ghost of his feelings for her. My ghost had left and it would seem his was just arriving.

Chapter Fifteen

Wyoming, Rhode Island, 2027

I blinked, staring at the candle and the shadow of her sleeping silhouette against the floral wall. Lana had been in for nine hours. We were testing it, just to see.

Her vitals were strong and her heart rate steady.

The machine was replacing sleep for us completely now. Her nine hours would turn to my nine hours. We would be awake and in each other's company the other few hours of the day.

A noise stirred in the hall.

I lifted my gaze, listening for it again.

The bell at the front gate startled me.

I sent the siren's call to wake Lana up and shot up from the chair, hurrying downstairs to the door. I peeked through the window, confused and wondering if I was hallucinating when I saw who it was. The sound of the bell a second time assured me I wasn't.

I pulled on my raincoat and hurried outside in my rain boots.

"Emma!" Marguerite waved at me through the wrought iron and vines. "You're here!"

"Marguerite, what a surprise." I couldn't lie and say pleasant.

"I tried calling but your phone's off. And you haven't emailed me back. So I drove out, hoping I would catch you here or at least get some clue as to where you were."

"Did you bring Lola?" I asked as I unlocked the gate using the large old skeleton key.

"No. She's with the kids, probably helping the babysitter maintain the chaos that is necessary for my house to run. We've moved, did you know?"

"No." I offered a smile. "I've been so busy." I glanced back at the house.

"Can I come in?" She laughed, hugging me.

"Sure." I hugged back, noting she smelled like perfume and soap.

"When did you get back from England?"

"What?" I scowled.

"You're speaking with an accent." Her eyes narrowed.

"Last week. I was there for a while. I always do that when I travel, pick up the accent. My old nomadic ear." I laughed it off and headed into the house, trying to sound American again. "How is Lola?"

"She's amazing. So spicy. She's a little monster in that tiny body. And what a garbage dog. I catch her in the trash more often than not. I have a video." She pulled out her phone as we got into the house. She paused and it took me a second to comprehend what she was staring at. I turned, seeing it through her eyes. "Oh, Emma." She gasped.

"Sorry, I haven't had the guys by to pick up the recycling. Like I said, I just got back into the country." I smiled, hoping we could move on. But she couldn't. I saw that too.

Her eyes fixated on the piles of magazines, newspapers, and bags of garbage that we hadn't ever taken to our bins. I didn't even know where they were.

The path that led from the front door to the kitchen was lined with stacks of newspapers and garbage bags. I hadn't noticed it in a while. I didn't know when I last had.

The kitchen was a sight as well. Old stained countertops and what appeared to be mouse poop met her as she turned the corner.

She swallowed hard, her fingers twitching and shaking as she flipped over the phone in her hand and struggled to get the video. When she did, I half watched it and her, smiling at my dog tipping over a trash bin and walking right inside, growling at whatever she had found in it. The smile wasn't enough for her. When I lifted my gaze to hers again, I could see that. She was worried.

"What's going on with you?"

"Oh, you know, the usual mad-scientist stuff."

"You sold the company, Em. Your mom called, that's why I'm here. They don't even know where you are. Hell, I didn't even know, not for sure. I came here because I remembered coming here before. And look at this place—look at you!" Tears filled her eyes. "Em, you need help."

"No, I'm fine. I'm doing well actually. I'm doing better than well. Yes, I sold the company to protect myself from the mayor—"

"I saw that in the news, the assault. He tried to sexually assault you in a library with two other men and I found out in the news. Your mother is devastated."

"He did what?" Lana came into the room with the spacey look in her eyes. "Marshall did what to you?" Though we had been together for years, I saw Lana for the first time through Marguerite's horrified stare. She was decaying before my very eyes.

"Mrs. Delacroix? Everyone is looking for you." Her eyes darted to mine.

"We've been hiding, avoiding the mayor." I tried to rationalize it.

"What did he do to you, Emma?" Lana sounded lost.

"He attacked me. He and some of his henchmen tried to get me to come with them, hold me hostage so you would come out of hiding. We were fighting and they ended up ripping at my clothes. So the librarian and the police thought they were trying to sexually assault me. I never told them the truth. I agreed and even gave a statement suggesting I believed they were going to rape me."

"The cut, that day you phoned 911 and said someone

recognized you. It was Marshall?" Lana's eyes flickered to the old faded scar on my arm. "That was from him?"

"Yes." I confessed, realizing how long it had actually been since that had happened.

"Oh, Em, why didn't you tell me?"

"I didn't want to scare you. The police took care of it. I believe he was found guilty." I glanced at Marguerite.

"Yes, he was. And a few other charges they'd been investigating him for. He paid fines and got away with no jail time. Em, you two look dreadful. Are you doing drugs?" Her eyes lowered to Lana's thin arms with needle marks covering them.

"No." Lana laughed. "I'm a diabetic." Her lie was so believable. "I test my blood a lot and give myself insulin."

"This house should be condemned. You can't stay here. You both need to leave." Marguerite's eyes were wide with concern.

"We can't leave." I said it firmly. "We're doing research."

"Research?" Marguerite sounded astonished. "You don't believe that. You don't believe this is research, living like this? Like animals? You don't even take the trash out, you leave it in bags in the middle of the room to rot. The smell in here is ungodly, and I can't decide if it's garbage or you two!"

"Thanks for stopping by." I'd heard enough. She didn't understand.

"Emma! Listen to me! You are dying in this house. Dying! You look fucking crazy! You're gray—not even just pale but gray! You leave your dog at my house for years and vanish. I don't hear hide nor hair from you and then you pop back up in the media after the mayor tries to rape you or kidnap you. You're hiding his wife, just like he said you were. And she looks like a hostage, not a friend. She has needle marks and she's filthy and you're filthy. What the fuck is going on?"

"We're working on the machine, trying to get the bugs out." I tried to sound like I wasn't getting angry, but I was.

"You still have the fucking machines?"

"Yes, Marguerite! I do. I invented them. They're mine. I can do whatever the hell I want. We're not hurting anyone living here.

We don't have kids or spouses. We're two lonely ladies, minding our own business, living alone. We work on the machines and stay here, enjoying the quiet. How is that so wrong?"

"She's right." Lana stepped forward. "We don't want help or interference from anyone. We're happy here. We like our lives. We might look crazy to you, but this is just a shell. The real world is up here." She tapped her head and I winced. I agreed, but I also didn't want Lana to get us sent to the nut house.

"You're both certifiable." She pointed at me, shaking her head. "We're done, Emma. Me and you. We're done. This friendship is over. I can't have this toxic bullshit in my life! I have been worried sick about you and searching everywhere. I came here as a last resort because it's so close to the place the mayor attacked you."

"Say goodbye to Lola for me." I blinked, not feeling anything about the sentence she'd said.

"You're a fucking bitch! We've all given you a break on life and being a terrible friend and person because of Jonathan's death, but this is it. The buck stops here. No more breaks. You're fucking crazy and I'm glad Jonathan isn't alive to see this hot mess," she spat and turned on her heel, leaving the house and slamming the door.

I sighed and waited for her to be gone before going out and locking the gate again.

When I got back inside I grabbed Lana's hand. "We need to look at the house, really look at it. Ready?" I stared her deep in the eyes.

"Okay." She sounded uncertain.

"Close your eyes." I closed my eyes and took a deep breath and turned us both, "Now open them." Opening my eyes and staring at the filth everywhere was worse than seeing it before.

"Yikes. No wonder she was so pissed. We need to get rid of this shit. If she comes back with doctors we'll be locked up. We'll never get back into the machine if they lock us up."

"You're right. I'll call a cleaning company and we'll sit in the attic while they clean."

"We could do it ourselves right now." Lana eyed up the mess.

"I don't think we have the strength to do it." I glanced at her skinny arms and then mine.

"No. This entire day has worn me out. I'm getting a snack. You want one?"

"Yeah. I'll call the cleaning company."

She walked into the kitchen, leaving me to stare at the mess.

Turning in a circle and taking it all in, I caught a glimpse of myself in the hall mirror. I didn't know the woman staring back at me. She was haggard and skinny, old-looking well beyond her years. Her hair was frizzy and yet thinner and her eyebrows were almost touching. I lifted an arm, wincing at the reflection. My tee shirt was rotten, stinking to high heaven.

I didn't know when it got this way but I knew it would happen again. We needed to consider the fact Marguerite had seen us. We needed to fix everything before she came back.

But I didn't want the solution to cut into our time in the machine.

Lana would never agree to that.

Chapter Sixteen

We turned at the old chapel and started back toward the house. Taking a turn around the garden with a navy man meant a long hike. Mary and Charles toddled behind us, whereas Henrietta and Louisa were ahead. When they started to run, Wentworth stood on his toes. "I think they're here." He grinned wide and grabbed my hand, squeezing tightly and making me run with him.

We hurried along the path to the driveway where two men on horses rode up. One jumped down with ease and the other climbed off awkwardly, allowing his friend to help him. He walked with a significant limp, using a cane to assist himself. The girls rushed up to them and we caught up a moment later.

The men, about my age, wrapped around Wentworth in a greeting that suggested a closeness brothers would have.

Louisa and Henrietta giggled, eyeing up the men in top hats and fine riding jackets.

"This is Miss Louisa Musgrove, Miss Henrietta Musgrove, and Miss Jane Dalrymple. Ladies, this is Captain Benwick and Captain Harville."

Harville glanced at me, smiling with a glint of something in his eyes.

Mary and Charles brought up the rear, with Mary gasping for breath.

"And this is Mr. Charles Musgrove and Mrs. Mary Musgrove."

"Surely, you've heard of my father, Sir Walter Elliot." Mary offered her hand to be kissed.

"Anne Elliot?" Harville scowled, his eyes darting to Wentworth's.

"My elder sister. You know her? She arrives within the fortnight." She frowned back, no doubt missing the connection.

"Lovely to make your acquaintance." He bowed at us all and placed a forced kiss on Mary's gloved hand.

Henrietta and Louisa looked about ready to murder Mary as they curtseyed to the officers. Charles began to speak to Benwick about shooting and the hunt and Harville took it as an opportunity to come to my side.

"Miss Dalrymple, you must accompany me for a turn. I have heard so many things about you," Harville insisted. "All good, naturally."

"Certainly." I smiled wide, unsure what he meant.

"Are you enjoying the visit to the countryside, miss?" Harville led me away from the crowd with his hand on my back.

"I am. How is your leg after the ride?"

"It gets sore after a long ride but a bit of a walk clears things up. Shall we go this way?"

"I'd love to." I slid my arm into his and allowed him to lead me around the garden.

"I haven't seen the old house yet. I am still in shock Frederick was given it. His loss of his brother was unexpected."

"I can't imagine." It wasn't a lie. I had no siblings to mourn. I supposed it would be like losing Lana.

"I must confess the meaning of this walk; I have to know, is it true Anne Elliot is coming?"

"Yes, she should arrive soon."

"Is there an understanding between Frederick and Miss Elliott?"

"I don't believe so. She has suffered a grievous loss and was invited to join friends here."

His eyes narrowed. "Frederick is one of my closest friends,

like a brother to me."

"I understand." I didn't.

"Forgive my candor after we've only just met, but his special relationship with you has me confused about why Anne Elliot is on her way here."

"Special relationship?" Now I was really lost.

"He has written of you, many times. Are you aware of his previous friendship with Miss Elliot?"

"I am. I think the relationship might be salvaged, if I'm to be frank as well. She is a sweet girl who he still loves. If she is coming, perhaps it is time they settle their grievances from the past and rekindle their love." I was questioning him by offering the answer, hoping he would spill how the captain felt about me.

"And your feelings for him and his for you?"

"My feelings are secondary to Anne's. She has loved him a long time." I couldn't believe he would be so bold.

"She never loved him, Miss Jane. Had she loved him, she would have married him, not let herself be led around by others. She's a fool and if he chooses to be with her after all this time, then he's a fool too. And if you let him slip through your fingers because of some old romance, then you're no better." He tipped his hat and limped away, annoyed with me over something that was out of my control.

"I was married once, before," I called after him, astonished at his behavior.

He turned with difficulty. "And where is he now?"

"Dead. He died in a fire."

"And you feel it would be wrong to find love again? Dishonorable even?"

"I don't know. I haven't given it much thought. I think I searched for my husband, hoping he would haunt me and that was all the focus in my life."

"And did he?" A flash of humor hit his eyes and lips simultaneously. "Haunt you?"

"He did. I saw his ghost. Here, in fact." I turned and looked at the house.

"What did he say?" He stepped closer, sounding like he believed me.

"He said goodbye, Captain Harville." My voice cracked.

"Then you're free. And my friend has genuine feelings for you, as much as he desperately fears love. His letters spoke too fondly of you for us not to make the trip."

"You made the trip to meet me?" I wondered what was in those letters.

"To suss out this situation."

"In case I ended up breaking his heart like Anne?" I was offended and yet understood.

"I can't watch him go through that again. He was so certain of their love. So certain she would leave with him."

"And she didn't." I nodded, sighing. "I adore my cousin, but I understand your apprehension toward me. It's why I told you I was married before. My trepidation isn't for anything beyond an old broken heart. There is no one who would advise me nonetheless."

"Your mother, the viscountess, doesn't have opinions on your marriage?"

"No. She doesn't. I am far past the age where a girl is told who to marry. So long as he's wealthy, they don't mind. Captain Wentworth has fulfilled that requirement, and now to be the landowner of this fine estate, I can't see it being an issue. But that isn't why I would consider him." I furrowed my brow, uneasy with the topic of conversation.

"I'm sorry if I've made you uncomfortable."

"No, you aren't." I laughed. "I think you enjoy making people uncomfortable, challenging them."

"Beautiful and astute. Interesting." He tipped his hat and headed back toward the house, leaving me in the garden to mull things over.

I took a stroll to the courtyard and wandered through the heather and arched pathways, thinking too much.

"Jane?"

I turned to find Wentworth calling me.

"I looked everywhere for you. Are you all right?"

"Yes, I'm fine, thank you. Just a little uneasy." I confessed awkwardly.

"About what?" He walked to me, his riding boots making the only noise in the garden.

"I am confused about Anne coming." It was a weak and petty confession I hated myself for.

"Why?" He was clearly lost.

"Because I know of your history with her and her feelings for you and it's all very complex. Yet I do not wish to abandon my cousin in her time of need."

"You fear we might hurt each other again?" He nodded, contemplating it.

"No," I whispered with an embarrassed smile. "I fear I might get hurt in the crossfire this time." My words were barely audible though his eyes widened.

"You're afraid I would"—he paused, swallowing hard—"I would discount the feelings I suspect we might have for one another because Anne is coming?"

I nodded my response, unable to speak.

His eyes were wide and bright, scared maybe, as he took a step closer, coming into the space I considered too close for a friend to enter. "I am enjoying our friendship. I think had I taken the time as a boy, to get to know the person I was about to ask to marry me, I might have spared myself a great deal of heartache. And now that I know your heart is also part of the equation and it's not my imagination running away with me, allow me to assure you there is nothing to worry about. Your heart is delicately placed within mine, protected." His voice trailed off into a whisper as he took another step, coming much too close.

I tilted my face up, staring into his expressive eyes, letting them do the rest of the talking. I parted my lips, exhaling slowly as he lowered his face to mine, pressing his torso against me. His breath tickled my lips, becoming part of the air I breathed as he hovered there.

I lifted ever so slightly, letting myself tilt back more as he came the rest of the way, finally sealing our mouths in a soft embrace. It was easily the most delicate kiss I'd ever experienced until the end when he pressed his lips to mine firmly, before he pulled back.

I opened my eyes to see him blushing. "Forgive me for being so forward, Miss Jane." He swallowed hard again and offered his arm. "It won't happen again."

"That would be disappointing," I whispered, noting the heat in my own cheeks.

"You are remarkably strange." He chuckled, squeezing my arm.

"You know that isn't a compliment, right?"

"I mean it in the most complimentary way possible." He bent and kissed my cheek once before we walked from the garden.

Chapter Seventeen

"So then I told Mary that if she spent more time taking a turn about the garden and less time popping sweets into her mouth she might actually be able to keep up with her kids."

Lana's eyes widened as she took another chip from the bowl. "You didn't. About time someone told her off."

"I wouldn't normally say anything about the amount someone eats, but she complains so much. I tire of it and her." I sighed and ate a chip with dip, being the pillar of virtue I clearly was.

"Has Anne arrived yet?"

"No. They think she might come in the next couple of days. She said a fortnight, but I suspect she'll want to get to Wentworth faster. She still loves him."

"But he loves you." She brushed her foot against my leg.

"Maybe. How is motherhood?" I asked, changing the subject.

"Wonderful. The labor was awful, as I imagined it would be. But Celeste is beautiful and sweet. She sleeps like an angel and I swear she smiles at me. The doctor says no, says it can't be a smile yet. Just gas. But I know my baby. It's a smile." Her eyes lit up.

"How does Danny love it?"

"He's amazing. I don't know what I ever did to deserve him." She gushed. "I wish you could meet him. You would get along so well." She grabbed another chip and my brain did its usual what if.

I sat back, pausing in thought.

"Shall I go first or you?" She remarked, not realizing she had spurned an idea in my mind.

"Emma, you or me? Who's first?"

I blinked. "You." My story could wait and it would give me time to think.

We went upstairs and I hooked her in, setting it for ten hours. We were able to go that long now. It was our full night's rest.

As Lana drifted off to sleep, I contemplated everything Marguerite had said and what we needed to do to fix up the house.

I'd gone over several contractors' business sites, choosing a few to have a meeting with.

I also considered having someone who would be here while we were in the machine. As it was, we only spent a few hours together per day, as each person was in for ten hours. It was like a married couple working shift work opposite each other. But if we had a helper who could put us in and monitor us, we could go in at the same time, a night shift. And then we could live and go on during the day, like normal people. Not to mention, the added bonus of going into each other's worlds.

The outside world, apart from our helper, wouldn't know how we spent each night. How we left this world for another, exploring and creating it together.

I combed through the résumés we'd received, unsure of exactly what kind of qualifications I was looking for. What exactly did this caretaker need?

One stood out.

Her face and eyes reminded me of Mrs. Humboldt at Wentworth's. She had a soft look to her, but maybe also that little bit of extra sass we needed in our lives. She would ensure the garbage never got piled up again and that we didn't spend all day lying about.

I opened my email and sent her a reply.

The pay would be over the top and the compensation would

be worth what she'd be doing, working night shifts, and a nondisclosure order was a lot to ask of anyone. Being a retired nurse in search of a job, she was perfect. She could administer the needles. She could see to us both nutritionally. And most importantly, she could understand the equipment.

It was a lot of trust to place in another person, but if Lana and I were ever going to be able to enter each other's worlds, we would need to be under at the same time.

The technology was there already. I'd used it years ago when sending family members and loved ones into the minds of coma patients and such.

It was going to work. Quite easily if we had a caretaker.

But first we had to fix up the old house.

We couldn't ever have a caretaker come to us in the house as it was.

No, we would fix the house up first and then get the caretaker to watch us sleep each night.

And if Marshall or Marguerite or Stanley or our parents ever showed up, we would be ready for them. We would be ready to defend ourselves. Not only would we be awake and revived during the day, but also the house would be tidy. Marguerite's stories of garbage and ruin would be seen as lies. Thinking her name nearly made me ache for my friend. Not just to have her friendship back but also for her understanding. I wished she could have gone into the machine so she would get it. But she was never a reader, hated fiction actually.

And now she had said we were over. I had to let that be the case.

We had the house in a not bad spot right now. Three days of cleaning teams had come in and junked out the house. We told them bad tenants were to blame. To which they'd replied that of course they'd heard of the witches who lived here.

Witches.

It was 2027 and witches were still a thing in Rhode Island.

I had to laugh at that.

Ten hours later when Lana woke, I had a plan. It was a smart one.

Lana sighed. "What a great day. We took a picnic and ate by the river. When Celeste fell asleep we made love by the water."

"Sounds divine." I lay in my bed, hooking myself up as she unhooked.

"Good luck with Anne," she muttered as she sent me off into oblivion.

I dropped into the world at the manor. I was on the stairs, going up to ready for dinner.

Louisa and Henrietta were giggling in their room down the hall from mine. I paused before walking past, hoping they wouldn't see me. I had little tolerance for their silliness.

"Did you see Charles fall asleep in his soup last night?" Henrietta asked, laughing.

"I did." Louisa giggled. I slipped past the parted doorway, hoping they wouldn't see me.

"Jane!" The door opened with both girls beaming out at me.

"Ladies." I curtseyed as they did.

"Will you go on the hunt with us tomorrow? Mary refuses and Charles says we can't go unless you or Mary accompany us." They blinked their eyes at me sweetly.

"Of course. If you want me to go, I am at your service."

"Thank you!" They leapt at me, hugging tightly. "You're so much like Anne," Henrietta whispered.

"And so not like Mary." Louisa rolled her eyes.

"Wherever would we be if I were?" I winked and hurried to my room.

As I changed clothes and had a sponge bath, I contemplated the idea of Lana here. She would be stunning in the gowns and jewels of the time. The baby would be adorable in the little dresses and boots and bonnets. And Danny would be a gentleman. He would be Daniel of course and she would be Lady Lana.

Then I glanced about the house and considered my renovation. Would I want our house to be like this one, or would I prefer a modern home?

I wasn't sure.

I supposed for resale's sake, something I would eventually have to consider, modern would make back the money I was going to spend.

The entirety of the renovation was just as Stanley believed it to be, worth millions of dollars. Millions I had stashed away, money I had never touched. I never needed. My life cost almost nothing, for I lived in here.

When I finished dressing again, I dusted some powder on my nose and hurried downstairs.

I walked through the dimly lit halls, listening for everyone else. A crack of a ball led me to the billiards room doorway. I paused when I heard the men speaking.

"Why I never fall in love with a simple girl, one who would be honored to be a navy man's wife, is beyond me." It was Wentworth speaking. He sounded upset. "The daughter of a viscount will never be permitted to marry a sailor."

"You're hardly a simple sailor now, Frederick. This place isn't exactly the inn in Lyme. It's an extensive property, a park even. And your parents bought your commission in the navy. Even removing the Spanish gold prize money, your family isn't exactly destitute." It was Benwick speaking.

"I don't understand why you have invited Miss Elliot back here, no offense meant, Charles," Harville spoke softly.

"None taken," Charles added.

"I invited her because her family is here and she's lost a friend. As much as I had a broken heart from her once, I am not so cold as to deny her comfort during this hard time. I wouldn't be cruel to her. I don't think I could be," Wentworth defended himself.

"It might be awkward, what with you pursuing the cousin," Harville pointed out. I agreed with him.

"Anne and I had feelings for each other a long time ago. I was a different man then. I was a boy, not even a man. Nothing will be uncomfortable. She is a respectable lady. Charles was nearly engaged to her once and there's not a moment of discomfort between them."

"Absolutely not," Charles agreed again. "And I will never admit to the fact I find her ten times more tolerable than my own wife."

They all laughed and played on.

I cringed, turning around and heading to the library to peruse the books.

I sat in the corner, pretending to read but really I was drawing the office I would need in the upstairs for us to do our work comfortably, when Wentworth entered the library. He cleared his throat to make himself known. "I believe dinner will be ready shortly." He spoke with the slightest of grins.

I glanced up from my book, narrowing my gaze but saying nothing.

"You don't appear to be anywhere near as excited to see me as I imagined you might be."

"Possibly it's because I too have come to the realization that my parents are important people, so I will likely abandon my feelings sometime soon and break your heart." I didn't even try to hold back.

He laughed, entering the library and closing the large door. "Using the secret passageways to spy on me?"

"Of course." I lowered the book and drawings.

"I do not doubt you or your affections, only your ability to be free with them." He pleaded with his gaze and words for forgiveness.

"No. That's a lie." I stood, putting down the book completely. "You doubt me because you had your heart broken. That would be the same as me doubting your safety in a house because mine burned down with my husband in it. You can't blame every female for the actions of one, just like I can't abandon living indoors because fires happen."

He parted his lips, visibly offended and then snapped them shut. He took a noisy breath and stepped closer. "I've offended you, and while the words were not meant for you to hear, you did. I cannot change the fears I have, only hope that you will forgive me for them and whatever strain they have caused."

"Maybe." I narrowed my gaze again.

He stepped closer, not testing my anger but maybe our restraint.

I took a step back, hoping he would give chase.

He did.

He came as close as he was the first time we kissed, but lifted my hands with his, kissing the backs of them delicately. "Forgive me," he whispered to my hand.

"Perhaps." A smile danced upon my lips as I thought about his other words. "You said you loved me."

"I did? Are you certain? It's hard to hear through the brick walls."

"I heard you. Verbatim, you said, 'Why I never fall in love with a simple girl . . . ?'"

"Hmmmm." He furrowed his brow. "That is not the way I intended to tell you I loved you. I imagined something more elaborate, perhaps a stroll in the gardens and a stolen moment amongst the hedges. Or a hilltop at sunset."

I bit my lip, wanting things I hadn't wanted in so long I wasn't sure they still worked.

"I do." He spoke one thing but his eyes wrestled with another. Perhaps the propriety missing from the moment. Neither of us was showing any. "I do love you. The moment I met you, I couldn't help but want to be near you. And now if I could wish one thing, it would be for us to never be apart. And though this is the wrong way to ask, as your father has not been considered in any way, marry me. Put me out of this agony I am stuck in. My hands and lips burn to touch you—be mine."

I exhaled, not just air but the subtlest moan as well.

The moment couldn't have been done better.

A fireside library proposal was one of my dreams. Forget sunset and hedges, this was gold.

I took two breaths before I could answer, savoring the seconds spent in this blissful moment, and of course we were interrupted on my second breath.

Chapter Eighteen

Wyoming, Rhode Island, 2028

"The house is over three hundred years old. I'm sure you can understand my worries about your experience with houses this old." I forced a smile at the man who wouldn't stop staring at me. He was the contractor I liked the least and most. His look was stern and his words abrupt, but there was something in his eyes. A gentleness I suspected he hid from the world.

"I get it. You wanna make sure the integrity is taken care of." He broke his stare from my face and started glancing around the house. "It's gonna take us three weeks to do the main floor including front porch and the stairs, two weeks upstairs, a week on the roof and attic, and then probably two weeks on the basement. And that's only if we don't find anything unexpected. Being so old, I'm assuming unexpected is going to happen. Did you go over the quote?" He turned back to me, again flinching when he met my gaze. "This work is going to take my entire team, forty guys."

"I did. It sounds fair. I will have fifty percent transferred into your account tomorrow, and as you make progress we will continue to add funds." I didn't want to spend the money on the old place when I first got it but it had grown on me. Not to mention the fact we had a very real fear that Marguerite would show up with a psych assessment team any minute.

It helped that Lana and I were attached now and the plans we had for it meant it would need some refurbishment. And if we were doing a little, we might as well do it all. Get it over with. There was no way we would be able to defend ourselves against any attacks on our lifestyle if we kept living the way we were.

"I have often wondered about this old place. I'm excited you're going to fix it up. It's a real eyesore with that garden and the front porch." He nodded and offered his hand. "My team will be here tomorrow. We'll start on the roof and attic first, ensuring it's dry up there. It's usually a good place to find the beginnings of trouble. We'll work our way down, doing the second floor next week. Sound all right?"

"It sounds great, Mr. Daley. Thank you." I got the door for him, noticing the way he stared at me.

When I closed the door, Lana popped out from behind a corner. "He's cute."

"Do I have something on my face?" I asked.

"No." She shrugged.

"He was staring."

"Maybe he thought you were pretty." She slung her arm over my shoulders and led me to the kitchen. "I can't believe we're finally doing the renovation. It's going to be a mess in here."

"I know. But it needs to get done. We're spending all our time here; we need certain things to keep our bodies alive. We need a gym and the vibrational machine will be helpful with the atrophy. And the spa tubs will help with circulation. We need to start budgeting our time better. Think of it as an office job. When Gilda, the new homeworker, starts after the renovation, we'll be in the machine ten hours at night, simultaneously. Then we have to learn to live in the normal world and get a workout in and try to eat something healthy, not just vitamins and protein. We need to be able to say we're not crazy if Marguerite comes back, and with how we and this house look, I don't think we'll convince anyone right now."

"I know. I just hate the idea of someone being here while

we're in. I like that it's just you and me."

"We have to learn to trust someone else. We won't be so tired if we're in at the same time and out at the same time. As it is, we're spending twenty hours a day with the machine, either in it or observing it. My back hurts all the time. I'm exhausted. We have to fix that."

"Fine." She gave in and opened the fridge. "How much is the reno going to cost?"

"He's doing it for two million seven hundred thousand."

"Holy shit, that's a ton of money, Em."

"I know but I had the house assessed and the value of it is almost two million with no renovation. Once we fix it up it'll be worth over ten million."

"Did you take it out of the company?"

"Not yet, I will. I'll transfer him the funds tomorrow. Fifty percent up front and the rest spread over the job, withholding five hundred thousand until the very end of the project. And paying upfront for anything extra he finds. I checked, this is a standard contract."

"Sounds insane." Lana rolled her eyes at me and grabbed a Lean Cuisine for us both, heating them up in the microwave. "But if it makes the house better for our health, then it's worth it."

"I am telling you, there's mold and mice. The air quality is awful. It's spring. We need to get this done. The basement floods all the time. There must be cracks in the foundation. It stinks down there."

"I never noticed." She shrugged, making a face. "Did you say it's spring?"

"Yeah."

"I never noticed that either." She laughed.

"That's not a bad thing."

"No, it's not." She smiled. "Six months since my divorce finally went through and it's spring and I feel amazing, apart from the aching back."

"He's remarried, did I tell you? Marshall remarried." I couldn't recall if I had or not.

"No. Is he? Who's the unlucky lady?"

"Some young thing, I think only twenty-three."

"Jesus." Lana wrinkled her nose. "He's fifty this year, or was it last? He could at least try for half his age. What's he doing now?"

"He's back on Wall Street, same job he had before the mayoral career."

"I can't believe they took him back after your charges against him and his criminal convictions." She scowled.

"I know. Money buys everything."

"When did you hear he remarried?"

"I was combing the papers online the other day, catching up on some things. I was searching for the company that bought Lucid Fantasies, checking to see if they survived."

"And?" Her eyes widened.

"They have. They've made resorts. Imagination Playlands is what they're called. You go and stay at the resort and hook in. It's restricted and carefully done, but similar to what we have."

"When?" For the first time in ages, she looked as if she might actually be excited about something beyond going into the machine.

"Three weeks ago." I didn't realize the time had slipped by so quickly.

"Good for them. We might have to try it out."

"Yes, once the reno is finished we should go on a vacation."

"We should." Lana brought the dinners to the table while I doled out pills, probiotics, and green supplements.

We ate, laughing and joking and daydreaming about the possibility of leaving the house. Something that likely wouldn't happen. Unless forced.

Chapter Nineteen

"Captain Wentworth, Miss Elliot has arrived. And she has a guest. A man by the same name," Mrs. Humboldt interrupted us as I was about respond to the proposal.

She held the library door open, expectantly.

"Of course. Excuse me." He bowed and hurried from the room.

I slumped back in the chair, the wind sucked from my sails.

I wanted so badly to say yes but I wanted that moment to last forever.

I left the library after a minute of pouting, and sauntered to the front door. As I expected, Anne was early. As predicted, she couldn't stay away.

When I got to the door Mary was gushing over some man, a very handsome man. He had dark hair and was as tall as Wentworth and Charles, both tall men.

"And this is our cousin, who you must know quite well, Miss Jane Dalrymple." Mary held a hand out to me.

I made eye contact with the man, of course knowing him exceedingly well. I recalled him and all our shared memories that had been written into the storyline as I blinked once. "Cousin William. How are you?" William Elliot, our dreaded cousin, who had always been a social-climbing and money-grubbing letch, was with Anne?

What a turn of events.

Clearly, the unfortunate Mrs. Smith hadn't had time to warn Anne.

"Jane, what a pleasant surprise!" William exclaimed and pulled me in for an embrace. We knew each other well. Quite well. I patted his back and pulled away, earning myself a rather scandalous stare from Wentworth and Anne.

"Cousin Anne, I am so pleased you have returned." I embraced her also. "I was sad to hear of your friend's passing. I am so sorry."

"Thank you. She was a dear friend." Her eyes darted to William. "To us both. William was a friend to her late husband."

In my head I recalled the friendship. William had not done his part with the husband's will and Mrs. Smith ended up destitute as a result. I wondered what lies he had told to account for actions toward the poor widow. Or lack of action.

"You must be tired. The ride is quite long." I laughed. "I'm afraid we will never leave poor Captain Wentworth again for fear of the carriage ride."

Everyone laughed.

Everyone but Wentworth. His eyes burned the way my heart did.

I stepped back once more, allowing for other conversations to spark up about the carriage ride, and edged over to stand next to Wentworth. I let the back of my hand brush against his, trying to tell him I was his. I wondered if it was me trembling or him.

Everyone made their way into the dining room, apart from Anne who went to freshen up. And Mary who went with her.

"It's a very nice property, Wentworth. I wasn't unaware this was in your family." William said it like he meant no harm, but I knew he did. He had all the Elliot countenance.

"My uncle was the one who inherited. He was older than my father. But then he had no heir, so it came to my brother and then me."

"Quite recently?"

"Yes." Wentworth was polite, the very essence of a

gentleman. Unless we were alone, then he was much more like a caged animal. "Similar situation for you and Kellynch Hall, is it not?"

"Indeed it is. I am set to inherit. Poor Sir Walter, losing his only son as a small child."

"Was there a son?" Henrietta asked, clearly following along in the conversation.

"Did you not know?" William feigned care.

"How sad. He lost his heir and his wife," Louisa remarked, also paying close attention.

My eyes lingered on Wentworth's, hoping he would signal for me to leave the room and meet him in the hall, and he would again tell me how much he loved me.

But he didn't even meet my gaze.

In fact, when Anne and Mary made their way back into the room, his eyes widened with delight, as did everyone else's.

"Thank you for hosting us all, Captain." Anne smiled softly, offering a sweet sigh. "It's a lovely home."

"Thank you, Miss Elliot. I take it you had an uneventful trip?"

"Yes, very quick trip over. Bath was—"

"Bath." He chuckled, mocking the city with her in their private joke. "You hate Bath."

"I hate Bath," she agreed. "It was busy and damp and my father insisted on visiting with everyone, but at our lodgings. There was no peace."

"And poor Mrs. Smith." Louisa put a hand on Anne's.

"Yes. That was a terrible shock. She'd had a bit of a cold, but it changed, and within a few days she was gone. Her nurse did say she had a weakened immunity of late. Catching every cold that was to be caught."

"I warned dear Anne, she shouldn't be visiting and risking herself." William sat next to Anne, placing his hand on the back of her chair. It was a possessive and comfortable pose.

I wanted to roll my eyes but I didn't. I sat stone-faced and watched as they interacted, laughing and eating and drinking.

After dinner, Anne played the piano and they danced. I

excused myself, confused by Wentworth's sudden coldness toward me. It wasn't a mystery, Anne had arrived. His first love. But as his latest love, my feelings were injured by the slight.

I walked to my bedroom and slid the fireplace back, taking a candle and creeping into the secret passageway.

I sat on the stairs and listened to the sounds of music and laughter.

Nothing about the day had turned out the way I'd hoped.

I wondered where the real Jonathan was, not hoping he would come to visit me, but what his life looked like now, what heaven was like.

What my heart looked like up there, tucked away with his.

The heart in my chest, the one being abused by Wentworth, wasn't my whole heart. Pieces of it had broken off and were safely tucked away in heaven with the first man I ever loved.

I told myself the pain in my chest would end. I would get over it. It wasn't whole heart pain. I couldn't possibly really love Wentworth anyway. He wasn't real and I wasn't really here, and as many times as I told myself it was real, it wasn't.

I got up and continued below, taking the tunnels down to the main floor.

"Jane!" Wentworth called after me from above. I turned to see him storming toward me. He appeared to be angry with me. "I looked everywhere for you."

"I didn't think anyone would notice that I'd left." I wasn't trying to start a fight, but I also wasn't about to pretend things hadn't become peculiar since Anne arrived.

"I noticed. I simply assumed you would be making your way back to us. It's been over an hour since you left."

"I wasn't in the mood to be jovial. Forgive me, my lord." I curtseyed and turned to walk away, but he grabbed my arm, knocking the candle from my hand.

It blew out on its way down, leaving us in the dim light filtering through the open doors. It was just enough light to see his face, his eyes.

He pulled me to him, roughly, and then softened his grip as

his arms swept me up into them. He gazed down on me, cupping my face. "I never received my answer, Jane. I've waited all night, impatiently for it."

"You seemed fine without it."

"Answer me," he demanded, maybe annoyed by my being purposefully reserved.

"Yes."

"Yes?" He scowled.

"If that is still your wish, then yes. My answer is yes." I hated that this was my response.

"If that's still my wish?" He sounded aghast. "I've been upstairs, entertaining more than half your bloody family, being the perfect host to that scoundrel you call a cous—"

"To a woman, you loved. You have been playing host to a woman you loved."

"'Loved' being the operative word, Jane. Loved. I haven't loved Anne in a long time."

"You light up when she walks in the room. I saw you."

"No, you saw me pretending to be happy. You saw me acting like a gentleman ought to when someone he can't stand is in his house, but he isn't permitted to be authentic. I can't stand to be around that man. Watching him put his hands all over you and Anne and even Mary, ridiculous Mary, makes me imagine doing all sorts of vile things. Acts gentlemen don't admit to once committed." He exhaled loudly as if defeated. "I love you and I want to marry you. You and you alone."

"Then I accept. I want to marry you, Wentworth. I want to be yours."

"You are, you're entirely mine." He lowers his face, brushing his lips against my cheek, whispering to me in the dark and creepy secret passageway. "I must confess, I am having thoughts not to be entertained." He placed a second kiss on my cheek, lingering too long and breathing hot breath on my ear and nape.

"You did mention you didn't want to be parted from me," I offered softly, having trouble keeping my own breath in check. "Does that include at night, when we must be separated?"

"Jane." He said my name as if declaring all the indelicate desire burning inside him with one word.

"Frederick." I said his, hoping I conveyed even half the lust.

Our eyes met when I pulled back, his seeking permission to do things nice men didn't do until they were married. I prayed my stare offered the consent he was requesting as butterflies had a ball in my stomach.

Seeing the assent he wanted, he lost the delicacy and sweetness. He unleashed a fervor sweeping me into his chest, lifting me off the ground and turning for the brick wall leading to his bedroom.

When we got to the bricks he placed me down. I glanced back at him as I entered the tiny space, sliding through.

The tension of what was about to happen pricked at me. His gaze, stuck on mine, sucked me in and made me wonder what exactly he was thinking about. He appeared crazed and possibly angry, but he wasn't.

When I got into his room I stood by the fire and listened as he scuffed his way through the bricks. The crackling wood tried to be louder than my rapidly beating half of a heart.

I gasped as he came into the room, stepping close to me again, becoming the delicate thing he thought I was. He reached for me, running his fingertips down my cheek, creating more heat than the fire shimmering off our faces.

I saw everything in his eyes. He made love to me with just a stare, far before he even took his next step closer. His fingers brushing my cheeks, cupping my face and tilting it to his, made me feel like I was a precious thing, a fragile creature.

I'd never been a sexual person.

I'd never been in that sort of relationship.

Jonathan and I were friends long before we were ever anything else.

But in Wentworth's eyes, I saw the promise of what was to come and I braced myself.

"Captain . . ." I whispered as he lowered his face to mine, gracefully placing a kiss on my cheek.

"Are you certain?" he asked breathily.

"Yes, Captain." Something about calling him that made my head spin even more than the dimly lit room.

"I love you, Jane," he whispered again, kissing the other side of my face with the same passivity.

I waited with baited breath as his fingers danced down and then up my arms, tickling almost. His lips pressed in, slightly firmer as he kissed my cheek closer to the ear. I closed my eyes, breathing deeply.

He kissed lower on my neck as his hands made their way to the back of my dress, pulling at the tie. The force of the knot coming loose and bagging my dress around my slim body made me gasp again.

My eyes shot open as I bit my lip, noticing he'd stepped back. A grin crossed his lips as he tugged my dress down my arms and past my breasts to the floor. It pooled around me. I shivered as the heat of the fire licked at my left side as he reached for my stays, both his hands touching the top of my chest, brushing against my flesh where it swelled out the top, as he carefully untied it.

His fingers reached between my breasts, slowly and moving with intention, tugging at each lace, loosening the stays until it could be glided off.

I stood in my sheer petticoat, naked beneath it.

His eyes traveled me as I slid my arm through one armhole and then the other, letting the petticoat drop to the floor with the dress.

His gaze widened as his breath hitched. "You're beautiful." He lifted a hand, brushing the backs of his knuckles up my stomach, making me flinch when he made contact. He dragged, digging into my skin with his, ensuring I felt every bit of him against me.

Once his hand neared my breasts, he lifted the other, and cupped, lifting my breasts into his palms. He touched so gently I didn't know how to respond as he weighed each breast, massaging carefully.

When his fingers massaged their way to my nipples, I inhaled sharply.

This was the official point of no return.

I lifted my hands, hurrying to take his uniform off, stripping him of his jacket and shirt and even undoing his pants. We paused, me naked and him partway there, both trembling and unsure of who would make the next move.

It was him.

He lifted me in the air, carrying me to his bed, and laying me down so gently but with such desperation. He kissed my stomach as he dragged off the rest of his clothes until he too was completely naked.

I glanced up, curious as to what sort of man the captain was.

He was much larger than Jonathan in build and everywhere else. His body was smooth and lean, perfect really.

I slid up the bed as he climbed atop it, hovering over me. My mind wandered over things like foreplay and protection and everything else I imagined would be a modern idea of sex.

Our eyes met and all the thoughts and questions faded. I reached up, cupping his face in my hands and pulling him down to me, to lie beside me. The warmth of our bodies made me shiver as I forced him on his back, kissing him with passion. My tongue brushed his lips as I led him into a much more desperate kiss. As his tongue entered my mouth, he pressed me into him and rolled me onto my back, sliding his hands up my torso to my breasts, cupping and massaging.

His lips traveled, leaving mine and adventuring along my neck and chest, joining his hand in caressing my breast. When his warm mouth landed on a nipple I inhaled sharply, tensing and remembering the feeling of a man touching me.

He suckled and flicked, rubbed and teased, until my entire body felt like it might explode. Then, with his cock bobbing between us, he hovered over me again, spreading my legs wide and pushing himself inside me.

It was all too much for a moment, too filling, too heavy, too satisfying.

I clawed at him, grabbing his muscled arms, feeling them

tense as he pulled back and pushed into me again, making moaning breaths burst from me.

He bent his head down, kissing me violently as he continued to slide in and out of me, pushing me too far.

My fingers dug into his arms and back as we joined, coupled with each other. Every long rhythmic stroke of him built more and more pressure in my body as our breath turned ragged and our need for pleasure drove us to move in and out of one another in grinding and rotating bliss.

I clung to him, desperately lost in the waves of pleasure that rocked me, me being the ship and he the captain.

When the pleasure climaxed, my body took over, tilting slightly as I reached around, grabbing his ass and pulling him into me, forcing a speed I needed.

I orgasmed violently, clinging to every inch of him.

He cried out, exploding inside me, groaning and gripping me, pinning me to him and him to me, pressing me into the mattress and yet lifting at the same time.

The violence of our affections cooled as we collapsed, both struggling to breathe and find space without leaving the sanctity of the moment.

"Holy shit," I muttered, not even sure that was the right word.

"Indeed, my lady. Indeed." He pressed a sweaty kiss against my neck and groaned again.

My brain made an attempt at firing a thousand questions off but my heart swelled, pushing them back.

There was no need to think, everything about this was perfect.

Chapter Twenty

During the first week of the men working on the house, I filled my ten hours of monitoring Lana by checking on her randomly as Mr. Daley and I went over plans. She spent the first shift in the machine and I spent the nights. Far more was expected of me with the reno than I'd been prepared for.

"This website is a good one. They have tons of decorating ideas. If you keep pressing 'Pin It,' it'll build pages of ideas. Good for referencing." Mr. Daley clicked on the word "save" on the picture of a beautiful rug I'd mentioned I liked.

"Okay, that makes sense. This one's nice." I pointed at the screen.

"Click 'save.' You have to know how to do this so you can get it done when I'm not here."

"Okay." I clicked it and tried not to take offense to the tone with which he spoke all the time. He was impatient.

"How are you finding the work being done?"

"Good. Your men work very fast and hard. It's impressive to see."

"That they do." Mr. Daley laughed almost bitterly. "They wouldn't be my men if they didn't. Jobs are hard to find around here. The economy's in the toilet, so I'm able to be picky."

"And as a paying customer I appreciate that," I remarked, also laughing.

"Well, enough of this chatter and wasting time, I need to get back to work. So you keep scrolling through these sites. You need to create a page, just like I showed you for each room. The decorator will help with a lot of choices and getting us the best prices once he knows what we're looking for." He got up and nodded his hatted head at me before leaving the grungy kitchen table.

We spent weeks this way—me, the website, and Mr. Daley's constant reminders to finish choosing décor for each room.

Even when I thought I had finished one, I would find something better. The sites that Mr. Daley had shown me were all easy to use and the pages I built on the Pinterest for each room were overly stocked with modern and beachy décor.

I recalled the thing Jonathan had said once about our house when we were fixing it up: he would finish it in a way that made him think he was in the Hamptons.

I tried to stick as closely to his taste as I could, honoring it as this had been his house before it was mine. It was a way of keeping him here without needing to see his ghost.

I had come to terms with the fact that he was never going to haunt me.

My husband had left the earth and gone to heaven because he had no unfinished business. It wasn't a scientific finding, but a common sense one. He loved me and had lived a wonderful life, doing all the things he wanted to when he wanted them. He never had a bucket list; he just acted when he saw something he wanted.

The very opposite of me.

I was the one stuck with the list of things I wished I'd done. I was the one with regrets.

One afternoon as Lana slept in the machine, something she did far more than I did now, I left the room to show Mr. Daley a site I'd found with handmade wooden furniture.

He was leaning against the kitchen table, mulling over a plan and speaking to a man. The guy offered me a wrinkled nose look, possibly one of disgust, one I'd gotten used to. But Mr. Daley turned and smiled. It was genuine and lit the room up. "Emma, how's it going?" His eyes darted to the disgusted man. "We're done. Go show them what I mean." His tone changed as he spoke to the man who left us alone. He softened again as I got closer. "How's everyone feeling?"

"Good." I smiled, offering the tablet. I noticed how dirty his hands were but his nails were clean and filed. I couldn't say the same for my hands. They were clean but my nails were chipped and stained. I didn't even know what it was; I hadn't done any of the construction. "I found this site, they make wooden furniture and I liked one of the desks. I couldn't save it on Pinterest, and I didn't want to order it without consulting the decorator." I laughed. "Seems foolish to have to ask permission to buy a desk, but I would hate to disappoint him if he has other schemes."

He laughed with me, nodding. "Safe bet there. Leave it with me and I'll take a look and see what he says." The sparkle in his eyes was only there randomly. Today must have been a good day.

"Thank you. They have beautiful shelves too, for the books. I'll have to go through them all and give some away. They won't fit in the office. I've got a hoarding issue with them if I'm being honest."

"You love books?" he asked like he was confirming.

"I love books. The traveling and the knowledge and the glimpses into a stranger's heart. Reading is the greatest escape there is. You don't have to leave your home, or worry about anything. You just crack a book and let it drag you inside. And now I have too many."

"But if you love something, is there such a thing as too many?"

"Perhaps not." I laughed and felt awkward as I lingered just a moment too long before turning and leaving him there.

I needed to wash my hands and file my nails.

Weeks passed and the house moved along. We could smell it in the dust and paint and drywall mud.

We never went upstairs, allowing for the surprise ending Mr. Daley suggested he wanted. It was odd imagining him wanting to surprise me, a person he barely regarded. I wished I could say the same for him but there was something about him I found challenging. I wanted to see him smile, perhaps be the one who made him smile. And not that bitter grin he offered, but a real and genuine one. Maybe because he was doing so much for me.

"The hammering is driving me insane," Lana growled on the third week of construction. "My head vibrates every time they start again."

"I know, mine too. But we're halfway. It's almost over. Once they move into the basement we won't even hear them," I lied.

"Yesterday one of them peed in the garden. I saw him from the window."

"Gross." I wrinkled my nose, disgusted and yet almost grateful they peed outside and not inside. "How is Celeste?" I asked, changing the subject.

"Wonderful. We're discussing a second baby, she's been so delightful. And you, how is Wentworth?"

"Breathtakingly perfect." Heat rose in my cheeks as I contemplated one of Jane Austen's men having sex. The fade to black just didn't do them justice, for what lingered in the dark was better than anything I'd ever had in the real world.

"You seem different."

"Oh, I am." I chuckled. "I assure you, I am altered from it all. A changed woman. I had no idea." I joked about Wentworth but truth be told, the renovation had started to inflict itself on my time in the story. And I wasn't going into the machine as often as before, and I was preoccupied with the renovation when I was there.

"Hmmmm, sounds perfect." Lana grinned with knowledge and confidence. She knew what I was talking about.

"Shall we?" I asked as I got up, bringing my tea and heading for the office we were working in on the main floor while the top floor was being completed. Mr. Daley had promised it was days away from being done.

The leaking roof and damp attic were fixed.

The floors had been redone upstairs and the plaster pulled

away, replaced with drywall and paint, no more wallpaper. I'd seen enough plaster and wallpaper to last a lifetime.

We had three ensuites added to the largest of the seven bedrooms upstairs and we had them make us a proper room for the machines and beds. I had asked that it resemble my old office almost perfectly.

The windows were new, casings and all, and the doorframes were replaced with modern ones, and no more doors that creaked and groaned with every movement.

As she walked to the office, I noticed Lana was filling out again. Our improved diet and forced time on the treadmill in the guest room might actually be saving our lives. I hadn't told her but the inactivity was essentially killing us. Every year spent sitting and lying about removed eight from our life span.

We needed more than the meager stroll about the house to get food or to use the bathroom. I was carefully and slowly implementing the changes. Having workmen about the house constantly was helping as well. We couldn't hide here and pretend everything was fine, distracted by a different world.

I pulled my thinned hair up into a bun and sauntered into the office, closing the door behind me.

She closed the drapes, another thing I wouldn't miss. The custom blackout blinds we added to the bedrooms upstairs were perfect, sleek, hidden when open, and clean. No more dusty drapes and ancient smells.

The main floor would be the hardest. The tiles were broken and needing replacement and the wood floors were damaged well beyond repair. We were stripping the entire floor: plaster, banisters, crown molding, bathrooms, kitchen, windows, and everything.

It was going to be a difficult three weeks. The demolition would be the worst of it. Dust and noise and constant shouting as they joked and laughed with one another. The crew seemed jovial enough, but they also appeared to despise the old house. Only Mr. Daley, the owner of the company, saw the older home for what it was.

The rest constantly spoke of lighting a match.

As Lana lay on the bed and began hooking herself up, I sat and turned on all the tablets and monitors. As the construction progressed, my time in the machine lessened. And when I did go in, it went by too quickly. Even Lana was doing short trips, four hours at a time.

Lana slipped off, no doubt enjoying the relaxing day spent with her husband and child, as I did a crossword puzzle by candlelight. The smell of the burning beeswax reminded me of home.

A subtle knock on the door lifted my gaze. I jumped up and hurried to the door before they knocked again, and opened it.

"It's done." Mr. Daley nodded his head at the stairs.

"The whole top floor?" I asked softly, slipping out into the hallway. I glanced back at Lana, certain she would be fine for the moment.

"Wanna see it?" His eyes widened, filled with emotion I hadn't seen before.

"Of course." I closed the door and followed him.

"We changed a couple of things: opened the attic up more so it's now a third floor and we removed the stairs that pull down. The halls are so large we had tons of space to create a new full set of stairs. Better for resale down the road. Especially if the new owners had kids or wanted to make this an inn. The attic is massive, over three thousand square feet." His eyes darted to my face the way they always did. "Are you feeling better?" he asked boldly.

"What?"

"Well, you two are sick, right? Like cancer or something?"

"Why do you ask?" I assumed he meant the hooking up to the beds all the time.

"Well, the treatments you get every day seem to be working. You look better. I think it's working. When I got here you looked pretty rough." He said this as if it were a compliment. "The guys thought you were witches. I think a couple still do."

My insides tightened, taking the verbal blow. "Yes," I lied. It was easier than explaining that our bodies lived in one dimension, barely acknowledged, while our spirits lived elsewhere, receiving all the sustenance.

As we got to the top of the stairs I noted they didn't wind me as before.

He smiled wide, expectantly. "Well?" He held a hand out and I brought my fingers to my lips. "It's perfect." The floors were done to resemble the color of driftwood and the walls were a paler version of soft sky blue, almost white blue. The doorframes were almost cream, matching the doors, done in an antique white. The knobs were antique style, but brand-new and chrome.

The sand-colored blinds were half drawn, adding softness to the hall. Each room was the same, clean and beachy. The ensuites were all done with white marble and antiqued cream-colored vanities. The showerheads were large, so the water felt like rain, with sand-colored pebble bases in the stand-alone showers with glass surrounds. The claw-foot tub in each ensuite stood off to the side, in front of the window he had matched in every room.

The floors in all the bathrooms were marble to match the countertops. Everything was crisp and bright and coordinated. The upstairs no longer smelled dank or moldy.

He led me from room to room, showing the small details he was obviously proud of. I ran my hand along the banister, an ornate wrought iron. I hadn't been able to picture the black complementing the space but it did. In fact, it became the showcase, looking like Spanish lace on a flamenco dancer's dress.

As we rounded the corner, I gasped again. The stairs to the attic were beautiful, done with the same banister and driftwood floor, they were wide and clean. I could see up into the attic perfectly, admiring the pale-colored cedar ceiling he'd put in with tongue and groove boards.

As we ascended the stairs, my mouth fell open. He'd made a library with massive round windows with benches in them. The walls were bookshelves, dozens of them. The enormous attic could have been a ballroom, but a library was better suited for us.

"You said you were a neurologist and I saw all the books

downstairs," he offered sheepishly.

"Neuroengineer," I whispered as I turned, tears flooding my eyes. No more words left my lips, just breath in bursts.

"That is the response I was going for." He beamed, folding his arms across his chest. He smiled in a way, the way I had wanted him to from the moment we'd met. He lost all the hardness and bitterness.

"Th-thank you," I stammered.

"You are more than welcome, Emma." His eyes glistened for a moment too as he said my name so softly. "I hoped this would make you ladies feel better. So random, two people with cancer being together. Did you meet at the hospital?"

"No." I chuckled through the tears. "No. We aren't together. Just friends. Sisters even."

His eyes widened. "You aren't married?"

"No." I laughed harder, gripping my side as a stitch hit.

"I think everyone here sort of thought . . ." He laughed too, wiping one of his eyes dry. "It doesn't matter. I'm glad you're on the mend and this library suits you. Wanna see the medical room now?" He grinned.

"Please, lead the way." He offered me his arm, suddenly less standoffish. Maybe less afraid of me now that I was no longer the dreaded small-town lesbian dying of cancer.

He led me back down the stairs to the second floor as I wiped my eyes. At the far end of the hall, the one we hadn't gone down yet, he opened a lock with a key. "I put a lock on this one." He handed me the key as he opened it and swung the double doors wide. The office was ten times nicer than the one I'd had before, very modern and sleek with white countertops and two beds. It had shelves and units for all our equipment and a bathroom with a shower off the back. There were no windows and the lights were dimmed.

"This is wonderful. Thank you." I reached up and placed a small kiss on his cheek. "This means the world to me."

"You're welcome, Emma."

I realized then, I didn't even know his first name. "What is your name? I always call you Mr. Daley."

"Mike." He took my hand and shook it delicately. The calluses and toughness to his hands felt foreign against my own. I had never shaken hands with a man who was so weathered. But his hands lost my focus as the expression in his eyes altered. The softness of the honey-brown eyes became inviting, almost as if asking to be stared into.

He had the sort of smile that could go either way. It could be gentle and sweet or sarcastic and rude. I wouldn't have ever crossed him or wanted to see him angry, which I imagined he was frequently in his line of work. But to see him become soft and kind was like being around a pet bear. He was a gentle giant.

He led me back downstairs as his men put plastic up, sealing off the upstairs from the main floor. "So you ladies will be gone now, for three weeks?"

"We will be." I nodded. "We will be back when the main floor is finished."

"We shouldn't even be three weeks. Our crisis timeline, where we add in the extra time for the unexpected, hasn't been used. We were four days faster on the roof and top floor. I'm optimistic."

"Thank you."

"No, thank you for giving us the chance to work here. I've always wanted to fix this old place up. I drive by it a lot. My wife"—he flinched—"ex-wife, used to want to buy it and make a bed and breakfast. She always said she would call it the Lost in Time Inn." He chuckled.

"You're divorced?" I asked before I could stop myself.

"No, she passed before the divorce was finalized." He scowled. "It was a car accident. Kind of random."

"Mine died in a fire," I offered, opening my chest and comparing scars.

"Fire?" He winced. "You were married?"

"Yes. My husband had an aneurysm in a fire." I shook my head. "Also random. He went back inside the burning house for my dog and suffered an aneurysm. The firemen said he died before he hit the ground." I had never spoke of that part. "I always wanted to believe it was my fault for letting him go in after the dog, but the truth is, he would have died on the grass in front of me if he hadn't been in the house, I suppose sparing me that moment."

"Emma, I'm so sorry," Mike spoke with understanding. "I don't know exactly how you feel, but I can relate. I always thought that if we hadn't gotten a separation, if I'd been a better husband, I would have been driving. I wouldn't have fallen asleep. I can drive for days without sleep."

"I'm sorry, Mike."

He sighed. "Guess we're two peas in a fucked-up pod." He pointed at the front door. "I better get going though. The guys want a midway celebration. Have a nice trip, Emma," he bid politely, sounding so different from the man I met originally. Even looking it.

I sauntered into the office where Lana slept, and sat in the chair, surprised by everything the past fifteen minutes held.

Chapter Twenty-One

My entire body felt alive and rejuvenated.

I sighed and pinned my hair, catching myself smiling in the mirror for no reason.

I felt like a schoolgirl, crushing on someone. The memory of his lips and hands and thrusting body changed my breath. It hitched and rushed from my parted lips as I swallowed hard and relived it all.

The firelight and the way our bodies had writhed against one another in the crisp white sheets would be a top memory for my entire life.

He created feelings inside me I never knew were possible. As a married woman who had loved her husband dearly, I never realized how plain our sex life was until this moment. I never knew it could've been more, had I asked for more, had I known to ask.

I regretted not living like that with Jonathan, wrapped in him and sheets and gasping for air and needing food. I'd never been properly fucked before.

It changed everything.

I craved it. I craved Wentworth. I contemplated our marriage, more so our honeymoon and how much sex we would have once freed to have it regularly and not sneaking around. I longed for the way his fingers felt against me.

Then I paused, wondering something so ghastly and awful that I hated myself instantly. I closed the thought off, pushing it away. But it refused to go. If the strong hands of Captain Wentworth felt as good as they did, what did the rough hands of Mike the carpenter feel like?

I brushed a hand along my neck, down into my neckline, imagining it. I cupped my breasts, all the while watching myself in the mirror.

I had strayed and dishonored Jane Austen in every way but I wasn't going back. I wondered often, had she been alive in my time, if Jane Austen would have become quite the sexual woman. Had she been allowed to write it, maybe she would have even described some of it herself. Though it was better the way she left it up to us, the reader. We decided what Mr. Darcy's cock looked like. We chose the tautness of Mr. Bingley's ass. We imagined the feel of Mr. Tilney between our thighs, suckling at our breasts.

And I knew the feel of Captain Wentworth thrusting into me, forcing words and sounds from me I did not recognize.

I exhaled through pursed lips and nodded. I needed a cold shower or a cup of tea.

I left the room, dressed and ready for dinner, though I suspected I might have been a bit too glowing.

Catching Charles in the hallway confirmed it. "Jane, are you quite well? You're flushed."

"I was struggling with my gown actually, Charles. Worked up a bit of a sweat." I winked and hurried down the stairs, leaving him mouth agape and eyes wide.

When I got downstairs Captain Wentworth's eyes met mine from the library where he proposed, the first time.

I smiled coyly and walked in a different direction, wondering if he would follow.

I hurried to the garden, walking more swiftly than was considered ladylike but enjoying the prospect of him chasing.

When I got to the arches, arms circled around my waist from behind, making me cry out with laughter. I spun, gasping for air and longing to be pinned to a bed again by the large man holding me captive.

"Did I really startle you?" he asked with a grin.

"No and yes. I expected I would get a little farther before you caught me."

"Did you?" He pressed my back against the rough brick archway and forced himself up against me, roughly. "I have been thinking about you all afternoon." His hands traveled my arms to my chin, tilting it up and lowering his face.

"And what were you thinking of?"

"I'd rather show you." He kissed. The gentleman was long gone and in his place was a madman, desperate for the very thing he shouldn't have had, not yet.

I broke the kiss off and whispered, "Someone might see us."

"Not likely. Mary's come down with another cold and poor Charles is stuck tending to her. Miss Anne and Mr. Elliot have gone for a carriage ride to see another school friend of hers who lives nearby. And the girls are occupying the captains with billiards. Apparently, they play quite well." He grinned. "So you see, no one will come upon us out here." He lifted my skirts, pausing when he felt no undergarments. I'd opted for no pantalets when I dressed earlier.

His fingers pried, roughly exploring my exposed body. The wetness I was producing long before I even met with him, sparked urgency in us both. He slid a finger inside me, pushing and drawing, sawing in and out of me.

I grabbed at his pants as soft moans escaped my lips, freeing his cock and rubbing my hands up and down it.

He moaned as I gripped firmly, squeezing as I drew near the tip. He lifted me, scraping my back against the rough wall and rested me on his parted thighs.

I grabbed his shoulders, helping him nestle his cock between my lips, and he shoved himself into me. I cried out softly in the cool air, clinging to his shoulders as he lifted my dress more, gripping my ass and thrusting in.

Each jerk brought with it a breathy sound from me.

I took no care of the gardens or the public nature in which he ravished me. I ignored the scraping of my back, or the muslin tearing as he pushed himself farther into me.

We made no love and confessed no feelings. Instead, we acted on primal instinct and need, behaving as animals would, defiling his beautiful garden like Eve and her snake.

He pummeled me, bouncing my body off his, spearing me with pleasure and passion until I climaxed, moaning and biting into his shoulder, trembling and twitching. His orgasm was similar, unbridled and violent.

When it was over, again we clung to one another, shocked by our own actions and lack of propriety shown. The respect a wife and husband demanded of one another in this time, didn't match the aggression we both showed sexually.

Slowly, he lowered me, removing himself from my body. "Forgive me." He stepped back, clearly horrified by his actions. His face—his expression—hurt me, making the act not just something naughty, but a regret. He regretted me, this moment.

"No, please, forgive me." My voice waivered and I pushed off the wall, fleeing for my room in my ruined dress. My shame wore heavy on my shoulders as I slumped them in the safety of my room.

It wasn't bad enough that we had bastardized the language of the Regency era, but also the morals. I prayed as I stared at the girl looking back at me in the mirror, the one trembling and flushed from pleasure, that Jane Austen wasn't rolling in her grave.

Though none of this story was Jane's. Characters and a few traits perhaps, but the rest was me.

I was driving the crazy train.

I was the one in charge.

I had tainted it all.

"Jane?" A knock at the door startled me. I winced as Wentworth opened it, remorse clouding his eyes. "I will not ask for your forgiveness again. I do not deserve it." He stepped inside and closed the door. "The lust I feel for you is insatiable. I fear I am unable to control myself with you."

"You wish to call off the engagement," I said, knowing it was I corrupting him and only a matter of time before he realized it. I was not the virginal girl he would've wanted to marry.

"No." His eyes widened. "I could never. I love you. I just wanted to assure you that I will work on remaining a gentleman at all times." He wasn't angry with me? He didn't want to know where I'd learned to have sex? He was truly disgusted with himself?

"No." It was my turn to speak. "If you aren't opposed to it, I prefer how things stand between us." I tried to think of a way to say it without actually saying it, the art of the era. "I enjoy the way we are together. You are a gentleman in every aspect of your life; if you wish not to be one when we are alone, I have no reservations about that."

"But you were so horrified." His eyes narrowed.

"Only because you apologized. I thought you didn't—"

"Think nothing, because my actions and my words are at war." He stepped to me, bringing me into his arms, cradling my head against his chest. "I have never felt this way about any woman, and I dare say I never will again. The way you awaken the man inside me, pleases me as much as it scares me."

I lifted my gaze, sighing into his jacket. "I love you, Frederick."

It was the truth.

The half of a heart I'd brought into the book was in love with him.

While I'd destroyed the innocence and purity of Austen's character, I'd used her story as a baseline to create my own. One I could live in happily. Even if it meant Captain Wentworth was now a bit of a sexual exhibitionist with an insatiable lust for fucking.

I mean, maybe she meant him to be that way all along. I wouldn't ever know the truth to that.

Chapter Twenty-Two

Three weeks in a hotel wasn't much different from three weeks at our house. But here we took turns sleeping for ten hours, dreaming and living. Our bodies were used to the long sleep. We used step counters to ensure we got ten thousand steps a day while the other person slept and ate healthy. And with no construction workers, we had no one to know how we spent our time.

I spent a few hours every day lifting some weights in the hotel gym, swimming, and lying in a tanning bed.

We didn't go outside. The new tanning beds really were safer than going in the sun anyway. We didn't interact with other people unless we had to.

I never noticed that like true addicts, we found ways to have our cake and eat it too, without giving up our time in the machine.

In front of the mirror in the hallway of the hotel, I pulled my hair into a bun, noting the dark rich color had returned as had the thickness.

For a moment, I had to pause, checking my reality to determine if I was in the machine or not.

I looked like me again. Not quite as beautiful as the me in the story. The one with flushed cheeks and meat on her bones. But this was an improvement, much better than before. I lifted an arm, noting my skin now clung to my body instead of hanging there.

I was getting healthier but Lana lay on the bed, still a bit gaunt.

Her cheeks didn't flush and her hair hadn't fully thickened. Her skin was tanned, no longer gray, but it was fake. Beneath the brownish coloring was a pallor no one would envy and her skin still hung. She took the health risks lighter than I did. But she was improving, if only marginally.

Being a researcher, I knew the problems the organs faced when the body stopped being active, the same problems patients with ALS faced. A better chance of getting flus and colds and even pneumonia.

I didn't lessen my time in the world, I improved my time out of it.

I read again, something I'd not done in ages.

I lived, as a regular person might. A regular hermit. That still bothered me, being around groups of people. But it had always bothered me. Jonathan had been the extravert who adopted me and made me social.

When Lana woke, we packed up, leaving a massive tip for housekeeping, as the room would need a lot of cleaning, and headed home.

My stomach was in knots at the excitement of seeing the house.

As we drove up and the cab stopped, Lana climbed out but I sat, staring. The veranda was new, redone with large beams and fresh brick, matching the façade of the house. The vines and creeping gardens had been torn down and manicured to look as they had likely been intended. The open wrought-iron gates were gleaming in the spring sunlight and the pathways were fresh stamped concrete.

In the circle drive a massive fountain spewed water into the air, creating rainbows in the middle. I wouldn't have recognized my house if I hadn't driven right to it.

I threw money at the driver and ran up to the entrance as he and Lana struggled with the bags.

She shouted something at me but I ignored it, desperate to see inside.

The front doors had been preserved, fixed up and restained. The hardware glistened as the gates did, polished and new.

Mike smiled wide as he opened the door, almost bowing. "My lady, your house awaits. We even got most of the basement done. I hired out the yard to a friend's company, so we will have to add that to the b—"

"You're ruining it." I lifted a hand.

"Sorry." He laughed and stepped aside, his face as eager as mine.

I lifted my hands to my lips, gushing. "Oh, Mike. Oh my God." I stepped inside, spinning in a half circle to try to see it all. "You even had the furniture delivered?" I gasped. The front entryway was like I never imagined it could be. I narrowed my gaze. "How did you do all this in three weeks?"

"We worked night and day." He laughed his bitter chuckle. "The floors are Italian marble with radiant heating. No more cold floors." He beamed with pride.

The white square tiles laid on the angle to look like diamonds were separated by a black circle at each corner. The black-and-white floor glistened with the daylight and brightened up the old space. I didn't recognize anything in the house. The walls were that same crisp blue-white as upstairs and the moldings were all the antiqued cream. The lacey banister and railings shone, tying into the floor and creating a focal point.

My shoes clicked across the floor as I made my way into the sitting room. It was done in teal and beige, creating vibrancy and happiness. It was the happiest room I'd ever seen.

The sofas were lush and thick, looking identical to the catalogues and websites I had picked them from.

Throw pillows and rugs made up the few accents we had.

The massive fireplace took up half of one wall, going floor to ceiling in river rock. It was beautiful and yet added that warmth the room needed.

We continued the tour to the dining hall. The huge industrial table sat twenty comfortably with a giant chandelier hanging over it. Mike had insisted upon the table, boasting about how the exposed steel bolts holding the table together contrasted with the softness of the fabric chairs. Adding the glittering chandelier was exactly the right touch. The fireplace in here was ornate and done in that same antiqued white as the rest of the trim in the house.

The flooring on this floor was the same driftwood as upstairs, but the walls were a slightly bluer color than the rest of the house.

As we made our way through a beautiful archway, the kitchen stopped me dead in my tracks.

My hands wouldn't come away from my lips as tears streamed my cheeks. Mike wrapped an arm around my shoulders, just holding me as I sobbed.

It was enormous, boasting double islands with Italian marble countertops to match those in the bathrooms and cabinets to match the antiqued trim and doors. The sinks were huge, three of them. The backsplash was made of translucent blue glass subway tiles and went up the entire wall and around the enormous window where the largest sink was.

A small glass table sat under the bay window in the far corner overlooking the garden.

Every bit of this would have been picked by Jonathan. It paid the perfect homage to his memory. But it wasn't Jonathan I was grateful to.

"It's perfect," I whispered, wishing I cooked more than Lean Cuisine and salad.

"I'm so glad you like it," Mike muttered, still holding me. His rough fingers against my bare arm felt more real than anything I'd had in a long time.

"There's more." He strolled me down the hallway to the butler's pantry and access to the five-car garage they were in the middle of constructing.

"I don't own a car." I glanced at him, confused.

"You might one day. Maybe you'll want to drive. It'll be the wrong side of the road for you, but I could teach you."

"Wrong side of the road?" I was lost.

"Compared to Britain. You all drive on the wrong side."

"Britain?" I almost said I was from Los Angeles, but I didn't. I hadn't noticed I spoke with an English accent.

Mike was real.

I was fake.

I swallowed the comment down and nodded. "I would love to learn to drive."

"And the bathrooms and billiards room are this way. I also took the liberty of adding a theater room. I wasn't sure how much TV you ladies watch, but it would make an excellent selling feature." He walked me down the other hallway, past the foyer where Lana was hauling in bags and glaring at me.

"You could help."

"We're doing the tour," I snapped back at her.

The bathrooms resembled the ones upstairs and the billiards room was more like a cigar lounge for men, not really a room I could see myself entertaining in.

The study was lovely, done in a shabby chic décor as we had planned.

The theater room was ridiculous. "Was this necessary? It seems a bit ostentatious, like I can't just go to the theater on my own."

"Says the lady with seven bedrooms, a living room that seats thirty people in two separate seating areas, a dining room that seats twenty, the nicest recreation room I've ever seen, a study, a three-thousand-square-foot library, nine bathrooms, and a five-car garage. Yes. A theater room ties in nicely." He rolled his eyes and I laughed.

"Are you mocking me?"

"No way, Emma. I wouldn't dream of mocking you." He chuckled harder.

"Have your laugh. I don't even watch TV." I turned us around and walked us back to the living room. The doors led to a spacious back deck that overlooked a huge backyard. There were several sitting areas, making it seem more like a fancy health club than a house.

"You need a pool. I know a guy."

"Of course you do." I sighed, contemplating the pool. "I do like to swim. Does it actually get warm enough for pools here though? Aren't they mostly indoors?"

"You've lived here for years—have you seriously not noticed how hot the summers are?"

"No," I answered flatly. I never went outside.

"They get hot enough," he answered equally emotionless. I glanced up at him, lost in his stare for a brief second. "You look amazing, by the way. If you don't mind my saying. So different. So healthy."

"I do?" I had hoped I would. If I were being truthful to myself, I could admit I had hoped he'd notice. I had showered and blow-dried my hair and put on makeup, makeup I had to have a private shopper buy for me since I didn't own a stitch of it. I even wore a bra that made my boobs look much better than the one Lana called my after-dinner bra.

"You do." His voice changed, lowering and yet becoming rougher.

"Thank you," I whispered, suddenly painfully aware of his hand on my arm and the rapid beating of my heart.

But this wasn't a story. This wasn't made up. It was real. His rough hand was really touching my soft skin and I had thoughts. Thoughts I shouldn't have. I was engaged to another man.

It was hard fought, and lost, but I couldn't stop. I noticed everything about Mike in a matter of heartbeats. His lips were slightly chapped, like he might be dehydrated. His eyes were tired, weeks' worth of work had made bags under each one. His dark hair was shaggy under his baseball cap, unwashed and filled with dust from building me a dream house I didn't even know I had dreamt of. And yet, I doubted I'd ever found another man as attractive as this one before me.

"How did you redo the house so well, to suit me? You didn't miss a single thing."

"I paid attention. Do you remember us going through the websites and shit, looking at décor, and I got you to use that site all the women love—?"

"Pinterest."

"Right. I joined Pinterest so I could monitor what you were picking and the designer and I chose from that."

"Thank you." I smiled weakly. "The fact you were paying attention means a lot to me."

"You spent three million dollars, Em. Three million. There was no way I was screwing this up." He brushed it off, removing his hand masterfully. "I'm just glad it worked out. You're on the mend, the house is no longer a rat hole, and my guys aren't scared of being here anymore." He laughed.

I smiled wide, wishing that moment of his arm being around my shoulders wasn't over. Something about his touch was better, it was more.

For the first time in a long time, this world was more.

"You were worth every penny," I offered, hoping to sound indifferent, opposite to how I felt.

"Thank you." He glanced around. "Me and the guys will be done for the weekend so you can get the furniture how you like and whatever. I had the designer arrange it so it's functional. I don't know if you're like my mom and have to rearrange the shit a thousand times before you're happy."

"No." I laughed. "I love it all. It reminds me of a luxury inn."

"Well, I'm glad. So we'll be back on Monday to finish the basement. Shouldn't be long, I don't know how long though. We have some concrete curing down there now, so don't go down there. It's still fairly disgusting. Oh, and I took the liberty of hiring the gardener full time. She's a lady I know. She's good and she won't gouge you. She did the yard and garden for us. Looks awesome, huh?"

"She's a miracle worker. To be honest, I never knew there was a fountain."

"No, me either. Took some work to get it running again. You have a cleaning team of some sort, right? When the basement's finished, this will be a fifteen-thousand-square-foot house, plus garage. I can't imagine you two will keep up with that."

"Let me guess—"

"I know someone." He grinned again, his eyes filling with all the spark they had before.

A spark I had come to enjoy.

Chapter Twenty-Three

Captain Wentworth held me tightly, kissing the top of my head. We lay, postcoital and satisfied and yet my mind wandered as it had been doing for weeks.

I had been struggling to come into the story at all and fighting the urge to be in my world.

Not this one that I had made up, but in the real world.

Something was drawing me back there. My thoughts drifted to the house and the yard. I wanted to take a turn about my garden and be in my bed.

It was outlandish that I would want to leave this all behind, that I was frozen in thought, constantly overanalyzing how this had come to be.

This world, which had been my food and comfort and health for so long now, where I was falling into a type of love, an intangible love, with a character in a book, was losing its appeal. And though it felt real, there was still a hollowness to it.

I wondered if it was the renovation or my inability to connect mixing with my previous career, preventing me from seeing the falsehoods all around me as truths. Unlike Lana, I wasn't able to come into this with a blank mind, that was already against me. As I lay there plagued by dissatisfaction, in the arms of the man who defined it in my world, I knew there was only one solution. I no longer needed la la land.

There was no joy in it anymore.

The joy got lost in the realization of what this place was.

The walls tightened around me and the air grew stale. The joy was false and the companionship wasn't quenching my thirst. I drank from a fountain that only made me thirstier. And I didn't want to end up like Lana, driven crazy by the fact that this place wasn't giving us what we wanted but making us want for it all the more. And we would never find our desires here, only a bottomless pit of need.

The worst of it was my regret in the ruin of a beautiful man, character.

Lying with Captain Wentworth, a man of honor, loyalty, and morals, suddenly made me feel something I hadn't really felt here, disturbed.

Here was a man whose moral compass had always pointed north with pride and certainty, and I had managed to change that. I had twisted all the things I admired about him and made him love me.

But it wasn't real love.

It wasn't the feel of rough hands against smooth skin.

It wasn't a man doing something out of character, but rather a woman shaping a man's character to fill a hole.

My hole was filled, in every way, even the ones I could say were not to be spoken of. But my broken heart would only heal halfway here on the stage where every so often the lights caught the strings from the puppets, revealing them for what they were.

Distance had grown between Wentworth and myself and I knew what had to be done.

I had to fix everything I'd ruined.

There was no bringing back Mrs. Smith but I could at least guarantee Cousin William wouldn't marry Anne. I could guarantee he was the only one left single and outed for his sins.

The sun rose through the heavy drapes, creating a line of dust in the air above us. It sparkled and danced and I sighed, contented for the first time in ages.

I climbed from the bed to dress and slip through the bricks back to my own room.

When I got downstairs, the men weren't at breakfast, which was nice. We ladies ate and laughed. Even Mary was more than civil and less demanding.

Afterward, I took a turn about the garden, wishing the grounds were back home, but if I were to leave this book behind, I had to fix everything I'd broken. I couldn't leave it this way, even if it was imaginary.

Once lunch was over, I discovered Anne sitting in a chair, staring out the window. I walked past her, noting the look on her face. I followed her gaze through the window to where Captain Wentworth was speaking with Charles and holding guns. They were back from the hunt. After we ladies had joined them the first time, we weren't invited back.

I took none of the blame in that.

The sadness in Anne's eyes was heartbreaking. She truly was the best person, nicest.

Not just a doting daughter and kind friend but also a selfless person who wouldn't imagine asking for one thing for herself.

Truth be told, she had always been my least favorite Austen girl. Well, she and Fanny Price tied.

I adored Emma's meddlesome antics. She did and said what she believed was right, even when it wasn't, and bore a stern and judgmental lecture with dignity.

Eliza Bennet was a proud and intelligent young woman who tried to do right by people, apart from Mr. Collins, but I imagined no one judged her for that. She followed her heart.

Catherine Morland was curious and immature, which for her age suited her. She daydreamed and imagined herself in scandalous situations, never truly living in her own world. I couldn't fault her for it and I was forty.

Marianne and Elinor were also favorites, but for differing reasons. I adored the loyalty and strength of Elinor. She was a true lady. And Marianne was her opposite, reckless and living life to the fullest.

No, Anne Elliot and Fanny Price were the two I disliked the most. One a spineless doormat and the other a lackluster scardey-cat.

But upon meeting Anne, and witnessing her family's behavior firsthand, I had to admit, the feelings of judgment faded. To witness a person be so good made it hard to think ill of them.

The silent way in which she loved Captain Wentworth, never allowing herself to believe they might rekindle, was brave and strong in a way I didn't understand.

I had never had to fight for a man or for a love. One was taken before it really had the chance to be anything epic and the other was a figment of mine and Jane Austen's imagination.

I didn't have the same characteristics as she did, not all of them, but I believed I still would have acted the same as Anne had. I wouldn't have chased a man or let my feelings be known unless I knew for sure how he felt about me.

I sat next to her, smiling softly. "Might I intrude?"

"Of course, please." She repositioned herself and tried not to let her eyes drift to where the captain was.

"You still love him?" I asked, boldly.

"Love? No, of course not." She forced another smile across her lips. "That was so long ago, I hardly remember the girl I was then. Or the man he was."

"You can tell me."

"You love him too, Cousin." Her gaze shifted and a strange characteristic I didn't expect seeped out.

"Not the same as you." I shook my head. "I think I love the idea of him. The loyalty and lengths he would go to be with the woman he loved. I love that he never really smiles, he's always grumpy, but then when he does, it lights up everything."

Tears filled her eyes.

"And I love the way he loved you." I hated the words but it was the truth. "He was devoted to you all those years, even now he fights it. The smallest of words from you, encouraging his affections, would end my relationship with him. He would choose you and he doesn't even know it." My eyes felt heavy as I glanced down. "Winning his heart that way, knowing it isn't all mine, doesn't seem right." I got up before she could reply.

I hurried up the stairs to my room and stared at myself in the mirror.

I was never going to get lost here to the extent Lana did. I would always see the strings on the puppets.

Being the creator changed things for me that Lana didn't even notice.

I could have walked from the story, leaving it all behind, but I didn't dare. I needed to see for myself that they got the ending they deserved.

All of them.

Chapter Twenty-Four

I moved the chairs along the house, creating a few more sitting areas around the two new fire pits I'd bought. They had pieces of glass surrounding the flames, designed to resemble sea glass, that would heat up and help create an atmosphere. It was strange but I had never had an outdoor fire before. I'd been to fires, the old-fashioned kind where people sat around burning wood. But that was a long time ago, before the burning of wood was banned.

It was even stranger that I was moving furniture. I'd found it soothing to rearrange it all, moving it to suit me more.

Lana spent ten hours a day in the machines again and Gilda watched her.

"We're all done, Em." Mike came out onto the deck, nodding his head. "I see you got the bug."

"What?"

"Rearranging the furniture. It's a female thing. Men don't do this."

"Really?" I cocked an eyebrow.

"Swear to God, not a single man I know who isn't a designer, does this." He chuckled and I had the impression it was at me and not with me as he folded his thick arms across his broad chest. His tee shirt, this one also stained and holey like the last one, stretched with him. "You wanna see the basement?"

"Not really." I grimaced.

He laughed again. "You're coming to see it." He grabbed my hand, holding it in his and pulling me through the large doors. "All that hard work and you're gonna scrimp on seeing it? I don't think so." He dragged me to the huge staircase descending into what I always avoided.

It was the worst part of the house. Dank and wet and infested. I wished he could have just sealed it up and made it so no one ever had to go down there, but he had refused and called it usable space.

My hand in his felt nice until we made it halfway down and then the grip tightened. Half afraid of what I would see and half stunned by what I was seeing, I paused on the stairs. "Holy shit."

"Right?" He gave me that smile, that one that sent my heart fluttering off like a butterfly.

"What the fuck, Mike?" I never really cussed, but if ever there was a moment to cuss, this was it. I ripped my hand from his and covered my eyes and shouted, "I am dreaming, right?" I rubbed my eyes and opened them, earning a smug look from him.

"Nope." He bit his lip and I swooned, over him and my basement.

"How is this possible, Mike? Is the staircase a wormhole to a different house?"

"Come on, crazy." He grabbed my hand again and pulled me down the remaining stairs. "We used the same wood as upstairs on the stairs but the floor is actually treated concrete with the radiant heat under it again. It's stamped and made shiny so it looks like tile but it's more durable. The walls had to be completely replaced, it's why it took us two weeks longer down here. We have new foundation walls in a few places; patches had to happen. It was rough. You had a stream going through here and had to redirect the water and add weeping tiles and a whole new protection system. This is a rec room, obviously." He held a hand out to the beautiful room. "The windows needed new wells dug, so we did that and actually made the windows bigger so more light gets in. And we cleared all the shrubs away so there's nothing in front of them, just sky. Each window well has its own drainage now too." He nodded, satisfied with himself.

My stomach was a mess, fluttering mess. I couldn't believe the changes in the room. It had large windows that looked out at the sky and window wells that were clean and steel, glistening.

The ten-foot-high ceiling was flat and crisp white with pot lights spattered everywhere.

The walls were also crisp white and perfectly flat. No more exposed wood and rotten pieces of wall. No more rodents and disturbing messes.

The house was pristine.

"This doesn't even look like a basement," I muttered, imagining seating areas and a reading area and rugs with plush underlay and maybe even some plants. It was light and beautiful.

"And this way, please. The tour has to keep on schedule." He gripped my hand and pulled me to the left. A large cedar door greeted us. He opened it, blasting me with heat, revealing a giant cedar sauna with two huge rows of benches and a proper stove. The walls and ceiling were all cedar, not the same pale stain as upstairs in the library but dark and comforting.

He closed the door and pointed to the black dial on the wall. "This is the heat control. The room is insulated very well but also has a ventilation system to prevent moisture. It's a dry sauna." He led me to the next door down the hallway, opening it. "And your spa tub." This room was different than the sauna, completely opposite. It was a dressing area, complete with a changing room and that led to a large glass door. Brightness filled the space as if lights were on inside the spa room behind the glass door but they weren't. When he opened it, light flooded in from a huge glass extension, a ceiling and walls made of windows like a solarium. He pressed a button on the wall and the windows opened, bringing in cool air and the smell of spring.

The tub was massive, big enough to fit six people.

The room was done in bright white tiles on the walls, ceiling, and around the tub and seating areas.

It was stunning.

I turned to him. "I think you're making this a hotel."

"What?" He shrugged. "It just felt right. I mean, you can't have a hot tub in an enclosed area. You need to feel the rain and snow, and this room is watertight."

"This is insane."

"You don't like it?" He cocked his eyebrow, calling bullshit on my statement.

"I like it. It's just crazy to see such efforts going into a spa tub. It looks like a spa."

"You never know, Em. You might decide to turn the old place into an inn. At some point. The option is there. Ya know? Now that you're all healed up and better, you can do anything."

I smiled politely, not sure how much longer I would be able to play along with the cancer patient lie.

It felt wrong to let him believe that, but I didn't know how to tell him the truth.

He led me through the rest of the basement, taking me to four more bedrooms, each with a small ensuite, and a huge laundry room with three washers and three dryers, all top quality.

The room was bright with stairs leading out back to the yard.

Even the boiler and furnace room were clean and updated.

I'd never seen anything like it.

"So?" he turned and asked me when we got back to the stairs.

"I am speechless."

His eyes dazzled me as he smiled wide, the smile I looked forward to. "Then I did my job right."

"You outdid anything I ever expected. By so much that I can't express to you how pleased I am."

"So what you're struggling to say, in British, is that you're overjoyed."

"Overjoyed," I agreed.

He stepped closer, coming into that bubble I considered too close for friends. "This has been my favorite job yet. I'm sad to see it end." He offered me his rough hand.

I slipped mine into his and smiled. "Me too. You will still come to visit, won't you?"

"I'd love to come to dinner and see that kitchen in action." He winked and I sighed.

"Does it have to be me in action?" I chuckled, biting my lip and staring at his.

"Yeah. I mean it. I expect you to learn to cook. You can't have a kitchen like that one and not cook in it. You need to create in there."

"Even if it's entirely inedible?"

"Yes. I grew up on a farm, I'll eat just about anything."

"Good to know." I tried not to gush but he was making me gushy.

I walked him to the front door, leaning against the frame as he put his work boots back on. His men had loaded the trucks and driven off, leaving Mike behind with only his truck in my driveway. I was so used to seeing his trucks that as he took a step back from me, I realized I was going to miss them. I was going to miss *him*.

It wasn't just the house being new or the fact I was no longer a shell of a human being that made me not want to go back into my story. It was him.

For him I showered and shaved and cleaned and changed. For him I put on makeup and clean clothes. In the beginning, it was just the essentials that I had stopped doing before. Over the months we worked together it became weights and exercise and trying to look like the girl I once was, maybe even more than her. And it was all for him.

But like Anne, someone I had judged so harshly, I remained silent, swallowing the feelings now choking me as he smiled wide and took another step back.

His mouth moved and I knew it was just formalities, polite words spoken when one was leaving another person's house and employment.

I wanted so badly to tell him to stop. I wanted him to walk closer and not farther away. I wanted to reach up and see if his face was as rough as his hands and if his lips felt the way I imagined them. I wanted to tell him that he had awakened me, like the evil queen disguised as Sleeping Beauty. Tears lodged in my throat as I nodded and smiled politely.

"Promise me you'll learn to cook just one meal. One fantastic meal in that kitchen."

"Of course. And then you'll be by for dinner?" I asked, struggling to speak and breathe under these conditions.

"It's a date." He offered his hand. "And if you wanna learn to drive, I can teach you. I can even take you car shopping and make sure you get something safe."

I placed my hand in his and prayed it wouldn't be the last time. "It's a date then."

He held my hand, not shaking, just holding. I think I trembled but maybe it was him.

I regretted and would regret for the rest of my life, not owning my feelings then and there.

I regretted it instantly.

How could I let such a man let go of me and walk away?

How could I be such a spineless weakling?

It was fear.

The same fear that kept Anne silent.

Fear that I was reading more into it than was there. Fear that I was seeing things that weren't happening. Fear that I had misinterpreted this friendship.

I stayed silent as he let go and turned, lifting his hat and rearranging it on his head, glancing back once and waving.

I waved, wanting too many things from the moment that was slipping from my fingers.

He left and I watched that spot on the driveway for too long. Imagining it all going differently.

That really was the only thing I was good at.

Chapter Twenty-Five

Captain Wentworth met my gaze, offering a seductive smile with a hint of desperation. I smiled politely back, not leaving the room or hinting at a tryst in the hallway. I had a plan.

It was an awful plan but it was all I had.

When Captain Benwick and Louisa had opened up about their feelings, I suggested a trip to Uppercross would be in order for her father to be asked for his daughter's hand in marriage.

Harville was heading home. His visit had lingered and his wife missed him.

Then I mentioned to Charles that he should be there when his father gave Benwick consent, as his father might need his word to speak for Benwick. Charles of course agreed, feeling self-important by the advice. He demanded he and Mary return home as well.

Anne suggested going to Uppercross also, pondering if she would be needed to aid Mary with the boys, but I suggested it was I who wasn't feeling well and would require her to remain.

Of course, Cousin William had no intentions of letting Anne out of his sights, not before he got up the gumption to ask for her hand, so he remained also.

The first night of the house being just the four of us was awkward and quiet.

Anne seemed distressed at staying but I wouldn't hear of her leaving.

We ate and I went to bed early. Captain Wentworth snuck into my room, hopeful that I would be interested in some company.

When I explained I wasn't well or feeling the need for company, he left, looking rather defeated.

It was the first phase of killing love.

Several days earlier I'd started something with him, not letting him finish and leaving him sexually frustrated.

I considered sneaking the dreaded cousin into the room to seduce and then have him propose to me also, leaving Anne and Frederick abandoned and sad. But then I came up with a much better plan.

I sent word to my mother of the scandal with Mrs. Clay. I told her that Cousin William had boasted to the men, when he believed no one else was around, that he had indeed seduced Mrs. Clay in the hopes of ruining any possible relations between herself and Sir Walter. I explained that he was coldly hoping to marry Anne but keep Mrs. Clay at his beck and call in London, as a kept woman.

I sent the letter, knowing my mother would refuse Cousin William in every way and the news would reach Anne's father who would forbid her to marry William. And Anne being Anne, would listen.

It wasn't my greatest plan ever, but it would work, and swiftly.

I slipped the letter to the maid in the night, explaining I needed the utmost discretion as the letter was going to my mother in response to her disapproval of my marrying Captain Wentworth. Of course the maid would tell everyone and the news would get to Frederick.

He would worry that I was distancing myself at the great risk of being cut off from my family.

It was simple. I just needed to spend more time with Anne, which was easy, and less time with him, also easy now that my heart was so inclined to focus on Mike.

The days went by, Frederick seeming more and more impatient with me and even demanding answers when he came to my room in the night.

I'd told him I was feeling unwell still, and that indeed my mother disapproved which was likely the cause of my illness. He left, unsatisfied and brokenhearted. It was awful to witness until the next morning when I caught him and Anne as they took a turn about the garden.

He laughed and nodded, I couldn't hear what it was about, but I knew I had done what I could. They would need to find the love for themselves now.

A letter from my mother, one most hateful and questioning on the rumors of my marrying a sea captain had reached her. She was outraged. I was to come home immediately to answer for the charges and prove my innocence. She had also mentioned that word of Cousin William's disgusting behavior had been sent to Sir Walter and he was most alarmed at the actions of his own family and the guest of his daughter. He had discovered the truth for himself that Cousin William had indeed set Mrs. Clay up with an apartment already.

When Wentworth and Cousin William went shooting, I packed my bags, acting humbled and distraught.

Anne entered the room, offering a look. "Jane, what is it?"

I handed her the letter.

Her eyes widened as she read, her mouth dropping open. "Jane!"

"I cannot believe Cousin William has fooled us all. Of course he didn't want your father producing an heir with Mrs. Clay. He won her over, her fickle heart."

"And your mother forbids your wedding?"

"She does. I am leaving." I lifted my hands to Anne's, squeezing her trembling fingers. "Do not make the same mistake I have. Tell Captain Wentworth how you feel."

"I can't. He's in love with you."

"Not nearly as much as he's in love with you." I leaned in and kissed her cheek. "You deserve this love." I embraced her and walked from the room, leaving the bags to be picked up for me.

At the bottom of the stairs, I glanced back at her. "I think you're my favorite."

She blushed. "Cousin?"

"Yes," I lied. She had become my favorite Austen heroine. I understood her now. I understood the type of strength it took to keep your mouth shut when your heart demanded things it might not be entitled to. She wasn't a doormat, she was like Elinor Dashwood.

"Safe travels, Jane."

I waved and walked to the study, leaving a letter to explain my absence. I left the letter on his desk.

Dearest Frederick,

As I am sure you know now, my mother has forbidden our marriage. I have left to deal with her and will miss your home and company. I hope you find all the happiness in the world. I suspect you know where to look for it first.

Your heart has always truly belonged to one woman, and she is here, with you now.

She is the one you love, always and forever.

I have seen that from the beginning, but I fooled myself, as did you, professing that you were over her. I know that you're not and never truly will be.

Jane

After, I fled to the carriage, to ride in the miserable thing as I stared back at the house for as long as I could see it.

When Lana pulled me from the world, I realized it would be the last time I ever entered.

I was no longer fleeing anything.

I was no longer addicted to escape and imaginations.

I was over it.

It was a strange and freeing feeling leaving the world behind. Like I'd tucked them all into bed and left them there.

They were neatly settled. All wrongs righted and intended rights fixed.

I opened my eyes and sighed.

"How is Frederick?" Lana smiled.

"He's with Anne." I nodded. "As it should have been all along."

Her gaze hardened. "Did you find Jonathan again?"

"No." I smiled like I had a secret. "I didn't. I think I finally let Jonathan go."

"That's ridiculous." She scoffed, leaving the room.

But it didn't feel ridiculous. It felt good to be back. Not back like Jonathan hadn't ever died, or back like I was half living with my half heart. No, I felt back like I was new, different because of Jonathan and his effect on my life. I would never be Emma who hadn't ever been destroyed and crushed and lost everything. I would always be that Emma.

But I was also Emma who had created something new from the ashes in which she found herself.

The renovation had started as a way to clean up in case my friends or family came looking for me. But it ended up renovating my life.

Chapter Twenty-Six

I stared at the pan, sizzling over the gas flame, and then back at the recipe. The picture on the screen didn't look like what was in my skillet, at all. The picture showed nice browned onions and garlic but mine weren't nearly as dark. I glanced at the heat again, nervously before turning it up a fraction. It licked the bottom of the frying pan, making my hands sweat.

I could program myself with microscopic computers to become the greatest cook in the world, but I couldn't make one lousy Italian dish on my own. Not over open flames. It was something I hadn't realized triggered me until this moment.

"Come on, Emma. Buck up," I whispered, stirring again and then checking the recipe as they cooked. I was doing everything right-*ish,* minus keeping the temperature hot which was screwing with the amount of time I needed to cook them before adding the wine.

I turned the heat up a little, and within a second, the onions and garlic went from barely cooking to burnt.

I winced and pulled the skillet off and turned off the burner. "Shit!"

"What are you doing?" Gilda asked, giving me the most confused stare.

"Trying to go on a date." I sighed.

"With the fire department?"

"Actually, yes. I was sort of hoping any one of them would show up and take me out for dinner instead."

"I thought all English women could cook."

"They deep-fry, and I'm not English." I grinned. "I'm from LA. We eat sushi and avoid gluten but don't know why."

"You sound as British as the queen, kid. I hate to break it to you, you're English."

"No," I replied as the queen might and the focused on turning it off. "I am American. I've spent so much time in the machine, in an Austen novel, I got a bit lost."

"Like Mrs. Delacroix?" she asked as she glanced at the baby monitor she used to keep track of Lana.

"Yeah, about that bad."

"She's got a problem." Her eyes met mine like maybe she wanted to talk. "And I don't know how long I can keep on taking your money to watch her kill herself. She's up to twelve hours now, wearing Depends undergarments in case she doesn't hold it. I'm seventy and I don't wear them. Yet my husband on his deathbed didn't wear them."

"Twelve hours?" I felt sick hearing that. I hadn't noticed her comings and goings. She wasn't speaking to me since I stopped going in the week before. And with Gilda here I didn't account for her whereabouts. Without the machine, we really didn't have anything in common. She was living in a pretend world filled with avoidances, and I was planting flowers and speaking with the zoning committee about this possibly becoming an inn and rearranging everything because, apparently, the bug was catching.

"I think you might need to have a talk with her." Gilda gave me the motherly look.

"She won't listen." I knew she wouldn't. She'd been years at this and was only getting worse. "I'm afraid we have one solution and I can't be the one to do it. I need to call her parents. This is all my fault. I made the machines and the monster."

"Emma, that's not how being an adult works. She chooses to

go into the machine. You went in, you liked it, most likely you got crazy with it. Then I'm assuming you realized you couldn't keep this up and left the machine. You don't go in anymore. She is making this choice, not you."

"I know, but I feel like I've enabled her all this time."

"Oh, that you're guilty of, kid, there's no doubt. But enabling someone isn't making them pull the trigger. She's doing this to herself. Have you considered rehab maybe?"

"She'll kill herself, she has tried before. This is the only thing that prevents her from self-harm."

"You're speaking with a British accent again."

"It's hard to go back." I forced myself to be American again.

"Just promise me you'll figure something out for Lana."

"I will." I nodded at Gilda.

"What's with the date?"

"The contractor who was working here, he wants me to cook him dinner and I'm afraid I've never been a cook. And this gas range makes me nervous, so I keep turning it down, and then the food isn't cooking right so I turn it up and things are burning so I turn it off. I'm on frying pan number four, and I still don't have a good base to add the chicken to. I go from uncooked or browned to brunt in seconds."

"Okay, well a good home-cooked meal for a local boy is a chowder in the winter and barbecue with salad and potatoes in the summer. Dessert is pie. I would order a pie, no point in ruining this pretty kitchen with you and a pastry recipe only to make something inedible that will likely choke the poor man. I'm gonna write down the recipe. Trust me, you cannot mess this up and I'll order you a pie from my friend. She makes them for all the fundraisers around town. Her freezer is full of them, and you can just pop it in the oven and voila, homemade pie."

"Really?"

"Absolutely. I'll bring the frozen pie with me tomorrow. This was my husband's favorite meal. You call that boy and tell him dinner will be served here tomorrow night at six, and he better shower before he gets here." She winked and left the room, glancing at the monitor.

"Thanks!" I called after her.

"Don't thank me, deal with Lana," she called back.

I sat and contemplated what to do about Lana and made myself a smoothie for dinner.

What would I have done had I still been addicted? I would have ignored the world, ignored my health, and hoped no one noticed.

Who did I fear noticing?

The answer to that was obvious, I knew what I had to do.

But I couldn't do it today. I needed to clean the kitchen and figure out her recipe. And figure out how to turn on the barbecue.

Fortunately, Gilda's recipe was easy and by the next day I had it all down pat.

When it was time, I started the barbecue out back and noted I felt better about the meal. I'd made the salad in advance, as she had recommended, and had the dressing off to the side so I just had to mix the two before we ate.

The meat had marinated all day so, supposedly, there was no way I could screw it up. I used chicken so even if it cooked a little too long, it would still be better than an overcooked steak.

The potatoes were simple. I sliced them up with onions and wrapped them in tinfoil with butter and salt and pepper and put them in the oven at a low temperature. I would finish them off in the barbecue when the meat went on.

It all sounded simple.

I had even gone to the store, myself, and bought beer, flowers, and sour cream.

That hadn't been as fun as I hoped. It was more how I imagined—feared it would be. People staring and wondering who I was. Maybe assuming I was the lady from the house on the hill.

I felt naked and my hands sweaty, but I came home with everything I needed. Mike didn't strike me as a wine guy and I wasn't a drinker. A small glass of wine with dinner was my max and only since I went into the machine where we drank wine and ale all the time.

I set the table outside. It was almost summer and the weather was sunny; not too hot but the chill in the air had lifted at last.

When the doorbell finally rang, I jumped, giving myself a once-over in the hallway mirror. I'd checked the house and myself about ten times but once more wouldn't hurt.

My dark hair was still pinned in a large bun, it had grown back thick and lush, and then some. My makeup was simple—daytime makeup was what the tutorial on the computer called it. My tee shirt and capri-cut jeans were simple, matching the meal according to Gilda.

She said you couldn't cook something fancy and dress down, the same way you couldn't make a man barbecue wearing a silk dress. It sounded strict but made sense.

I loved having her around.

She'd turned out exactly as I had expected her to be, no nonsense and yet motherly. She even licked her fingers and wiped food off Lana's sleeping face once. It was a satisfying moment for me.

I slapped across the marble in my sandals. Smiling and taking a breath, I opened the large front door. I still enjoyed the heaviness of it. The realness of it.

Mike smiled, appearing cleaner than he had before. There was no baseball hat, his hair was brushed, and he was wearing a clean tee shirt with no holes. Even his jeans looked newish. I snuck in a slight smirk when I saw his dirty work boots.

"Hey, Em." He leaned in lowering his face, kissing my cheek. My body reacted to the kiss, leaning in. It had been a long time since a man, a real man, had done that.

I held my breath, grinning even wider as I pulled back. "Hi. I'm so glad you came."

"Me too." He handed me a bottle of wine. "This is for you. It's my favorite white, which is saying a lot because I'm not much for white wine."

"Favorite?" I glanced at the bottle, surprised by the label. It was a California white I'd never had before, or heard of. It looked trendy and it wasn't beer or in a can. "Come on in." I stepped back, making room.

"Thanks." He took his boots off outside, like always, and then stepped in. "How's it going?" he asked.

"Good. I got the medical office all set up and I actually started considering maybe taking a cruise. One of the ladies at the bank downtown gave me a brochure and I've never been on one."

"A cruise!" His eyes widened. "You must be feeling a lot better if you're looking at cruises and you went to the bank."

"Yeah, well the bank was forced on me," I agreed, guilt hitting me.

"You look incredible. I wouldn't even recognize you from before. It's almost like a miracle. Amazing what drugs can do to save us while killing us off, huh?" He followed me into the kitchen. "I had a friend who had colon cancer and when I saw him mid treatment he looked like he was dying. Then I saw him afterwards and he was a new man."

"It's pretty crazy," I agreed, needing a new subject.

"How's Lana?"

"The same," I offered, my brow growing heavy.

"That's too bad."

"Yeah." It was, but like Gilda said, she was the one making the choice. "Can I pour a glass of this for you?"

"What are we having?"

"Barbecued chicken, a Mexican salad, and grilled potatoes and pie."

"Wow, sounds amazing. I take it you've been cooking up a storm." He sat at the counter and shook his head. "But I'll take a pass on the white wine with barbecue. Why don't I find something from the wine rack that better suits? We need something stronger, maybe a Malbec." He got up and walked to the butler's pantry.

"The wine rack?" I cringed, following him. "I haven't had a chance to pick any—"

He paused as he got there, scowling. "Emma, this is shameful. All these empty racks."

"I have beer," I muttered, hoping I wouldn't be offending him.

"What kind of beer?" His honey-brown eyes narrowed.

"The Stalk. The green label was pretty," I replied weakly.

"Stalk isn't bad but next time get the Captain's Daughter. It's a weird-looking label but the beer's decent."

"Next time?" I smiled again.

He took a step closer. "Oh yeah. There's going to be a next time, Em." He lifted his hand and brushed some wispy hair from my face. "And another next time after that." He leaned in, grazing my lips. The kiss was the sort that whispered of possibility but reeked of self-control. He gently feathered his tongue against my mouth as he pressed into me. The attempt at open-mouthed kissing was hinted at and then dropped before it could be discussed further.

He pulled back, giving me a look that suggested we were having a conversation, silently.

I swallowed hard, needing to be out of the tight pantry before I did something unladylike.

Something I might regret.

No, I wouldn't.

But I would regret rushing it.

No.

I doubted I would regret that either.

I moved forward with each thought, flinching and then recoiling. I bit my lip, struggling with the idea of having counter sex with the man I'd come to adore. But the barbecue was running and the salad was sitting on the counter, and we hadn't even discussed the fact we were attracted to each other. And he called me a witch once. Maybe more than once.

"Are you okay?" He wrinkled his nose. "We don't have to rush into anything. It can just be dinner."

"I haven't dated in the modern times, in a really long time so I don't know what's right or wrong. I don't wanna look desperate, or slutty, but I think I might be." I listened to myself and then started to laugh.

"Trust me, Em, I am as green as you are at this. I went on one dating website for three months. In that time, I learned about something called the head-and-shoulders picture which automatically means the girl is a minimum of thirty-pounds overweight. I discovered the bootie call which means she doesn't want you to talk and only messages you to come over after ten thirty. And my personal favorite was the girls who dated multiple guys at once. They never stopped having a profile once you started seeing them. They texted other guys on the date. Not to mention, because I'm forty-five, I'm supposed to date down in age. The girls messaging me were the same age as my nieces. I gave up. I don't really selfie or Snapchat, and I never Insta anything." He stepped closer again. "And I don't think you're slutty and even if you were, I wouldn't care. I just wanna eat some barbecue and laugh and drink some wine, obviously less wine than I thought we would be, and maybe see if this is what I think it is."

"Okay." I was flushed, burning up. Desire, humiliation, and awkwardness engulfed me. But I took his hand in mine and led him to the kitchen, enjoying how real he felt.

When we got to the kitchen, I turned, pressing my lips together and pushing away half of everything I learned about being a lady in the Regency era. I lifted on my tiptoes and wrapped my arms around his neck, placing a kiss on him. It wasn't the possibility of a kiss or a whispering of what was to come. It was a kiss, not to end all kisses but to declare feelings.

And when his arms encircled me, lifting me into his chest, squishing me slightly, I parted my lips, sliding my tongue into his mouth.

He was going to be a gentleman until I told him he didn't have to be, not completely, and then he kissed me like he didn't have a single other thought in his mind but devouring me.

Our tongues danced in our mouths as our chests pressed into one another. He sat me on the counter, leaning in as I wrapped my legs and hooked them into his.

We kissed until I was breathless and tugging at his tee shirt.

His skin was warm against my fingers, burning me even.

He kissed and licked his way from my lips to my cheeks and neck. His fingers lifted my shirt too, dragging up and down my back, massaging.

We clawed at each other for several moments before he pulled away, abruptly. "I promised myself I wasn't going to do this." He scowled. "I like you. A lot. And I understand you were sick, and I don't want to pressure you—"

"I wasn't sick," I blurted it before I thought about it.

"What?"

"It wasn't cancer. I didn't have the heart to tell you when you assumed." I closed my eyes, unable to look at him as I said it, "I wasn't sick. Lana isn't sick. She's an addict but she isn't ill. Not conventionally."

"Oh shit. You're a couple of druggies," he groaned.

"No." I opened my eyes, noting he was even farther from me. "I'm a neuroengineer. My name is Dr. Emma Hartley. I'm from New York, well, Los Angeles." I took a deep breath. "I used to own a company." I wasn't making sense, I was panicking too hard to think.

As his face grew angrier and angrier, I hopped off the counter and offered my hand. "It's easier if I show you."

He eyed my hand like it was the most disgusting thing he'd ever seen.

"Please, give me a moment to explain," I pleaded. "Please. It will all make sense in a moment. I swear."

His jaw was clenched so tight he couldn't speak, but he nodded once. I dropped my hand and sauntered to the stairs. I walked up them to the medical room, pausing and slumping, not looking back at him. I didn't need to. I could feel his eyes and hot breath on me, like a dragon. "I never meant to lie. I just didn't know how to tell you."

He was silent so I turned the handle, shaking my head at a confused-looking Gilda.

"This is Gilda. She works for us. I think you met her before. She's a retired nurse who monitors us, well Lana, in the machines." I turned back, hating the cold expression on his face. It was breaking my heart, my whole heart. "It's an alternate reality based on literary works."

"Like a video game." Gilda tried to help.

"Right," I winced as I continued. "We enter a reality created for us and live as the characters we love."

"Are you fucking kidding me right now?" He sounded lost but not less angry.

"No. Do you have a favorite novel?" I asked, defeated and desperate.

"No. I don't read."

"Nothing?" I swallowed hard.

"I guess when I was a kid I liked a fantasy series called A Wheel of Time."

"By Robert Jordan." I knew it well.

"Yeah." He sounded so disinterested.

"If you lie back, I can show you. I promise it's not harmful in any way. I will put you in and take you out within minutes, just so you can see what I mean."

Gilda scowled. "I don't think that's a good idea." Her eyes widened like she was trying to tell me something.

"Why?" he asked.

"The machine is addictive—"

"Well, that's not entirely true. Loads of people use it and don't have any issue." I defended my work; I still defended it. "Lana and I had problems because we lost someone we desperately wanted back."

"Lost someone you wanted back?" Mike folded his arms across his chest.

"My husband. I thought maybe I could find him in the story and live a life with him. I wanted to live in the story and ended up stuck there. For a while."

"Jesus, Emma. This is sick." He stepped back, shaking his head. "This is what you were doing? Living in the fucking filth this house used to be, covered in weird sores and smelling like death because you couldn't be bothered to clean or change your clothes? You're still letting her live this way? You might have cleaned the house up, but it's still just a dirty crack shack. This is fucked up." He turned and stormed down the hall.

"Wait!" I hurried after him. "Mike, wait. Please." I ran down the stairs after him, grabbing his arm at the door. He ripped his arm from my grip.

"You let me think you had fucking cancer. You let me think you were sick. What kind of terrible person does something like that? A sick and twisted person. A selfish person. The fact that woman is up there, rotting away in front of you, still using that machine, and you just tried to hook me up to it, makes me think you're not just selfish. You're fucking nuts. I don't need any more crazy in my life. Jesus." He turned and stormed to his truck, slamming the door and driving off like a madman.

I dropped to my knees, hating the realness of this world and the truth in everything he'd said.

Chapter Twenty-Seven

I tapped in the number, the one I'd planned to call. The one I'd avoided until Mike left. The one his unkind words made me see needed to be called.

I'd tried to talk to Lana before calling, give her the chance to stop on her own.

I had showed her the mirror; I made her look at herself.

I had forced her to get on the scale.

I'd even tried to tell her the machine wasn't working or the electrical in the room was acting up.

She refused to listen, having fits and screaming in the bathroom with a razor in her hands, the girl who would never cut herself. The crazed look in her eyes suggested she might.

She twitched and pulled her hair out, and I paid Gilda more money to stay longer, for one week.

I'd lost control of my friend and I needed her to see there was no going back.

As the phone rang, I glanced at the monitor on the counter, the one watching Lana sound asleep in the machine.

An older woman answered with a hesitant expression on her face. "Dr. Hartley?" She was perplexed. I sensed it.

"Hi, Mrs. Nervier, I'm calling because I need your help."

Her eyes widened as I floundered, trying desperately to find the words to explain our situation.

"Lana is addicted to the machine I made. All along I thought it was impossible. I even joined her on these journeys for some time. But I can't help her and I can't force her out of it. She threatens to hurt herself and I'm ill-equipped to handle the situation. I'm more of a numbers and code sort of person."

"What do you mean addicted?" she asked. "What are you talking about?"

"She lives in the machine, like the mayor said she did. He was right." The words are whispered and hoarse, but I force them out nonetheless. "Everything he said was true." Including the part where I was to blame.

"Lives?"

"Has a life with Danny and their children. A fantasy world she has created in which she is still with him."

"Jesus Christ." She paled, her skin losing color so noticeably that I could see it on the tablet. "What have you done?"

"I don't know." I had nothing. I was responsible. I should have stopped her. I should have forced her. But I didn't. Stopping her would have been admitting my machine was faulty, my science was faulty, and that I had a problem.

Before Mike, before the house, that wouldn't have been possible.

But I saw clearly now.

I saw the flaws in the machine, the ghosts we put in there.

I regretted everything and nothing simultaneously.

"I thought the machine could heal her. I thought she was better. She's sick, Mrs. Nervier. I don't know what to do with her. I'm thinking about committing her, but I can't make that decision. I'm not her next of kin. What should I do with your daughter?"

"We don't have a daughter anymore, Dr. Hartley. She's been gone for years. Do what you have to, but leave us in peace." She disconnected the call, leaving me holding the tablet with my own face staring back at me.

And then there were two faces. I frowned, not certain Lana was really there.

"You bitch!" Her face wrinkled as she screamed.

I turned to her and then looked at the monitor, as if to check that the reality in front of me were real. Her absence from the picture proved this was indeed real.

"Lana, you need help. I love you, I just want to help you. You're not even talking to me anymore. And I don't know what to do. It's time to help yourself."

"You fucking bitch! You dare to try to commit me, when you know how much they need me? You would keep me from my family?" Her bloodshot eyes were wild, matching the way her hair frizzed out everywhere and the baggy tee shirt with stains on it and loose-fitting jogging pants. It was like seeing the "after" of a drug picture, only she was real and raving in my kitchen. "You backstabbing bitch. You think you're so much better than me, 'cause you don't need the machine anymore? You think you're so great, when even your husband wouldn't show up in your dreams? Even he didn't want you. And that fucking Wentworth douche knew who to pick. He never loved you. He always loved Anne. You're pathetic. For a smart lady, you're dumb as shit. Marshall was right about you—sad fucking spinster who needed to get fucked."

Venom poured from her chapped and cracking lips.

"You think anyone will listen to you, why? 'Cause you took a shower and got your hair dyed? You still look like shit, Emma. You always did. You're a plain Jane. You should have kept that name like your phony fucking accent. That's why Mike left. He saw what a fraud you were." She ranted and paced, screaming at me.

I was so lost in her words, letting each one hit me just a little harder, that I missed the blood on her hands for several minutes.

When I saw the crimson droplets hitting the floor, I scanned her rail-thin arms, searching for a cut but there was none.

My eyes darted upstairs.

"What have you done?" I rushed past her, leaving her to scream and shout. I ignored the vile things she said, bursting up the stairs. She couldn't keep up and was still shouting from downstairs when I got to the medical room, pausing in the doorway at the scene before me. "Gilda!" I screamed, pressing a number on my phone and rushing to her. I dropped to my knees, seeing the warm blood pooling under her.

"She was a meddlesome bitch. She was cutting me off, Em. She was limiting me, giving me less and less and fucking with the clocks so I thought I had more time than I did. Stealing time from my kids. She tried to give me a sedative." She leaned in the doorway, rubbing her hands over her face, smearing blood and wheezing from the stairs. Her voice changed back to wimpy and whiny, trying to manipulate me, "She tried to trick me into regular sleep." Her eyes darted to the needle sticking out of Gilda's old arm.

My phone call was picked up and someone spoke.

I hid the phone next to Gilda and shouted, hoping my cries would be heard, "You killed her, Lana. You killed Gilda."

"She deserved it. It was an accident," she whined and then shouted, "She tried to cut me off!"

Someone shouted my name from the phone but I hung up, hoping it was enough.

"Lana, we need to call the police." My voice broke as my hands touched the warm body of my deceased friend. I gripped her, hoping for some of her strength. "We need to call 911. We need an ambulance. She might not be dead." I glanced at the scissors lodged in her neck and knew she was.

"Don't touch her, Em. We can leave her here and get the machines and leave. We can call and say we were on vacation and someone must have broken in." Her eyes widened, showing the bloodshot whites. "They were trying to steal the machines. It was Marshall I bet."

Her ability to lie was uncanny. She was already starting to believe the lies she spun.

"Okay." I nodded, terrified and yet never clearer. "You need to get cleaned up. Wash your hands. I'll go and pack a bag and you pack a bag. And it'll look like we were on vacation."

"Yeah, and then we'll call and tell them the alarms went off or something. Say our housekeeper didn't check in today, which is weird. She always calls us on vacations." She spun so fast even I could see the details stitching together in the air around us.

Hot tears leaked from my eyes but I nodded and tried to sound normal, "Okay, so let's clean you up. You need to wash your hands first. I'll wait here with Gilda—"

"Don't say her name!" she shouted, sinking into the doorway. "Don't say her name, say housekeeper. She was a housekeeper." Tears flooded her eyes too as the predicament she'd put us both in began to build around her, walling her in.

It was strange to watch it happen. She'd been so big and loud and terrifying a moment ago and then it changed. She shrunk, sinking into the doorframe and falling to her knees. She pulled in her shoulders, getting smaller and smaller, hugging herself and rocking. "Say housekeeper. Em, say housekeeper. Okay? Say housekeeper. Don't say her name."

"Okay."

"Emma!" she shouted at me. "Help me!" She clawed at her head, smacking it over and over. "You have to help me!"

I glanced back at the syringe on the counter filled with the blue liquid, the carrier for the nanobots and then to the scissors in Gilda's neck. I didn't know which one was a crueler fate, but I knew which one I was capable of. I grabbed the blue syringe, holding it up. "You need this. You need Danny," I spoke softly, walking slowly to her. I didn't need to get her worked up.

"I need Danny." She nodded, her eyes wide, lost in the beauty of the incandescent blue light.

I tried not to shake when I took her thin arm and stabbed the needle in, pushing the liquid into her. "It'll be okay."

As I sent the nanobots, the tension in her arms and legs lessened.

She smiled as she relaxed. "Thank you." She gave me a last look. Her eyes were filled with knowledge, some of it gratitude and some of it fear.

I dosed Lana Delacroix for the last time.

She was drifting off, completely gone, only not.

It was over.

"I have to call the police, Lana," I whispered, my voice now filled with everything I was trying to hold back.

"I know." She blinked a tear down her cheek. "Let me die in here."

A shadow crossed the floor of the hallway behind her, and for one second I wondered if it was Gilda, already haunting the house. But the face of the man I'd called, rounding the corner, lifting a finger to his lips, made more tears fall from my eyes. I nodded, losing the control I had on myself. I exhaled as he crept up behind her, holding her as she fell—succumbing to the nanobots.

I collapsed too, falling to the floor, sobbing.

The tears and sobs weren't just for this moment. Most of them belonged to a woman standing in the yard as her husband was carried away. She never cried then—I never cried then. I never sobbed like this, the purifying tears one needed to grieve properly.

Mike laid Lana down carefully and lifted me up even more so. He held me to his chest, whispering into my ear all the lies I needed to hear.

He held me through it all: the police, the ambulance, and the psych ward attendants who came and took Lana.

She was as still as could be when they strapped her into the gurney, restraining her hands and feet and administering an antipsychotic.

She wouldn't need it. Ever.

She would never have an episode for them.

She wouldn't come back for them, and they wouldn't know what was wrong with her.

The needle marks and the dying body would suggest enough.

Like a coward, a villain, I never told them about la la land. I never told them who I was. And with no one to care for Lana, or about her, there was no one asking questions.

She was a crazy woman, just as her ex-husband had declared her to be.

And all the guilt of her situation rested on me.

She would live out her life in la la land, lost forever, and I would be stuck with the bill. Only I would never have the amount needed to cover it.

Chapter Twenty-Eight

Palm Springs, 2030

I sat in the window, watching the gray day as the rain came down.

Her reflection and mine were so close, our eyes almost matching in the lost stare we both had. Her gown was the difference. That and the gauntness of her face.

Lana sat in the chair, permanently gone. The dose of nanobots was in her, letting her live, freeing her, taking over her brain.

Her mouth was slack and her eyes dead, her skin gray and her nails peeling. Her lips were chapped and if you looked closely enough, they moved. She whispered to you the secrets of where she was. She told you of what she'd done that day, and she let you into the most intimate of moments. Sometimes a flush hit her cheeks or her lips almost puckered.

In her eyes, the day and nights moved at a pace she dictated.

In the real world she withered, sitting in front of a false window where it always rained and it was always gray, neither awake nor asleep, just gone.

It broke my heart to see it, to feel the lifeless touch of her hand in mine.

But at the same time, I told myself, she wanted this. She

wanted this end. She wanted her family and her life there.

The real world was lost to her.

Lana Delacroix had climbed the icy banks of the shore, saved by the man who would be swept away seconds later. She met his eyes as he bobbed once, just above the water for a second. She saw the lifetime they might have shared slip away with the freezing muddy water. In that instant, he'd pulled her with him. He'd taken her heart, her whole heart, with him to his icy grave. He'd saved it, protected it in heaven.

But Lana was not like me. She could live without a heart.

She coasted and floated and acted like a person.

She married someone her parents needed her to.

She bought shoes and perfume and had sex, never making love.

She lived as a shell in a half life, already a robot when the nanobots found her.

They had brought her back.

They alone gave her the life she had witnessed once in a flash, before it was taken.

And now Lana sat, alone, truly a robot.

In the reflection of the window, I saw it all. Me here, me sitting next to her. Not holding her hands, but slumped in my seat as well. In one version of this tale, this cautionary tale, we matched, she and I.

My hospital gown was baggy and my hair was thinning. My skin was pale and my heart missing. The spark in my eyes, the one that suggested I had thoughts and feelings and hopes, was gone.

I too sat, staring out at the gray world, the one where it was always raining and cloudy.

I too saw the world passing by in the flecks of my eyes as I lived in my mind, a host to a whole world. A world with a real moon, stars, and sun and a son, daughter, and husband—a whole galaxy living inside the flecks in my eyes.

This was my nightmare. A ghost I had brought out of the machine with me.

Every time it rained, I checked, to ensure I wasn't in the

machine. I wasn't sitting in front of the rain wall in the hospital with Lana, lost in the dreariness of it all.

There was always a chance that I'd gone in and this world was a figment of my imagination.

And I wondered what I would want.

I contemplated the syringe in my bag, the one that linked to the tablet next to it. The one that would bring her back.

The one that would ease my guilt.

I could wake her up and she would be forced back to the land of the living, and she could choose how she lived or died.

She wouldn't be a slave to the games played with her mind, the games she was playing.

It would ease my guilt to know she was alive and whatever harm fell upon her was her choice.

I reached into the bag, touching it, feeling the cold glass of the siren's holder, and I contemplated for the longest second of my life.

I glanced back at Lana once more, putting the syringe back at the bottom of my purse.

"I am so sorry, Lana. I want to wish we'd never met." I blinked a single tear and stared out at the rainy day once more.

The selfish truth was that had I not met Lana, I never would have found my heart again. It would still be lost in la la land, buried. I'd had to crawl through the levels of hell to find it; punish myself enough for everything that I'd fucked up, to dig it up from the ashes where I'd left it. But now that I'd found it, I didn't entirely regret sacrificing her to have it back. For the truth in all this, was that I was the evil queen and she was the sleeping princess.

Had I not joined her in the trip to rock bottom, I wouldn't be clawing my way back up to the land of the living.

But she would be different too. Maybe alive. Probably not. But Gilda would be.

Gilda.

Pushing it all away as a cold shiver of self-hatred crossed my body, I squeezed her hand once more before letting go and getting up.

I walked for the door, taking my guilt with me and leaving her the freedom she had so badly wanted. If my peace of mind over what I'd done to her couldn't be gained through time and healing, it certainly wouldn't be gained by bringing Lana back.

She would never recover from being away from her kids in la la land.

I left the hospital in Palm Springs and went directly to the airport, with the window open and my face in the fresh air. I no longer feared the rebirth of spring or the bloom of summer. I no longer hated the feeling of being alive.

Life was for the living and I was amongst them again, a place Lana never wanted to be.

I lived it for Jonathan and Danny and Lana.

I lived it for the kids we would never have and the lives that would never be real.

My heart was no longer with the dead. Splintered little pieces of it remained, but I felt them returned to me in the night when I slept, truly slept. Jonathan or God or maybe the devil himself, returned them with every real dream I enjoyed or suffered. I woke most days refreshed. Sometimes I woke sweaty, shaking with a nightmare, but even those moments were better than being in the dream.

Those nightmares were my regrets and guilt overwhelming me, a feeling I deserved.

Gilda had been a great woman and her death was partially on my hands.

I should have acted sooner.

I should have cut Lana off.

I should have had her admitted.

I should have acknowledged to myself that my machine was evil, that I was too.

I just never did the things I should, not soon enough.

I got lost in numbers and codes and what-ifs and possibilities.

When I landed back in Rhode Island, exhausted and yet enjoying the sensation of being so tired my eyes would hardly remain open, I was jolted awake by a smile from across the airport arrivals gate.

It was the one I had grown to love.

We were friends, and that was okay.

It wasn't my place to ask for more.

I hadn't earned the right to more.

Like Anne Elliot, I had chosen the wrong thing, costing me the love of a man I deeply respected.

Mike waved me over as I headed down the arrivals ramp.

"How is she?" he asked, still concerned about my sending Lana to the hospital she had always enjoyed, the one with the window that lied and showed you what you wanted to see.

"I couldn't do it. I couldn't bring her back. She's stuck awake and sleeping. Exactly as she would have it." I had nothing else to say about that. She was nothing and everything at every waking moment in my life.

All my guilt. All my possibility. All my warnings.

Most of all, she was my reason for destroying the remaining machines.

She was my reason for taking down the beds and making the room into a second office.

She was my reason for selling my home.

But he was my reason for staying in Rhode Island.

I linked my arm in his and walked to his truck. "How does the old place look?" I asked, acting casual about it. There was nothing casual about selling my house. Nothing casual about the fact that I couldn't sleep there. Nothing casual about Gilda's murder. Nothing casual about the blood on the floor and the crazy woman who had lived upstairs.

"It looks good." He lifted his phone and flashed a picture of the new sign. It had daisies on it and a whimsical name. "Apparently, they're putting in a pool."

"Wind Swept Inn." I smiled, almost laughing.

The poor house. It had been such a scary old Gothic mansion once upon a time and now it was a beachy luxury inn. I wasn't sure the bones would agree with the change, but it was done.

"Will you miss it?" he asked as he got my door.

"No." I knew my eyes betrayed me with the lie I told.

"I will too." He shrugged. "But I think you need a fresh start."

"The new place is so small," I joked, forcing us to move on in the conversation.

"Yeah, it is. But you'll get used to five thousand square feet of beachfront property." He rolled his eyes.

"Are you mocking me?" I narrowed my gaze.

"Of course I am. If I don't, who will?" He nudged me.

The truck ride was occupied with fillers. Small talk and laughing, fake laughing. He kept me at arms reach and I understood, grateful to even be this close.

When he dropped me off, I pointed at the house. "You wanna come in?"

"No, I have to work in the morning. Have a good sleep." His tone when he said it killed off a piece of me. I hated that he only saw the liar and the villain. He didn't see the person behind her. The one I was sometimes. The one I was now. The one who had gotten lost. He didn't understand, and I didn't know how to make him see. "Night, Em."

"You called me a hag and a witch," I spoke before I could stop myself. "When I met you, I didn't know I'd gone so far the other way. I needed a renovation because a friend had come by and she saw us and lost her mind. We thought maybe she would bring doctors and straightjackets and lock us up. So we called you to come and fix the house, so at least we weren't living in some run-down shack." Tears filled my eyes. "But we weren't fixing the house up for ourselves. It was so the machines wouldn't get taken away. All my decisions were for those machines, for that world. Lana's too."

"Emma—"

"Let me finish, Mike. I didn't know what I looked like. I was this broken woman, a shell of a human. I was living in the machine and pretending this life was the lie, and I didn't look in mirrors or see the house because this world had nothing for me. There was nothing here for me to stay for. I could have died and no one would've noticed except Lana, and only because she needed me to bring her out." The cold hard reality of it burned like acid in my throat but I pressed on, "And then you came and I started to notice things. You might not have seen me, but I saw you. I saw myself through you. Those stares, the horrified stares. They changed everything. They killed me. They forced me to take a hard look. And pretty soon what was in the fantasy of la la land wasn't better than what was in the real world. Because of you—you, who called me a hag and a witch and told me I looked awful. And when you assumed cancer, I didn't have the heart to tell you how or why I was so ugly. I just kept trying to fix it. And then you started looking at me like a normal person, sometimes even more than that, and I couldn't go back. And it was wrong and I'm sorry. I never meant to mislead you or try to evoke your sympathies. I was just so ashamed." I stepped back, closing the door. I turned and walked to the house, hating that I couldn't get through it without sobbing.

"Emma, wait." He jumped out after me.

"No. You don't have to add anything. I don't need a lecture, Mike. I'm not ever going to forgive myself for what I did. I don't need you to hate me for it too. There is nothing you can say or do that will make me feel worse than I already do. My best friend in the whole world has disowned me. My other best friend is a vegetable who killed her caretaker, a sweet old widow I was really starting to love. And that is on me." I held my hands out as if to show him the blood on them.

"No, Emma, it's not." He walked to me, grabbing me by the arms roughly. "You didn't choose for Lana. She chose for herself."

"I could have stopped her."

"No, she was a junkie. She would have found a way to make it happen for herself. She would have found her way back into that world. Or she would have killed you in the process of trying. You didn't kill Gilda and you didn't force Lana to go into the machine. And I shouldn't have called you a hag and a witch. I say the worst shit when I'm nervous and trying to be funny. My mom says I'm nowhere near as funny as I think I am."

"Please don't." I stepped back, shoving him off. "I just wanted you to know I didn't want to lie to you—I didn't know how to tell you the truth. I know I'm not a good person."

"You're not the bad one you think you are."

"I'm also not the one you think I am."

"Emma, I don't think you're a good person or a bad one. I think you're a human who fucks up like the rest of us. You make mistakes. You're real. This is the real world."

"My mistakes cost lives."

"Yeah, they did. So did mine." His eyes welled too. "I can't do this anymore." He admitted it like it was a great secret. His voice cracked and his eyes flooded with emotion joining the tears. "I love you. I have loved you for a long time. Not the moment I met you"—he laughed that bitter chuckle—"but sometime after that. I built that library because I loved you. I spent nights on that stupid Pinterest, going over everything you pinned, smiling and plotting. I thought about you, long before I realized. And when you called me and sounded so terrified, and you said Lana had killed Gilda, I have never been that scared in my life." His voice cracked again, making more tears spring from my eyes. "I drove across town like a madman. I couldn't bear the thought of something happening to you."

"I'm so sorry, Mike. I'm so sorry."

"It's not okay, I'm not gonna say it's okay. It's fucking insane, is what it is." He laughed again but this time it sounded like a sob. "But if this pile of insane shit is your burden to carry through life, then I am here to help you carry it. I am here, because I can't stay away. I know I should. Your baggage puts the head-and-shoulders mom of six kids from five guys, saying she's an average build, to shame." He stepped closer, lifting a hand and wiping away a tear. "But I love you, crazy baggage and all. And I will never be as sorry as I am right now for the way I spoke to you and treated you. It was honestly meant to make you laugh, not tear you down."

"Mike," I whispered.

"Shut up, Emma. You love me and you want to share your burden and your life with me. I already know that. I'm already carrying some of it for you." He scooped me up into his arms, pressing his lips against mine.

It was hands down the worst declaration of love in the history of declarations, but it was true.

I sobbed into the kiss and the embrace and he held me. He sat on the bench until the tears slowed and eventually stopped.

He carried me inside, like crossing the threshold of the house after a wedding, kicking the door closed and turning for the bedroom.

Being alone in the house, with no one but my ghosts of course, meant leaving the bedroom door open as he laid me on the bed.

He stood over me, maybe checking my puffy eyes for the permission gentlemen sought before.

I didn't reply with words but chose actions. I started to drag my jacket and tee shirt off as I kicked off my shoes and hauled my jeans down.

He sprung to life as well, grinning in a way that made my heartbeat hasten more than it already was.

He stripped completely naked, completely at attention, and climbed over me, hovering there for a second. "You are so beautiful." His honey-brown eyes dazzled me, but he wasn't trying to be charming. He was being earnest.

"So are you." I pulled him down onto me, letting the weight of him become the only weight in my life as he pressed me into the bed and brought me back even more.

Sex in a fantasy was based on all the things you wanted in another person. Sex as an adult in the real world was based entirely on sensation and experience, of which Mike clearly had loads.

We became a mixed-up jumble of sweat and moaning, lip biting and groaning, silhouettes of writhing pleasure against the backdrop of the sea. The sounds and feelings reminded me of la la land but the pleasure wasn't the same, it was truer. It was intense and satisfying, and when I caught a glimpse of myself in the mirror, astride his cock, riding him with his hands cupping my breasts as I leaned back, I didn't look the same. We didn't look the same, as in la la land. We were real.

And when it was over there was no awkwardness or rules or polite society. There was a shower filled with laughter and exploring each other's bodies more.

He had scars, loads of them. A large one on his back from falling off a roof onto a saw bench. His hands were rough and callused but the feel of them against my soft skin was exactly as wonderful as I had imagined. His knees were bad from years of construction, and his heart was bruised from an ex-wife who cheated on him with a workmate before she left him and died.

He didn't easily declare anything and he never offered his feelings without provocation.

He snored and ate terribly.

But he could cook and he loved his mom who he talked on the phone with every week.

He feared his dad who had died years ago but still haunted him in some ways.

He worked too much and laughed too little, but the moment you won that smile from him made up for all the grumpy faces you endured in his presence.

He was real and flawed and that meant he was perfect.

We made love, we didn't fuck. All the things he didn't say were explained there, physically. His hands and his lips and the way he held me so tightly to him that I thought I might burst, enlightened me to the way he felt.

Chapter Twenty-Nine

Middleton, Rhode Island, 2031

"Emma, you burning those steaks?" Mike called out to me on the deck.

I jumped up and ran for the barbecue, carrying the book I was reading with me. When I lifted the lid of the smoker barbecue he'd insisted we needed, I winced. I flipped them quickly and added more barbecue sauce. It was Gilda's recipe and quite good.

"Nope," I shouted at the screen door. Catching my reflection in the window, I grinned. The girl—woman—looking back at me was so altered I might not have known her. Altered in all the best ways.

Her hair was long and braided at the side. She wore a black-and-white sun hat and sunglasses and her shoulders had freckles. She wore a sundress and held a book, and all the cares in the world blew away in the sea breeze coming off the ocean.

Nothing lasted here—not weather, not feelings, not moods, not pain. Love was the only thing hardy enough not to break on the rocky shores or get swept away in the wind that never really died down.

I'd had no idea I needed it, the ever-changing ocean and the constant wind. I had no idea how therapeutic it was. Even when it was soft, it reminded that changes were coming. Some were good and some were bad but they were always coming, mixing it up and keeping it from ever getting stale.

He came out with a plate and a disappointed scowl. "I can smell the burnt meat."

"No, you can't," I lied a little, grabbed the plate, and raised the lid, revealing completely uncharred steaks.

I lifted them off and put them on the plate, carrying them inside, hoping the sauce was enough to cover the burnt taste of the other side.

He pressed himself against me, kissing my neck and encircling himself over me like a bear. "You smell good. Like ocean air and meat." He kissed again.

"It's weird you find that combination attractive." I handed him his plate, which he'd already done up for us both but was waiting on my single contribution: not burning the steaks.

As we sat on the deck at the large table that never felt empty, he lifted his glass of wine. "To you, Em, for thinking you fooled me by placing my steak burnt-side down and hoping I might not notice. And because you lost, you don't get to read your book while barbecuing, like I said you shouldn't."

I laughed and lowered my glass. "Shut up, Mike."

"I love you, even if you're trying to kill me with carcinogens and can burn steak on a smoker, which shouldn't be possible." He toasted me and drank. "That's good wine."

I took a bite of the salad, also Gilda's recipe, and nodded. "Good salad too."

He tilted his head, frowning. "You still don't say 'too' right. Too and darling."

"As well," I said as American as I could. I didn't tell him that I still read with a British accent.

"Much better." He winked and cut the steak, flashing the darker side at me. "You're seriously considering cooking school? Right? I mean, not as a professional, but more like a survival thing. The fact you're even using the barbecue is amazing. But you need to overcome the whole gas-burner thing."

"I have thought about it."

"You really should think about it. If you went in the evenings for something simple, I'd go with you."

"You don't need to learn to cook."

"I know. I'd go in looking like a big dumb construction worker and then surprise them by being the class star." He gave me that bitter grin.

"Oh my God." I rolled my eyes. "Your humility is awe-inspiring."

"I know." He chewed and took a sip of wine. Watching him eat was a pleasure I'd never enjoyed in another person before. He chewed and flexed his jaw in a way that made me pause in the middle of eating and stare. "You're doing it again." He scowled and swallowed the bite with difficulty.

"Doing what?" I played dumb.

"The staring thing, where you zone out and watch me eat." He hated it but I didn't care.

"Oh." I continued to stare. "Just lost in thought."

"Speaking of which, how's the new book?"

"Good. Suspenseful and funny." I bit my lip, about to confess something I never imagined in all the worlds I would. "I have been meaning to tell you something."

His expression instantly grew nervous. Our trust had only gone so deep, both of us scared of the level of commitment we were in.

"I'm writing a book." I took a sip of wine and let that sit in his head.

"About what?"

"All of it. The whole story. It's so far-fetched I think it might make a great story. I'm co-writing with an author. I sent the story to an agent, just the first couple of chapters and the whole synopsis and she liked it. She knows an author who would be able to add the extras. She said the first draft, the meat and potatoes, should be written by me and then the extras would be done by a professional writer."

His eyes widened. "Holy shit, Em. That's insane."

"I know."

"That's amazing. Are you scared of admitting the truth of it all?"

"Yes and no. I'm finding it cathartic to write it all down."

"Add cathartic to the list of things you say wrong." He shook his head, grinning. "This is insane but I'm excited for you. I think you're right; this is cathartic, cleaning even."

I didn't bother telling him that cathartic meant cleansing. He was too cute.

"And will you publish it while Lana's still a zombie?"

"No. I will wait until she's gone." I shook my head. "The book isn't about her anyway. It's about me."

"Are you the good guy or the bad guy in the story?" he asked carefully.

"Which do you think?"

"In your head?" His eyes burned right through me. "You're the bad guy. The better question though is, am I in it?"

"You are." I lost my appetite but forced a bite of salad into my mouth. "Is that okay?"

"No." He tried to sound serious but a smile crept up and it wasn't even the bitter one. It was the one I loved. "But the story might not be the same without the charming construction worker."

"It would be very dark without the light," I agreed.

"Add light to the list." He tried to sound as though he was joking but all the humor had left the meal. "Burns the steaks and rains out the game." He cocked an eyebrow. "I think we might have to start setting rules for things you're allowed to discuss during happy time and what you have to save for your therapist."

I never did tell Mike, but his mom was wrong. Once you got his brand of humor, he was very funny. Maybe even as funny as he thought he was.

"You know I only tell my therapist lies." I grinned, saved by the light again. "I prefer to hear about his problems anyway. They make mine seem like nothing."

"I know. How is old Frank these days?"

"Well, he's confirmed that his daughter is pregnant, which he's suspected for months now. She's showing and well past the point of options, and his wife is going to church again, which he didn't sound excited about. She gets a bit fanatical. And his son has dropped out of football and is dating a girl Frank doesn't approve of. Her parents let him sleep over so Frank isn't letting him leave the house. It's a mess. And his blood pressure's up, so we switch it out, sometimes I take the couch and sometimes he takes it."

"I cannot believe you pay him to let him tell you his troubles and then lie to him about yours. You have the weirdest life I've ever heard of." Mike chuckled and started eating again.

"I know it."

The rain clouds I'd brought to the table left, carried away by the wind. This was our dance. I was gloomy and he was light. And then he was serious and grumpy, and I was cheerful and mocking. And we switched it up, helping each other carry the load.

His burdens became mine and mine his, and together neither of us ever had to take on too much.

I loved the realness of this world, and the truth that was so large inside him that it overshadowed all my lies.

Chapter Thirty

Manhattan, New York, 2032

The dress felt wrong, too tight and not long enough. The mirror had lied when it showed a dress to my knees and slightly baggy.

"Is it hot in here?" I asked Mike.

"No, stop asking that and quit fidgeting with your dress. You look great, calm down." He sounded annoyed, but I didn't recall asking him if it was hot before this.

My eyes darted nervously, searching the crowd for the one face I dreaded seeing. One I hadn't seen in so long I didn't recall it the way it might've been, only the way it was when he screamed at me and tore at my clothes.

A sea of dark clothes and gloomy faces filled the small church on Pierre Street.

When her parents made their way to the front of the church and sat, heads held high and eyes dry, I felt sick.

They'd abandoned her, sold her into marriage to save their livelihood and then abandoned her when she needed them most.

I hated them and didn't even know them. We had never met, except that one phone call, that one cry for help.

Lana's coffin sat at the front, closed casket naturally. By the end, she'd been hardly more than bones and skin.

Her death lay heavy on my heart, and shoulders, so I leaned on Mike as I wondered about things. Things like had I left her unresponsive, all those years ago when she first got lost in la la land, would she have ended up here sooner? She could have avoided the entire tragedy by remaining unresponsive and slowly fading. My conscience wouldn't be clearer, but Gilda would be alive.

A man I didn't know but assumed was the priest, got up and began speaking. His words floated in and out of my ears as I stared at the vibrant photo of her, taken before she'd met me. It was black and white and almost like artwork. But if you looked close enough, in the flecks of her eyes, you could see the moving pictures. You could see the world she lived in. You could see she was already lost, well before she met me.

That didn't soothe my aching heart. I was the villain of the story. For a time, I told myself the mayor was. I thought the machine might have been and perhaps we were victims of it together. Sometimes on stormy nights, when thunder and lightning struck and I jumped, scared of the shadows around me, I thought maybe Lana was the bad guy. Lana with her scissors and her empty chest.

But those were lies that villains whispered to themselves.

The fact I had the brass balls to show my face at her funeral said things about my ability to lie to myself that I hadn't considered until now. In fact, none of us deserved to be here. We had all failed her.

The man holding my hand, feeling the sweat on my palms and the hellfire licking at my soul, he knew the truth. He knew that I was the villain, I was the bad guy, I was the one pretending to be something I was not.

I was never a friend to Lana.

I was never a doctor to Lana.

And I most certainly didn't save Lana.

I condemned her to a death that she asked me for, a death I had no right in granting.

Like loads of scientists and doctors, I had acted like God. I had acted like I knew better than he did. I had acted like the grim reaper, doling out services in the name of science.

And now I sat in *his* house and I listened to *his* words, I burned a little from my guilt. But it was nothing compared to what I deserved.

Lana had died quietly in her sleep, her vegetative slumber. Sleeping Beauty who would never be kissed awake by the handsome prince. For sleep was her prince.

I was the old queen, the haggard witch, who had used magic to transform herself into something beautiful. After she cursed the princess to sleep evermore.

I glanced at the huntsman next to me, the one who knew of my evil ways, and sighed.

He scowled, knowing full well what was happening in my head. His eyes obviously went back to the priest's as if telling me to pay attention, and homage.

But I didn't.

I couldn't.

For the moment I'd turned my head to his, eyes caught my stare. Cold, hateful eyes. They shot arrows at me, trying to pierce my heart, but like the clever queen, I rarely walked around with my heart in my chest.

I'd given it to the huntsman to safely keep with his.

Seeing the mayor in the corner with his henchmen made me realize I'd been wrong about one thing. I always told myself the reasons Jonathan couldn't come to me in la la land was that my level of denial wasn't as strong as Lana's. But the emptiness I felt when I stared at the accusatory glare suggested I was wrong.

All along I'd been in denial, cold sociopathic denial.

I took no more blame than I'd allowed myself from the start, even though he tried to give it all to me. No, I believed that the mayor had his share in this too, and I would be damned if I would take the entirety of her death on my shoulders.

I glared back, sneering a little even. I was no longer afraid of him. I'd brought my own henchman.

We were all guilty, all of us, some more than others and the mayor wasn't anywhere near innocent.

I turned around and feigned listening, as a man who didn't know Lana spoke on her behalf. He was the only one who did. Not a single other person spoke, for no one knew Lana in the end. Even I had lost her.

When it was over, I didn't stay and offer condolences to anyone. I didn't need to. Who did you tell you were sorry for helping someone commit the suicide they'd always longed for? Her parents who had done nothing to prevent it? Her ex-husband who had tried to fake it once for her and had driven her to try to commit it in the first place? Or myself, the person who had been closest to her but dragged her so far down that she committed murder?

No, none of us were owed anything.

I left the funeral with the ending of my book firmly in my mind.

Lana was finally freed to go to heaven and see the real Danny and tell him all about the life they'd lived together in a world of her making.

I linked my arm with the huntsman's and let him lead me past the mayor who I subtly flipped off when we got to the door.

The shocked look on his face became the one I recalled. I lost the image of him ripping at my clothes and tearing my skin and replaced it with absurdity and hatred. I catalogued him that way.

In the end, I would vilify him in the novel. I would lay more of my blame at his feet. The end of the book would do Lana justice as the victim and the mayor the horned devil. I would place the syringe in his hands and have him be the one who shot her full of that last dose, the one she rode out the remaining years with.

I would make her a true Sleeping Beauty, a true Snow White. I would build a glass container and place her in it, frozen as she dreamed of a different life, but captive in this one. And the vile mayor would be the one holding the old-fashioned key.

It was a good ending.

It did my story justice and left the reader with a pain in their heart. The reader could choose the ending they liked. Either seeing the girl trapped in the casket surrounded by the rainy day that never seemed to end, listening to the droplets ping off the glass case.

Or, ending the story as she did, in the world she created.

It was exactly like Choose Your Own Adventure.

And when the asshole mayor read the story, which I knew he would, he would understand that I blamed him far more than I blamed myself.

Another lie, but who was counting at this point?

Chapter Thirty-One

Manhattan, New York, 2033

The crowd made me nervous, even though I was hidden from them behind the curtain. What had I gotten myself into? How had I been so insane as to agree to this? Where were my sociopathic tendencies that enjoyed a narcissistic boosting that swelled the ego as this surely would?

"Emma?"

I turned, feeling all the color drain from my face. "Marguerite." Her name tasted like ash and yet I'd never felt so excited to see her face.

"You look so good." She burst into tears and ran at me. All the time, all the years and hateful words between us, melted away. Her hands around me, clinging to me, felt exactly as they had before. As they had on that day when I saw myself through her eyes.

"I'm so sorry, Marguerite," I whispered. I had longed to say this but it was her that had walked away, declaring the finality of the friendship. I never had the courage I needed to mend this. As always, I was afraid it would be rejected, that I would be.

"I'm sorry, Emma. I abandoned you and you needed me." She stepped back. "I wasn't strong enough for you."

"No, you were exactly what I needed in that moment. You

saved me. Did you read the book?" I asked. I had to know if she saw the part where the friends showed up and suddenly the narrator realized the fall she had taken.

"I did. It's beautiful and tragic and I suspect all true." She tried to smile but it came up a grimace through the tears.

"Thank you for being there when I needed it." I hugged her, noting the shake in my hands. They never did this anymore. I never shook like this. "How's Lola?"

"Gone," she whispered. "I should have called. I wanted to." She started to cry harder. "She passed peacefully last year. Sweet and feisty until the very end."

That was when my tears hit. "Gone?" I'd wasted so much time on myself that I had missed my own dog's death. Even if she wasn't my dog anymore. "I'm so sorry," I offered, wiping my face. I wasn't certain how I would sign books with puffy eyes and a runny nose, but it was looking like I would have to.

"Me too. She was a good girl. The kids made a grave for her in the yard at the farm. You should come out and see it."

"I would love that."

"Where is he?" she teased. "Where's the huntsman?"

"Mike?" I cleared my throat and wiped my face some more. "He's not here. He hates bookstores and large groups of women and wearing clean jeans." I tried to sound as if I was recovered from the shock of her being here.

"I'll wait around for you, after."

"No!" I nearly shouted it. "Don't go. Stay. You can sit at the table with me. I was supposed to have some assistant I don't know, but this is better." I was terrified she might leave. "We have so much catching up to do. How are the kids and Stan?"

"Good. The same. Honestly. Life with kids means things stay relatively the same for a long time. We do sports four days a week, volunteer for school shit, I work, I make dinner, I do laundry, Stan works, we try to have sex on the weekends and sometimes Tuesdays. I drink way more wine than I ever have, sometimes out of to-go coffee cups at the sports things. Sometimes in the bathroom while I eat candy that I hide from everyone else." She laughed and hugged me again. "I have missed you, friend." Her fingers trembled like mine did.

"I missed you too." I kissed her cheek, and pulled her to the curtain. "Stay with me, okay?"

"Okay." She smiled wide, not grimacing but looking like herself again. In her eyes and face I saw something I'd not noticed before.

We were older.

We had both aged, not a lot but enough to notice. She had aged with kids, even sporting some gray hairs. And I had aged with grief, self-denigration, and torment.

But we were on the other side. Her kids were older and my grief had thinned, some of it washing away completely.

As some random person announced my name, the curtain opened, and I beamed at the very large crowd of eager fellow bookworms. I waved and sat as the line started. Each woman telling me about their experience in the brief moments they were given to speak.

I signed and laughed and tried to be as real as the story was, allowing each person's interpretation of my work and their experience as the reader.

It lasted for hours.

My fingers cramped.

My butt hurt.

My back ached.

But my heart swelled.

Not only was Marguerite at the signing, and by my side, but the bookworms accepted me and my book.

It was a great moment, humbling even.

The cowriter who had made the work shine smiled at me, nodding his head as if letting me know what a good job I'd done.

I smiled back, grateful for his way with words and scenes.

As we left the shop, I was full. My heart and soul felt as if they were glowing. I linked arms with Marguerite and listened to stories of kids and Lola and all the shit I'd missed being a selfish and horrid person.

The stories were vibrant and visual but the nagging sense of disappointment was always there. It was my villain's cloak, something I never really took off. And if I did, it remained close by, hung up and waiting for me to put it back on. Waiting to drape me again in the weight of a lifetime worth of misdeeds and villainous choices.

We hurried to the bar where Mike was watching a game and many beers deep into his tab. He offered a confused and lazy smile, a drunk version of the one I loved. "Emma, there's my girl. How was it?"

"Amazingly ego boosting. I suspect I'll be ridiculous to be around for at least a month."

"Add month to the list." He winked and offered his hand. "Marguerite, how are you?"

"Good, Mike. And you?"

"You know each other?" I stepped back, sensing some sort of betrayal lingering in the air. I was always ready to be wronged.

"Yeah. I hunted her down and told her you missed her, but you were too much of a stubborn baby to admit it." He nodded. "You're welcome."

I laughed, hating the feel of this in my throat but Marguerite corrected him, making me feel marginally better. "We were both being stubborn."

Mike handed the barkeep cash and oozed off the barstool. "See, it all worked out." He slung an arm over my shoulder and directed us out of the bar. "I need to take a piss." He headed to the alleyway, close enough to us that we could hear him behind the dumpster.

"I did not see that as a possibility for you." She pointed in his direction.

"No," I agreed, still a little annoyed if I was being honest. "No, me either."

"He loves you a lot," she spoke softly.

"I know. I think he's my Stan. I always believed Jonathan and I were soul mates. And when he died I thought for sure my soul was missing. And I was lost."

"I think we have more than one match for our soul, Em. Jonathan and you were good together, but you were a different person then. You hadn't gone through any of the things you have now. You're different. You look like it and smell like it and feel like it. There's a haunted aspect to your eyes but there's also love in there. A type of love I don't think you felt before. Your heart didn't go missing when Jonathan died, it got bigger. It had to make room for sorrow. So it felt empty and someone like Jonathan wouldn't have filled that hole. You needed someone bigger to fill the bigger space." She grinned, her eyes shining with light as she watched Mike amble down the alley, zipping up his pants. "And that guy is larger than life. He probably even makes your heart stretch a little bit so he fits."

I burst, unable to contain myself, covering my eyes with my hands as I sobbed. She wrapped around me, blanketing me in love. It wasn't unconditional, it wasn't some fluffy bullshit love that pretended to understand you when everything was wrong. It was the kind of love that carried you when you couldn't walk anymore. It was the love that called a spade a spade and told you when you were wrong. It was the love that didn't need tending or building. It was lifelong, taking breaks and being inseparable but carrying on the same as always. It didn't change or grow, it was constant.

We'd been apart for years and still, no one knew me the way she did. Not even Mike. Or if he did, he couldn't ever explain it to me like her.

"Jesus, I'm gone two minutes and you're blubbering?" He wrapped himself around us both, draping and weighing too much. It was my turn to carry our burden, but an unexpected person was there to help me. A person I should never have counted out.

Chapter Thirty-Two

Seated at Lana's grave, one of the old-fashioned ones that had to be purchased decades ago, I stared at the grass that had grown over her, sealing her in.

I'd left Mike at the hotel to come be alone with her once more. Footsteps came up behind me and I tensed, wondering if perhaps I was about to be stabbed in the back or neck or murdered as Gilda once was. There would be some sort of irony in the death.

"Dr. Hartley," the mayor spoke softly as he sat next to me on the bench.

"Mr. Delacroix." I almost called him Mr. Mayor but that wasn't his role anymore.

"She's finally in the ground, huh? Dead for half a decade almost and only now in the ground."

A thousand bitter words floated in my mind but I didn't speak them, I think surprising us both. "If they knew her, they never would have put her in the ground."

"No. Lana needed to be free. On the wind. I tried to tell them that. She needed to chase the rain." His voice cracked and when I glanced at him I could see the emotion in his eyes.

"You loved her?" I was stunned by what I saw.

"I did. Always." He swallowed all the venomous things he wanted to say back at me. "It wasn't enough." He meant he wasn't, but I didn't need him to say that, and he was never going to. He turned to face me, square in the eyes. I could see the hate he held back, all of it. But his words made me suspect not all that hate belonged to me. "I should have told you about Danny and her attempts on her life." He nodded. "I read your book."

I was the villain of this story again. His blame was lessened by his love and his pride and that made mine worse.

"I should have warned you that she didn't match your guidelines."

"She never told me a thing until it was too late," I defended myself weakly, like every villain did at some point.

"I know. And that's why you're still alive." He sighed and got up, leaving me with that haunting threat. "We both know she wouldn't want to be in the ground, Dr. Hartley, and we will always share the blame in how she got there." He walked away and I never saw him again. Not in the real world. In my mind's eye, he would always be this: a long dark shadow eternally walking away from me after laying more guilt at my feet.

I turned and glanced back at her headstone. Almost smiling at the ridiculousness of her life and death and this moment. It played out like a movie, one that would eventually become a movie. She would have smiled and laughed at Marshall. She would have called him a bully and told him he was fucking insane with his possessiveness and how he smothered her.

It was harder to hear her voice here, even though I was right next to her and knew that was what she would've said. So I sat, recalling all our conversations at the table, eating and laughing and sharing about our secret lives.

I imagined her kids, wishing I'd gone into her world just once to see what she'd created. My images of them were older now, they were grown and living an amazing life. I spent a second on this, as if I was in the world and the lie I had made was making a truth. In this world, if I were the one in control, Lana would be alive and with Danny and I wouldn't be sitting here at this grave.

Instead, I would be with Jonathan.

But then I couldn't be with Mike.

One of those things was unacceptable and it canceled out my desire for the other. And here at her grave, I realized it meant she was also expendable.

The path that led to Mike, the one I'd stumbled down, clawing my way back up onto the banks of, was the one I wanted in the end.

I had the ending I wanted.

The story was bullshit and made up of lies I wished weren't truths.

I glanced at the sky, having always assumed God lived up there, and nodded as a second dose of irony hit. I hadn't just been looking for Jonathan, I'd been looking for a way to peek into heaven and hadn't even realized it.

I wanted back something I didn't think should've been taken and so I had cheated the system to get it.

But what I got was this moment here.

I chuckled a bit. My cheating and sneaking into heaven to retrieve my heart, ended up sending me to hell. And the reward for surviving hell was the light that had brought my heart back to life. For like Marguerite had so poetically explained to me while the light of my life pissed in an alley, my heart had never been missing or broken off. I didn't need to venture into heaven to get it back, or suffer the wrath of hell. I needed only to find the right person to fit and fill the space. But I had to go through all that to find him.

I got up, not necessarily forgiving myself for the sins but definitely unloading some of the blame.

Lana and I had both wanted into heaven and she was finally there. And I was finally free of the desire to go. I was done being the conflicted scientist who wanted to find heaven, even if she had to make it. Of course, I had made a hell, a place that gave you a drink but never quenched your thirst. I lacked the talent, ingenuity, and skill set God himself had. I was limited to math and science.

I turned to walk back to the hotel when I saw the smile I loved more than anything in the entire history of the world.

He sauntered over, hungover and wearing a tee shirt with a beer label on the front and a pair of jeans I'd picked out for him and snuck into his closet. He'd never looked sexier.

"You all done?" He sounded groggy.

"I am." I sighed, so much lighter. "I am finally all done."

"Thank Christ." He slung an arm around my shoulders and turned us around, leading us back to the hotel. "I tried to eat my way out of this hangover, but I think I might have to go for some hair of the dog." He rubbed his bearlike chest, wincing from what I had to assume was heartburn. "How's the mayor?" He snuck a side-glance at me.

"Still an asshole." I laughed.

"Am I allowed to kick his ass yet?"

"No, he's suffered and like Marianne Dashwood once said, 'If his present regrets are half as painful as mine, he will suffer enough.'"

"That is mighty poetic of whoever the hell Marianne Dashwood is."

"Remember the Jane Austen movie I made you watch after I won the bet on the football game you made me watch?"

"Oh yeah, the one with Alan Rickman. I liked him."

"Me too." I laughed and snuggled into his chest.

"That movie was awful though. You cried through most of it. And always when that one chick was just looking out windows." He chuckled and rubbed my shoulder.

"Elinor Dashwood is the woman I strive to be. Unfortunately, I'm much more of a combination of Anne Elliot and Emma Woodhouse, with a little bit of Catherine Morland thrown in for good measure. And then you take all that and make a smoothie with all the evil witches from Disney movies and voila!"

"That wouldn't even scratch the surface, Em. You're complex and weird in ways Disney hasn't had a chance to make up yet." He kissed the side of my head and walked us back to the hotel.

He was right, he was always right.

Chapter Thirty-Three

The tiny grave was perfect. The rose bush was the touch it needed. I sat on the lawn, the dampness of the grass cooling me through my underwear and pants.

"Lola was a good dog." Seraphene, Marguerite's eldest daughter, smiled. She was so grown I wouldn't know her but for the look in her eyes. It was her mother's.

"Thank you so much for taking care of her when I couldn't." I had nothing else to offer. What did you say to a child when you were trying to explain that level of darkness? She might have been eleven years old, but she was still too young to understand that overwhelming darkness could lurk inside a person.

"We were just glad you gave her to us. Mom said you lived in kind of a crazy house and Lola would have hated it."

"She would have. This was a better fit for her." I nodded, swallowing the acidity in my throat. Crazy house was an understatement.

Marguerite carried over a couple of glasses of wine and sat next to me, handing me one. "Mike is officially my favorite person in the world and if you break up with him, I will murder you, for real."

I held my glass up to hers and clinked it as a response.

Seraphene got up. "Mom, you're so weird." She turned and left.

"Probably." She wrinkled her nose at her daughter and then turned back to me. "And if you do, he's mine. I am calling shotgun on him now. If Stan dies, I also get visitation rights." She winked.

"You're drunk." I laughed and sipped the wine.

"I'm happy." She leaned into me. "This is the life I knew you would one day have, so fabulous and smart and kinda refined and yet trashy at the same time. I just never imagined you would date a construction worker, I guess be common-law with him. How many years has it been now?"

"Dating or living in sin, as his mother calls it? Three. Which is nuts. I agree. I never imagined this was how my life would be."

"Hey, you said imagined normally like a Yankee should," she beamed and turned back to the guys on the huge back deck, laughing and talking like they'd been friends for decades. "She said imagined normally."

"Oh my God." I shoved her.

"Still says God weird though." Marguerite laughed, nudging me back.

"You should hear her say cup of or spot of. That'll never be normal again."

I lifted my middle finger in the air at Mike.

"Ladylike." He scoffed. "And in front of the children."

"Mommy tells Daddy to piss off." Kara, the youngest daughter laughed.

Marguerite's eyes widened as she burst out laughing. "Stan! Deal with your kids."

"Yes, because I'm the one cussing in front of them in traffic." He chuckled and spoke quietly to Kara, letting her know that piss was a bad word.

"They're gorgeous, Marguerite."

"I know." Her eyes squinted as she smiled hard. "I never imagined this would be my life either. You remember that apartment we had before the kids? God, I loved that place. I was so smug then. So blissfully unaware what life really tasted like.

What pain and hate and disappointment were."

"We all were."

"No, you'd lost Jonathan already. You were filled with misery then. But I was still smug and foolish. I had so many ideas about who and what I was."

"The word you're looking for"—I took a big gulp before I said it—"is insufferable."

"Asshole." She laughed and stared at the rose bush on her small farm. "Come on, let's go inside." She got up. "I need to put out some snacks before we all get too drunk."

I took her hand and followed her inside. She went into the kitchen, but I sauntered over to the dining room, sitting at the same large industrial table that they'd had for ages. I noticed now it had scuffs and marks and even something resembling crayon on it. There was food in the crevices and no fancy tablecloth or runner. No bowl of pretentious dried acorns or yarn balls made out of grape vines. It had a stack of plastic tablemats that weren't particularly clean and a stuffed bear who seemed like he was a bit lost.

But none of this had brought me to the room.

It was the painting I had come for.

The one spread across five canvases, the one of the beach grass and the boardwalk. I sat and stared, stunned that the beautiful painting was still here.

I could still smell the grass and sea and hear the waves. I could hop from canvas to canvas. But this time I didn't want to get lost in the beauty of a world where I could flee my troubles. I pondered if Mike would want to go to the beach. I desired to snuggle into his arms around the fireplace with the weird broken glass pieces and listen to him tell stories. Or walk on the beach with him, my hand safely encased in his.

I glanced outside quickly to check and see if it was raining as I wondered for a moment if I was possibly still in the machine.

It happened frequently when it rained, especially if I was sitting in a window. I would gaze around, double-checking.

This painting was the full circle moment, the pinnacle of me sensing I was reliving something.

But unlike the first time I saw the painting, I didn't listen to the siren's call. I didn't let it tempt me into a fate I believed was better than this one.

I turned my back on it and smiled at my friend. "You need help?"

"Sure. Can you lay out the crackers to go with these dips. Did you ever try these?" She held a container of dip up. "It's from Costco, I love it. The kids don't, so more for me." She chuckled.

We set out food and when the guys came in to get some, Mike planted the biggest kiss on my lips, pinning me to him. "Don't get drunk, Em. I have plans for you later at the hotel," he whispered in my ear.

"Take your own advice." I bit his lip.

"I've been drinking the kids' grape juice for hours. I'm getting a stomachache from it but that's about it." He laughed and grabbed some food.

I put my glass down on the table and forgot it inside.

I wanted whatever his plans were.

At the end of the night, he drove us to the hotel. I had the window open, sticking my hand out in the warm summer air.

"They're nice, huh?" Mike remarked, sort of randomly.

"The best." I grinned wide.

"Did you know they split up for a while?" He puzzled, making me bring my arm in and close the window.

"What? No."

"Yeah, the reason I got so drunk that night in New York, at the signing, was him. He came and kept me company while she went to the signing. He got hammered too and needed a walk back to the hotel a little early. On the walk over, he told me the story. She had an affair with some guy, some big shot from the city. She thought she was pregnant and he found the tests. I guess he got the snip-snip so he knew it wasn't his. They broke up for a while. He took the kids and she moved into the city for a bit. Came back about six months later and they got back together. Heavy counseling and shit, but back together. He still sounded crushed though. She would go like weeks without seeing the girls."

"When was this?" My insides were on fire.

"I don't think he mentioned—"

"Don't lie!" I could smell the lie seeping from him. Liars always knew their own kind and Mike wasn't one of us.

"Right after you girls had your thing. I guess she had a bit of a crisis and it went downhill."

"Oh my God." I felt sick. I hadn't imagined that my state and how I'd acted would have affected her. Typical villain. "She never told me."

"Yeah, I assumed as much. I thought you should know. Maybe cut her some slack on the whole way she treated you before; she was obviously going through something."

"You think I am offended by how she treated me?" I leaned away from him, wondering if he really knew me as well as I thought he did.

"No. I know you blame yourself for it all, but we all have self-preservation, Em. And yours is sometimes really good at pointing at the other people in the crowd and hinting at their blame so you don't feel as bad."

He knew me. He knew me better than I knew myself.

"And you don't need to blame anyone else, or feel guilty about everything you've ever done in your whole life. No one is holding it against you, except you. And I suspect if you stopped counting them and holding them in such high regard, you'd forget your problems were even there. Maybe not always, but some of the time." He reached over and rubbed my arm. "You think I hold myself hostage on every shitty thing I've ever done?"

"No?" I asked.

"No. I don't. I have a list a mile long of horrible shit I wish I could take back. Everyone does. I lost my virginity when I was sixteen to my neighbor because I knew she was in love with me and I just wanted to do it. She told me she loved me, and I didn't give half a shit about her. I screwed her and she told me she loved me again, and I said thanks and then I never talked to her after that. She was kinda easy so I thought why not?" He didn't sound as remorseful as he should. "My mom found out like five years ago and beat the hell outta me. She actually hit me with a wooden spoon, around the kitchen table, shouting like a madwoman. Over twenty years after the fact." He outright laughed at that. "And truth be told, I deserved way worse. And that isn't even one snowflake on the damned iceberg of bad things I've done. Your inability to deal with guilt is ridiculous. If I knew your parents in any way, I'd blame them. But your twice-a-year phone calls don't reveal much." He laughed at me, doing that mocking thing I hated, where we laughed but really it was only him.

He pulled into the hotel and I lost my interest in whatever it was he wanted to do.

I couldn't believe Marguerite had gone through all that alone.

Her statement about being smug before, it meant so much more now. So did the wine and candy in the bathroom, alone.

My perfect friend with her perfect life and her perfect marriage wasn't so perfect.

I glanced over at Mike as he pursed his lips, checking for the valet slip before he handed over the keys. I smiled, seeing all the things I knew were flaws but loved him more for having them, even laughing at me for mine, which I hated. My annoyance dissolved.

"I love you," I blurted.

"I know you do." He turned and gave me that smile. "And I love you."

I leaned in, giving him a soft kiss before hopping out when the attendant got my door.

Mike and I held hands up to the room, clinging to each other.

The sadness for my friend slowly lessened as we got there, but my passion for him didn't come around. I needed a hug and the ability to lay some of my troubles on him, if only for the night.

His plan for the night was ruined, but we still spent it in a perfect ending to a flawed and chaotic day.

Chapter Thirty-Four

I stood on the deck, overlooking the gray ocean and sighed into the wind. It was glorious, having it blow in my face and clean me off. The visit to New York had been amazing, but the solitude of our house was what the soul needed.

"Em?"

I turned, confused at the suit Mike had on.

He scowled at my capri pants and tee shirt. "You know we have dinner in like an hour, right?"

"Dinner?" I bit my lip.

"Yeah, you have the dress already laid out. Hurry up!" He glanced at his watch.

"Shit! I forgot!" I blew past him and raced for the bedroom and changed my bra and underwear before pulling on the lilac knee-length dress with empire waist that was draped across the bed. I slapped on makeup and threw my hair into a messy but stylish bun.

I pasted on some quick lip gloss and gave myself a once-over before I donned my black heels and headed out. I lifted my armpit in the hallway, checking for smell, satisfied it was still linen and lavender and not one of the times I had forgotten to put on deodorant.

When I got out on the deck a dinner had been set up, with two metal covers overtop the plates, obviously keeping it warm.

There was unopened champagne and flowers and Mike.

He was kneeling.

My heart stopped. "You shit," I whispered, realizing he'd used my lack of remembering everything against me. "We didn't have dinner plans."

"We did, you just never knew about them." He spoke in a way I hadn't heard in a long time. His voice cracked and his eyes flooded with emotion. "Emma Marie Hartley, when I met you, I thought you were the weirdest lesbian I ever did meet. You and your hermit of a partner were scary, beyond all reason. The famous witches of the old haunted house on the hill." We both laughed as he continued, his hands shaking just a little with the Tiffany's ring box clutched tightly. "But as I got to know you, the magic spell you were under faded until I didn't see it anymore. You showed me the beauty and intelligence of the person inside you and made me love you far before I ever knew I was attracted to you. And yes, I know how this sounds. I'm not good at this stuff, we both know that." We laughed again. "But I knew from the moment I finished your library, my heart was yours. And it won't ever stop being yours. I know this because if I die before you, you'll come hunt me down, almost killing yourself to be with me."

I laughed, hating and loving him not even close to equally.

"Make me the happiest man on earth. Marry me?" He didn't budge.

"You can't call me out on my shit in the middle of the proposal. Lemme see the ring first." I pretended not to be impressed.

"No. Say yes." He laughed with me.

"Yes." I tried not to sound like a gushing schoolgirl as I said it, and failed.

He flipped open the box and stood, towering over me.

Inside was the most perfect ring I'd ever seen. "The lady said it was the one that resembled the era—"

"You're ruining it." I lifted my hand.

"Right, sorry." He slipped the ring from the box and placed it on my finger, of course fitting perfectly. It was stunning: a large square-cut diamond with a halo of small pink ones and clear diamonds going down the platinum band. It suited my finger dreamily, delicate and yet bright.

His fingers shook as he lifted his hands and cupped my face, staring into my eyes. "I love you."

"Craziness and all?" I asked.

"Wouldn't have it any other way."

"Then I have one condition: I want one thing for our honeymoon, and you have to say yes blindly and agree to the entirety of it."

"Okay." He suddenly sounded nervous.

"You're fine. Don't be a baby. I said yes. That's the hard part." I lifted onto my tiptoes and kissed him, smearing lip gloss on his lips and leaving him mussed.

"Hungry?" He glanced at dinner.

"Not for that." I grabbed his tie and led him to the bedroom. On the way, I glanced out the window to make sure it wasn't raining. I needed to be sure this was real. It was dry and sunny and warm.

Epilogue

He swallowed anxiously as they strapped him in, but acted as though he was trying to hide his nervousness. "I can't believe this is what you wanted, and you didn't even tell me until now." He growled, looking sexy in his hospital scrubs.

"I just want you to see it once. And if you still hate me in three hours, you have plenty of time to get an annulment."

He lifted his middle finger from the restraint.

"I love you, Mike."

"I don't feel loved, Emma."

It was the last thing he said to me before the drop.

When I opened my eyes, I didn't see the bright light of the load into the machine. They'd fixed that. It was loaded already as we landed.

I grinned at Mike's Rand al'Thor costume. He had on a white blouse, a brown cloak, and black breeches. There was a small sword at his hip, nothing fancy. This was Two Rivers Rand. He was still a boy. So Mike looked young, maybe twenty.

He blinked for a minute, confused and starry-eyed before he peered down at his outfit, lifting a black boot from the ground. "Holy fuck."

"Welcome to Two Rivers." I grinned wide. The Wheel of Time series, the one he had told me about, was popular in the nineties and early two thousands. I'd read it then and recalled my favorite character was actually Matrim Cauthon.

"Are you Egwene al'Vere?" He tilted his head to the side as if confused. "I kinda always had a thing for her."

"Yeah, I guess so. Simple green dress, no knives, and these stupid boots. Glad to see they didn't fix the footwear." I gave him a grin. "You wanna go see the town?"

We stood on a dirt cart path, a road of sorts. Smoke rose in the distance from where the forge was likely put.

He spun in a circle, taking it all in. "This is nuts, Em. Nuts. I can taste it, the wood smoke. I haven't tasted that in years." He beamed and I folded my arms, giving him my best Egwene smug-ass grin. "Okay, okay. I get it. This is off the charts. I get it. It's amazing and you're an engineering genius, and you didn't make something to lure people to the dark side," he offered weakly, almost sounding like Rand. "Come on. I never want to come back in here so let's see everything we can."

"If it's the start of the book, shouldn't the carnival be coming to town?"

"I don't remember. It's been a long time, and I'm super anxious right now and overwhelmed. Is my heart beating fast to you?" he asked, holding his chest out.

"Oh my God, come on. And get into character." I grabbed his hand and dragged him toward town.

He started out rocky, struggling to fit in and earning some strange looks, but by the time we were sucked from the machine, he was grinning like a kid.

"That was fucking awesome." He sat upright, bright and awake.

"I'm glad you enjoyed yourself, Mr. Daley." The lady monitoring us smiled brightly, a little too brightly. Her gaze turned to me after a moment. "And how did Mrs. Daley enjoy it?"

I barely caught what she said beyond my name. "It was magical." I winked at Mike.

"Yes, we do love the machines. The experience is one of a kind." She helped us up as we were served refreshments and taken to a room to come back down in.

"I get it," Mike muttered as he ate his cookie. "Mrs. Daley. I get the appeal. If I went in that machine before, before when I was in the middle of my divorce or after she—" He paused. "I wouldn't have been good in there. I actually played enough *Call of Duty* that they offered me a job testing the data. I didn't sleep so I played. I see now, this is the same thing. Only better."

"Thank you." I needed this. The villain in me died off a little as vindication was offered. Not all of it, but the motives with which I made the machine were no longer in question.

"Now promise me, we won't ever come back here. I have an addictive personality, and I think I could get into this. Kinda seriously."

"I promise, Mr. Daley. We won't ever come back here." It wasn't a lie. It wasn't even a slight exaggeration.

"Mr. and Mrs. Daley, I like how that sounds." He ate a bite of my cookie and kissed me with his crumby lips. "What's your big plans now?" He sighed, sounding satisfied.

"I was thinking pretty seriously about those cooking classes." I smiled. "And getting a dog."

"Cooking classes sound amazing. A dog sounds like me going outside to make sure he takes a crap and then I have to pick it up."

"I'll make you yummy things to win you over so you don't mind the dog crap."

"Deal." He kissed me again. "What kind of dog?"

That I didn't know the answer to. "When we get home we should go to the shelter and see what they have."

"Okay." He stared deeply into my eyes, making me smile. "What are you thinking about?"

"Nothing," I lied. I didn't want to tell him that I was feeling complete, like I'd come full circle. Part of the reason I needed to go back in was to let go. And I had.

When we got to the car to drive home from Imagination Playlands, I pulled a copy of my book from the backseat. I had a few extra copies on hand for family at the wedding. They cared more about the stupid book than they did the wedding. Second weddings were never as entertaining for people. Except Mike's mom who was relieved we were finally right with the lord. Like he and I would ever be square.

I started to read the first couple of pages, remembering how it felt to be this woman, so long ago.

How it felt to be so troubled.

I closed the book and tossed it in the backseat where it belonged.

"So what kind of cooking classes?" he asked as he got in and started the car.

"I was thinking about taking beginning baking first."

"That sounds like the right place to start. My favorite place anyway." He lifted my hand and kissed it.

The huntsman had become the handsome prince and the evil queen had become the princess.

And they lived happily ever after.

As happily as two people with a lifetime of ghosts ever lived.

Because this was the real world. It was messy and ugly and scary at least some of the time. But that was what made the beauty and love and kindness so much more worthwhile.

The End.

If you liked this book, try In The Fading Light, also by Tara Brown.

Lost in La La Land

Tara Brown

I believe growing up in a really small town gives a person a little advantage when it comes to the imagination. You need one or you go mad.
Needless to say, mine saved me. After it got me into trouble first, that is. That's the problem with a vivid imagination, all the lies you tell.
I am happily married with two girls.
I have two giant dogs, two savage cats, and a penchant for a glass of red.
Also, I drag my bread through the sauce. I can't help myself, bread is life.
According to my age, I am meant to be a responsible adult, but it isn't going well at all. I would still head off to Hogwarts tomorrow and I suspect there isn't a single wardrobe I haven't crept into, hoping to find the door to Narnia. And don't even get me started on the King's Road, I get lost.
Fortunately, I am an international bestseller so I have wormed my way into the "Quirky" or Eccentric" category.
Thank God for that.
I am represented by Natalie Lakosil from the Bradford Literary Agency and published traditionally with Montlake Romance.

Other Books by Tara Brown

The Devil's Roses
Cursed
Bane
Hyde
Witch
Death
Blackwater
Midnight Coven
Redeemers
Betrayers

The Crimson Cove Mysteries
If At First
Second Nature
Third Time's a Charm
Four Crimson Corners

The Born Trilogy
Born
Born to Fight
Reborn

The Light Series
The Light of the World
The Four Horsemen
The End of Days

Imaginations
Imaginations
Duplicities

The Blood Trail Chronicles
Vengeance
Vanquished

First Kiss
Sunder
A Royal Pain

Tara Brown

The Seventh Day

Made in the USA
Columbia, SC
08 November 2017